Wisdom Tooth And The Awful Truth

The Tooth Fairy Chronicles

Book Four

Victoria Rocus

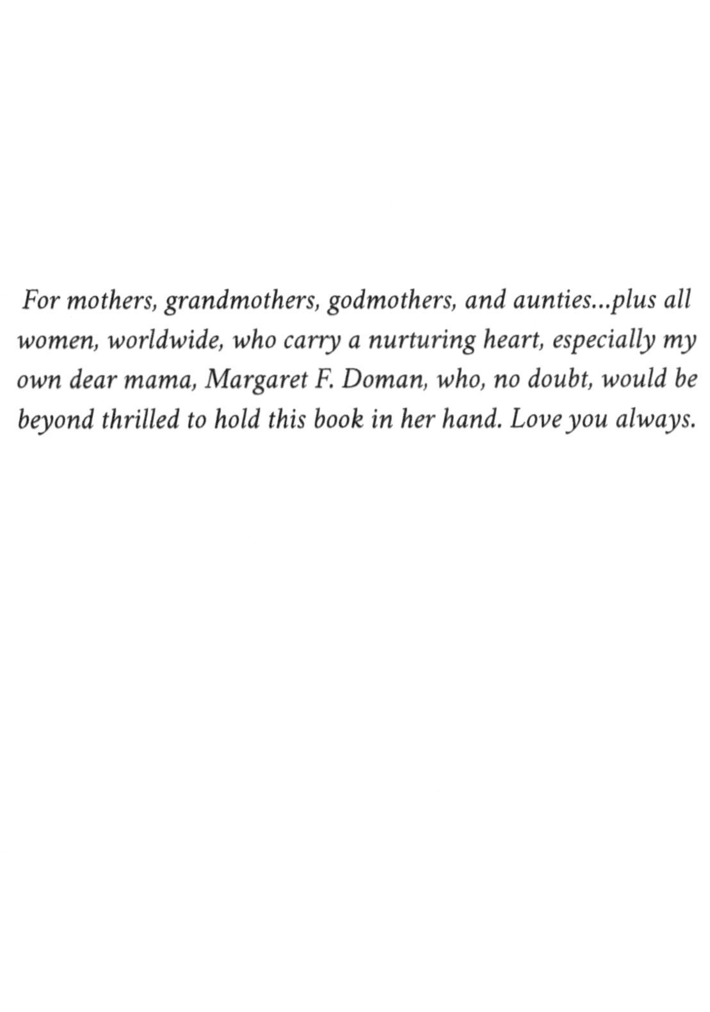

For mothers, grandmothers, godmothers, and aunties...plus all women, worldwide, who carry a nurturing heart, especially my own dear mama, Margaret F. Doman, who, no doubt, would be beyond thrilled to hold this book in her hand. Love you always.

GLOSSARY AND PRONUNCIATION OF ANCIENT OTHERWORLD GAELIC

Ag spochadh - (*åh spa-whoo)* – teasing

Ailm – (al îm) – an ancient Celtic symbol that represents inner strength

Aingeal milis – (an-gål mil-ish) - "sweet angel" – a term of endearment

Alainn – (ah lin) - beautiful

An Banna Siorai – (On Bon-nå Shear-ē*)* - "The Eternal Bond" - an unbreakable vow of commitment that follows a fated couple into the Afterlife

Anraith – (ón-ray) – soup

Aoibheann - (Ay-veen*)* – a feminine name meaning "radiant beauty"; the name of *Crann Bethadh's* head housekeeper.

Ardaigh mo stor – (ar-daw ma store) – "my darling rose" – a term of endearment Declan uses for Rosie

Asgard – (As- gart) – A *Nordboerne* Otherworld Elven kingdom north of *I Idir* and ruled by Odin; currently not on friendly terms with *I Idir's* monarchy over their opposing stand on Mundanes crossing the Veil. Pronounced (As-garter) by its citizens.

Athair - (ă-hair) - "father" - when capitalized, used as a formal title

Athame – (ă--thaym) - ceremonial knife used for ritual magic

Badh – (bod) – an ancient *Tuatha de Danann* House that serves as part of *I Idir's* Ruling Council. The Morrigan originally descended from this line before starting her own as Otherworldly Queen of *I Idir*

Bairn- (bĕrhn) - baby

Banphrionsa – (bon frún-sa) – royal title of Princess

Balor – (ba-lor) – a giant, one-eyed supernatural being of ancient origins; leader of the Fomorian race of hostile monsters

Beltane – (bee-awl-tin-ya) A sacred Otherworldly holiday held on May 1st, halfway between the Spring Equinox and the Summer Solstice, celebrating fertility and new growth.

Bhrocaire – (bru-câra) – a dog breed within the terrier family

Birgit – (beer-gît) – a variation of the name Bridget, meaning "help" or "salvation; The name of Dylan's *scathach.*

Breagadoir – (brig-a door) – a liar, or deceiver

Bricfesta – (brick- fas-ta) - breakfast

Bronntanas – (brawn-ta-nis) – a gift

Buachaill – (bow-hill) boy

Buaf – (boo-êf) – toad; the name given to the orphaned kitchen boy at *Dun Siorai*

Buime – (bwî-ma) – nanny; nursemaid

Bwca (boo-ka)– an Otherworldly House formed by a *Sidhe* race of Welsh Fae who are known for their domestic talents, especially in the area of cooking and food service.

Cait leanbh (câwt ya-nov) – translates to "baby cats" or kittens

Caladbolg – (Kăl-uv-bŏlg) - an ancient Otherworldly Fae sword with magical powers given to the *"Ridre Dubh"* (Black Knight) of *I Idir* to protect its people and the monarchy; currently in the possession of the reigning Black Knight, Theodore H. Beckett (Myrdynn), the 27th Merlin

Caoimhe – (kwee-va) – a feminine name meaning "gentle noble"; the name of one of Declan's five sisters

Cara – (kar- a) - friend

Carraig an Bhroin - (kăr-ig ĕn frăwn) - "Rock of Grief" - a treacherous out crop of cliffs overlooking the Gorm Sea; the land is part of House *Nuada's* holdings and is infamously known as being the location of choice for those Fae wishing to commit a quick suicide by breaking their neck

Chaturanga – (chaa-tr-aang-guh) – a game focused on battle formations and an ancient form of chess still played in the Otherworld

Cillian – (Kill-ee-an) – translates to "bright-headed" in reference to war or strife. Cillian *Mac Badh* is the young heir to House *Badh*, a cousin to the Queen of *I Idir*, and Declan's long-time nemesis.

Cistin – (kíst- shin) - kitchen

Cluidin – (clew-jean) – a diaper or baby "nappy"

Coinin beag milis – (coo-neen bag mel-ish) – an endearment meaning "sweet little rabbit"

Corvot – (Kor-vêt) – Lady *Siobhan Nuada's* page; an Other-worldly citizen with Elven heritage and a surly disposition

Coisir – (có-shure) - a party

Crann Bethadh - (Krŏn Bĕ-hĕ) - "Tree of Life" - the royal seat of The Morrigan, Queen Maeve, built out of a giant, ancient oak; sometimes referred to as "The Raven's Nest"

Croi – (cree) – heart

Crios – (krîs) - belt

Cuach an Fhithich – (Coo-ha en If-itch) – "Raven's Hollow" The estate belonging to House *Badh* which is in close proximity to the Royal Seat of *Crann Bethadh*

Daidi – (dá-dee) - daddy

Danu – (Da-noo) – Celtic goddess of nature and fertility

Deaglan - (Dĕk-lĕn) - "full of goodness" - the Otherworld spelling of Declan

Deamhan – (jewm) – demon of an unspecific nature

Dithreabhach – (dee-how-ack) – hermit

Duais – (do-ish) – a prize or reward

Dubnos - (dŏv-nus) - the Fae version of the Underworld

Dun Siorai - (Dune Shear-ē) "Eternal Fortress" - House *Nuada's* ancestral home

Epona – (uh-pow-na) – Celtic goddess known as the protector of mares and foals

Fear beag mó chroi – (far-bag-ma-raw) – "Little Man of My Heart;" a term of endearment Declan uses for Dylan.

Fadhbanna – (fie-bána) – problems or troubles

Fearg iarmhrach – (far-ig ear-var-ah) – lingering anger or resentment

Fiacail Chisteain – (fee-a-kil kris-teen) – translates to "Tooth Treasury;" the government building in *I Idir* that houses the teeth retrieved from the Mundane world by tooth fairies

Formorians – (fó-mor-ee-ans) – an Otherworldly race of violent, monstrous giants who are always at battle with the Fae.

Gadai – (gâ-dee) – thief

Gloanna na fola – (glena na faw-la) – translates to "the blood calls"; the Fae metaphysical and spiritual belief that members of a family bloodline are "soul connected" through all the generations

Gruaim – (grew-em) – a grumpy person

Him leanbh a anom – (ham va-nov ê ênom) translates to "child of her soul," stipulates a very intimate bond.

I Idir - (ē ēdar) "In Between"- the Fae kingdom in the Otherworld ruled by The Morrigan, Queen Maeve, as its monarch.

Ladhar an diabhal – (leered on dowl) – translates to "devil's toe;" how the superstitious Fae describe the genetic quirk of having an extra toe on the foot.

Lamh claoimh – (láv clêv) - translates to "sword arm;" refers to a Liege Lord's Second in Command.

Leimneach – (limb- a nock) – a state of anxiety; jumpy

Leithsceal ceart – (lash-kil kar-sht) – a proper excuse or reasonable explanation

Lioncs – (lionx) – an Otherworldly lynx-type animal

Lonad mo Chroi – (lond ma kree) translate to "Center of my Heart:" a term of loving endearment

Lugh – (loo) – a god-like warrior king in ancient Otherworldly history; patron of the arts

Mac- (mc) - "son of"- a title given to an eldest son and heir of a Ruling House

Madra – (mod-dra) - dog

Madra diabhal – (mod-dra dowl) – translates to "demon dog;" the nickname given to the kitchen boy's unruly dog

Mairead – (MAH-rayd) – meaning "pearl," it is the Gaelic version of Margaret

Mathair - (mă-hair) - "mother" - when capitalized, used as a formal title

Mhamo – (ma mó) – informal term for "grandma" or "granny"

Mo Shiorghra - (mō hear-gra) - "My Eternal Love" - a fated mate in magical Fae tradition, wrought by a magical spell.

Nead an Fhithigh, - (yad en fifth-edg) – "The Raven's Nest" – the informal name for *Crann Bethadh*, home to Queen Maeve of *I Idir,* The Morrigan

Nuada - (new-a-da) - the name of an ancient Celtic king who possessed a silver arm; a major House from his bloodline within *I Idir's* Ruling Council that currently has Declan's father as its Lord

Oillpheist – (Ellie-fayst) - a serpent like monster in the Fae Otherworld

Ostara – (oh-star-ah) – an Otherworld Fae holiday celebrating the spring equinox and symbolizing fertility, rebirth and renewal

Piog biabhoige – (pee-õg bee-vôg) – rhubarb pie, Lord Nuada's favorite spring time dessert

Saoirse – (sur-shuh) – the name of one of Declan's younger sisters; it translates to "freedom"

Samhain – (sow -win) – an Otherworld sacred celebration marking the end of the harvest season and the beginning of the darker months; it is also the time when the Veil between the Mundane and the Otherworld is at

its thinnest and easiest to pass through. Mundane
Halloween traditions have their roots in *Samhain.*

Seamus – (shay-mus) – the Otherworld name for "James"
or "Jamie;" the name the kitchen boy, Buaf, gives his dog.

Sean – (shawn) – a male Celtic name meaning "the gods
are gracious"

Seanathair – (shin-a-ver) – grandfather, capitalized in
formal terms

Seanmathair - (shin-ma-ver) – grandmother; capitalized in
formal terms

Scathach – (skah-hak) – an elite group of trained Fae
female bodyguards hired by Ruling Class Houses to care
for their infant heirs. These positions are usually passed
down through a bloodline.

Sidhe - (shē) - the term used for the Fae race in Celtic
mythology, as well as the forts and mounds they once
lived in during ancient times; the *Sidhe* possess higher levels of magical skill, and thus are considered part of
Fae higher society

Siobhan - (shiv-awn) - a Celtic female name meaning "gracious gift"; the name of Declan's Mother

Slainte – (slawn-cha) – meaning "health," the word is used
as a toast before a salutatory drink much in the same way
as the word "cheers" is used in the English-speaking
Mundane world.

Smeara gorma – (smear-ya garm) – a blueberry like fruit of
the Otherworld

Spiedog – (spee-dowg) – translates to "robin;" the first
name, spelled "Robyn," of Dr. Brannagan, who is a Prince
of Avalon. His great grandmother many times removed is
the legendary Lady of the Lake and ruler of the Kingdom

of Avalon, as well as a good friend and ally of The Morrigan.

Tarraingeoir fiacail - (tar-a-gore fee-a-kil) – translates to "tooth puller;" a derogatory *Sidhe* title given to Rosie in her capacity as a dentist

Teaghlach – (chye-lukh) – a family unit or household

Tuatha de Danann - (two-ha de dan-an) "The Shining Ones"- a magical race of ancient, metaphysically gifted Fae with royal bloodlines. They compose *I Idir's* ruling council under

the Monarchy of The Morrigan, Queen Maeve

Uan beag – (ou-in be-og) – "little lamb;" a term of endearment used for Dylan

WISDOM 1

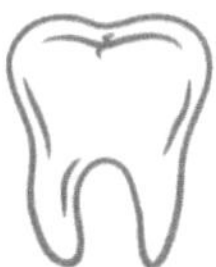

As Fate Would Have It

CARRAIG AN BHROIN (ROCK OF GRIEF)

The boy wedged the toe of his leather boot in a narrow crack and lowered himself down with the most precise of movements. The soil and rock on this side of the cliff bore the brunt of the blustery gales from the northeast, while the sea spray from the churning waters below left its face perpetually moist, sometimes crumbly, and always dangerously unpredictable. A single bad choice and he'd find himself at the bottom of the wall far faster than safety allowed, but that was only if his body wasn't broken on the way down by the jagged rocks that stuck out in random angles.

Buaf (toad) could still hear the small dog whimpering

over both the roar of the waves and the high-pitched whistle of the wind blowing through the breaks in the crags. "*Seamus*…ken' ya' hear me, boy?" he shouted above the duet of wind and water. "I'm comin' far' ya', doggo. Just sit still a bit longer. I'm on me way."

The bottom of his bare right foot was torn and bleeding. Without the benefit of a second boot, his tender skin was at the complete mercy of the sharp, cutting rocks. It was because of this very boot that *Buaf* and *Seamus* found themselves in such a dire situation. Up until that moment, the lad had followed each and every dictate his Lady had set forth regarding staying clear of the estate's large staff and avoiding interaction with people outside the family circle. But it was one of those perfect spring days and the freedom of the moment was too much of a temptation to trudge straight back to the closed rooms despite how grateful he was for the shelter of them.

While he'd been relaxing on a stump watching the dog sniff at a dead bird, *Buaf* had removed his new boot to shake out a stray pebble, forgetting that his young pup had an insatiable affection for anything made of leather. Before the boy could react, *Seamus* had abandoned the dead bird and snatched up the shoe, taking off at a remarkable speed and leaving his owner to follow in hot pursuit. There was no way the lad could admit to his newly found family that he had carelessly lost one of the expensive boots to an animal he had promised to train better.

"'Tis all ma' fault. I should've never chased after that feckin' dog," he muttered under his breath, gripping the rough outcrop in full sweat despite the early spring chill.

"'Specially knowin' he's a *madra* (dog) who loves a game even more than me. If only I'd been smart enough ta' coax him with a bit of biscuit, then perhaps the hell hound would have abandoned ma' boot for a much tastier treat." Now, because he'd not thought the whole plan through, both he and *Seamus*, the name he'd given the rascally mutt, found themselves clinging to treacherous precipices in a spot normally claimed by hopeless jumpers.

From this lower position, *Buaf* could finally catch glimpses of ginger colored fur through the early budding trees that had managed to take root among the rocks. The *bhrocaire* (terrier) sat pressed against the craggy wall of a narrow ledge, nearly a foot to the left of where the boy was now positioned, with the missing boot firmly tucked between his front paws. *Seamus* must have sensed his master's presence, for the pup stood up, yipped a shrill bark, and wagged his tail, causing him to drop the boot, which then slid perilously close to the edge of the rock.

"Stay still, *Seamus*. Stay, boy! Don' ya' go movin' a muscle," *Buaf* hollered. Without warning, the stone under his still booted foot shifted, and bits of rock bounced down the side of the cliff. It took all the boy's arm strength to keep from sliding further down the cliff on his face. "Feck!" he swore. "I should just leave ya' there and let *Balor* (Celtic monster) carry ya' ta' hell, ya' mangy mutt. Ya' had no business stealin' ma' boot when I was nice enough ta' give us some fresh air." The dog yipped in response, his barks changing to frightened whimpers as pieces of earth and stone loosened around the edges of his ledge and tumbled down to the surf below.

Buaf's heart beat faster in his chest. With the doggo's

rock shelf crumbling, the boy surely had no more time to move in the careful manner he currently was attempting. He repositioned the booted foot to a more secure holding when a fresh thought came to his panicked mind. Eyeing a tree with low hanging branches, the small boy deduced that he was probably close enough to grab *Seamus* if he could just swing himself over to the dog's spot rather than tediously climbing across the perilous rocks.

He unknotted the twisted rope belt holding up his breeches. Making a loop in the belt using a knot the Hound Master had shown him, *Bauf* swung the line over his head and attempted to lasso the closest branch. It took at least a dozen attempts before the boy was able to secure the other end of the cord to a tree branch in order to use it as a rope swing. Dropping a prayer to *Danu*, the Fae mother goddess, *Buaf* grabbed tight to his end of the line and pushed off from his spot toward the ledge with the dog.

It wasn't until the third full swing that the exhausted boy was finally able to reach the place where *Seamus* and the missing boot had taken refuge. Panting with exhaustion, the lad squatted down and hugged the dog to his chest, then tucked the pup inside his buttoned tunic. "I gotcha, boy. Yar' safe with me. Now all we have ta' do is figure out how ta' get back ta' the top. I wonder how in *Dubnos* (Celtic Hell) did ya' get down here in the first place?"

The grateful pup began licking his chin in response, making the boy laugh and wiggle. That was all the movement and extra weight the ledge could bear. The stone outcrop broke away from the cliff wall with an echoing crack. Child and dog instantly lost all sense of balance, tumbling down, bouncing off smaller ridges and outcrops, the boy cushioning the terrier with his own body. Though it seemed like an eternity to the young adventurers, the fall lasted no more than seven seconds. *Bauf*, with *Seamus* still inside his shirt, landed with a thump on a soft patch of beach below. For a second, neither of them could move, the wind knocked completely from their lungs. Finally, the young boy sat up and rubbed at a wound on his head, confused and dizzy, and as of yet, unable to get his eyes to focus. "Are you okay, *Seamus*?" he mumbled. The terrier poked his head out of the boy's shirt and sniffed at the oozing scratches on *Buaf's* face. "'Tis a lucky thing this ground is soft, doggo, lest we find ourselves with broken bones to mend," the kid murmured to the pup as he patted its furry head. It was only then that the lad noted what had broken their long fall to the beach. With wide eyes, *Buaf* looked down at what sat under him, or rather whom; it was the cold, still body of a young *Sidhe* woman, blood coming from both her nose and ears, and her head twisted completely around the wrong way.

WISDOM 2

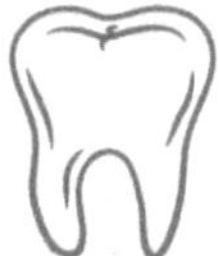

Heir and Spare

THREE WEEKS EARLIER...

It was a bad idea from the get-go. Our little family of three had been in the Otherworld less than a week. I had yet to organize the new nursery that'd been hurriedly created in anticipation of our arrival, nor had I completely unpacked the limited Mundane necessities I'd been allowed to bring along for our exile. Exhaustion followed me like a winter shadow, as I was still not back to my normal self so soon after Dylan's birth. Sitting for long periods of time was an uncomfortable exercise in futility, not that there was much time for the luxury of reclining. Perhaps if Declan's asinine father had waited just a few more weeks, the *Mac Nuadas* might have been more open to being put on display like prize hogs at a county fair, though, in truth, I doubt I would ever be comfortable with the Fae need for pomp and ceremony. Our personal feelings mattered little to my self-serving, jerk of a father-in-law. When his Lordship Callum Fitzpatrick *Nuada* told you to jump, you were supposed to gratefully ask how high.

That whole incident of my going over his Lordship's head to The Morrigan in regards to where I'd give birth put an even larger rift between the Tax Man's *athair* (father) and me, one I expect never to be completely healed. I was upfront with Declan about what had gone down, regaling my husband with the shocking story of how I'd summoned Her Majesty to our Salem home in order to assure that our son would be born in the Mundane world as we had both planned. In all honesty, there was no other choice but for me to come clean. The fact that his normally acrimonious, disagreeable *mathair* (mother), whom I made no secret of detesting, was present at Dylan's birth by my own request, did not go unnoticed by my husband. However, I did leave out certain parts of the story; like how his Lord *Athair* insisted my missing husband was dead, even going as far as attempting to officially name our baby House *Nuada's* heir, while at the same time plotting to rid himself of a troublesome tooth fairy daughter-in-law by marrying her off to the youngest son of House *Badh*. The Tax Man was in no shape, physically or mentally, to hear such stomach-turning details.

Because I knew I was already on his Lordship's hit-list, when he came to us with his plan to throw a huge "Welcome Home Heir and Spare" party, I smiled sweetly and thanked him for his graciousness rather than giving him the good sock to the gut he deserved. Even Dragon Mama, who normally never passed on the opportunity to show-off to the neighbors, seemed reluctant over her mate's idea and questioned whether it might be more prudent to wait until Declan was more physically and magically healed. Despite his body repairing itself faster in the Otherworld, my husband still bore the marks of his horrible experience in North Korea, and his magical energy was nearly non-existent. Lord *Nuada's* response to his wife's suggestion was as selfish as the man himself. "'Tis a good thing for everyone to see how much House *Nuada* has sacrificed for The Crown," the bastard replied, "lest the others forgo the respect we deserve."

From my own perspective, "House *Nuada*," sacrificed nothing. It was Declan, and Declan alone, who stood as oblation for the safety of the Otherworld. Still, I was also finding it difficult to understand my husband's sense of shame and embarrassment over the injuries he sustained while being a prisoner. It wasn't as if any of what happened to him was his own fault. The blame for that rested solely on the shoulders of one person...that evil bitch, Marcy Kilcrabtree. It also seemed odd to me that since we'd returned to *Dun Siorai*, my *Mo Shiorghra* was being increasingly reluctant to leave the privacy of our quarters, taking meals alone with just me as company, and only meeting with a very small circle of friends. With this being his mindset, it was beyond my understanding as to why he agreed to his father's grandiose celebration, an event where he'd be so publicly on view.

Despite any and all reservations, Lord *Nuada* went ahead with his overblown *coisir* (party). Declan and I were expected to stand for hours while most of *I Idir* flowed past us, offering gratitude for my husband's service and congratulatory gifts meant to honor the birth of House *Nuada's* newest heir. In complete contrast to Mundane customs, where sleepers, blankets and diapers are traditional gifts, Fae protocol declares that silver is the trademark gift for newborns, and the collection of shiny cups, spoons, baby rattles, coins and jewelry next to us grew to a sizeable pile that I knew would ultimately be melted down and its revenue added to House *Nuada's* treasury. We were dressed in *Nuada* gold and maroon, and, as his Lordship had specifically ordered the staff, our clothes were made to the same sizes we wore on our handfast day the previous summer. Thus, Declan's tunic and pants hung on his gaunt, starved frame, and I, with my postpartum figure, found myself busting out of my gown, my nursing boobs leaking and leaving a stain on the dark fabric every time Dylan whimpered. I didn't even want to begin to contemplate my father-in-law's reasoning behind us wearing ill-fitting clothes, though I have no doubt he felt it somehow benefited him or the image he wanted us to present to his all-important guests.

The turn-out for the event was more than respectable. The *Sidhe* Lords and Ladies of the Ruling Council, along with most of their heirs, were in attendance, as well as a trove of *I Idir's* top movers and shakers. Much to my father-in-law's annoyance, Her Majesty, Queen Maeve, along with her immediate family and inner circle, sent regrets, saying they all would meet with Lord and Lady *Mac Nuada,* and their new son privately at a later date. I was relieved for Declan's sake, as I knew how self-conscious he would feel facing his Queen in the abused state he currently found himself in.

After nearly two hours of mindless meet and greet protocol, I was about to excuse myself to go and nurse Dylan, when chaos itself waltzed through the wooden doors of the main ballroom. The Tax Man noticed them first, and I could hear him murmur, "Feckin' hell," under his breath.

I looked up from Dylan's cradle to see my husband's long-time nemesis, Lord Cillian *Mac Badh*, making his way toward the line snaking up to the dais where we were standing. *Mac Badh's* presence was bad enough, as it was no secret that he and my husband didn't get along, the animosity between them recently made worse by Duncan besting Cillian's man with the long sword. Still, it wasn't the pompous young Fae male that caused the reaction it did, but the woman on his arm, the one and only Marcella Crabtree.

WISDOM 3

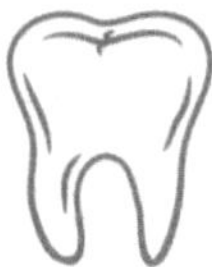

The Good and *Mac Badh* of It

PICKING the baby up from the cradle, I pivot toward Declan to comment on Marcy's surprising and very unwelcome appearance. That's when the whole scenario turned even more nightmarish. Trailing through the door behind the unwelcome gruesome twosome was Cillian's younger brother, Connor...the very same brother who so ungraciously offered to take me off House *Nuada's* hands when the Tax Man went missing. I had no doubt whatsoever that the dumb-ass kid would bring up that ridiculous story about handfasting me in front of Declan. *Sidhe* folk seem to have no boundaries regarding polite conversation and there was no way this could end well. All I could do was stand in horror and observe the train wreck that would certainly happen while hoping against hope there weren't too many casualties when this runaway locomotive got to the station.

As he is years younger than my husband, Lord *Mac*

Badh touches his forehead in the Otherworld protocol gesture of respect, but the solemn motion doesn't match up with the smirk on his face. There's not even a remote chance Cillian doesn't comprehend the utter contempt Declan and I hold for his escort. His bringing Marcy to this event is meant as a direct insult to the Tax Man, and the noise in the space drops a decibel or two, as all attention is now focused on the scene unfolding in the front of the room.

"I see the Universe continues to bless ya, *Mac Nuada*," the young Lord says. "A hero's welcome home AND a new heir far' yar' House. That is surely more than one man's equal share, don't ya' think? You must reveal to the rest of us which of the goddesses grant you such abundance."

"Aye, *Mac Badh*. I surely have felt overly blessed…until this moment. This is low even for you, Cillian. You shame your House with behavior of this sort." The Tax Man's voice is calm and even, but lowered by several octaves, a sign I've learned signals that he's angry.

"I ken' no' begin ta' understand what ya' mean, *Deaglean* Fitzpatrick. I've only come ta' welcome you back ta' the family fold and ta' honor yar' new son." *Mac Badh* then turns and addresses his vile escort. "Present our gift, won't you, *A Stor* (Darling)."

"Of course, my Lord." The Crabtree bitch smiles sweetly and digs into an expensive leather bag slung across her shoulder. At first glance, the gift looks similar to all the other silver baby rattles in the pile. Then, I note the extra details on each end. I put our son safely back in his bed before addressing the situation. "Hand that wretched thing to me," I growl.

"As you wish, my Lady," Marcy says with a grin as she hands me the token.

It takes my agitated brain a second or two to process exactly what I'm looking at, and I feel the flush of embarrassment rise from my neck upwards to my face. As I had noted, the rounded ends of the rattle were graced with detailed silverwork of exceptional quality but without the benefit of any decency or good taste. On one end, a Fae man's face peered up at me, the high cheekbones and arched eyebrows a match to my husband's. The mouth forms a grin, open wide like a clown's, a fool's cap sitting atop its head. The other end of the rattle is undoubtedly supposed to represent me, a woman's head with curly hair and overly round cheeks, a pig's snout where a nose should have been and a mouth full of pointed teeth.

It's such a cruel, horrid thing that I act without thinking. "You evil, whoring bitch," I mutter, then fling the rattle back at her, catching Marcy square in the lip, as the hideous toy bounces off her face, falls to the floor with a loud ping, and then rolls off the dais. Chaos immediately erupts. Crabtree goes after me, slapping at my face while I jab at her with closed fists. Both men do their best to reign us in, with Declan grabbing me around the waist and pulling me towards him, while *Mac Badh* does the same to his horrible partner in crime, but in the heat of the moment, feminine fury reigns.

"Get yar' Lady in line, Fitzpatrick!" *Mac Badh* yells at my husband.

"I would advise ya' to do the same, Cillian, but the woman ya' hold is surely no lady!" my husband counters.

It's a slam-dunk comeback, but before I can congratulate the Tax Man on his witty repartee, Crabtree hits me with a sucker punch to the right side of the face. I'll no doubt be sporting a black eye by the following morning. "You're gonna' be sorry you ever messed with me, you nasty *breagadoir* (liar)," I swear at her. By this time, both Lords are also involved in their own pushing and shoving match while other guests begin to take sides and shout encouragement from the sidelines. As I grab a handful of the bitch's braid, I catch sight of Declan's *athair* standing alone on the side of the room, his arms crossed, face expressionless, and, strangely enough, doing nothing to stop the escalating mayhem.

It's Dragon Mama who takes control of the bedlam. She steps between the four of us. "Enough! All of you!" Her voice is low and full of venom, holding to the promise of an especially virile tongue-lashing that will no doubt follow later this evening. Powerful magical energy crackles around her, reflecting her anger, and confirming to all in attendance that Lady *Siobhan Nuada* is no slouch in the magic department. Taking in her unspoken warning, the four of us stop our fussing and step back before we get a good taste of Lady *Nuada's* magical wrath.

She narrows her eyes at Declan and myself, giving us a look that would turn stone to ash. Then, she faces the gawking, stunned guests and announces, "I think we are all due for refreshments. "Tis nothing here that a good meal and fine ale can't fix. Come, let us all retire to the dining room for the evening repast."

Mac Badh opens his mouth to speak, but Lady *Nuada* stops him with a raised hand. "I will hear no more from you, Cillian McDougal. You bring this woman into my home while my only son still wears the marks of her stupid, dangerous games. Then you add insult to injury with your disgusting baby token. Take your low-born paramour and leave my home. Your presence is not welcome here. You can be assured I plan on speaking to your Lord *Athair* and Lady *Mathair* regarding your abominable behavior."

The young Fae takes a step toward Declan's mother, his face red and his hands curled into fists. "You overstep your station, Lady *Nuada*. Do you not understand who I am?" *Mac Badh* mutters as he invades more of my mother-in-law's personal space.

Bad move on Cillian's part. "Come no closer ta' ma' Lady *Mathair, Mac Badh*, lest I kick the vera' shit out of ya' in front of all of *I Idir*, let the law be damned," Declan growls as he steps in front of his mother. "Ya' know I ken' do it, even in ma' current condition, and I will gladly accept all of the Black Knight's consequences far' poundin' ya' into the ground. Take yar' foul leaman and go back ta' *Cuach an Fhithich* (Raven's Hollow). As ma' *mathair* has said, yar' presence is not welcome here."

Lord *Mac Badh* is a lot of things, but stupid isn't one of them. Declan is nearly four inches taller, and even starved as he was, has more muscle mass than the younger *Sidhe* himself currently possesses. It's also common knowledge that my husband has been personally trained by one of *I Idir's* deadliest warriors, the Black Knight himself, and is considered one of the most skilled street fighters in the Knight's A-team. Even on his best day, Cillian McDougal *Mac Badh* is no match for D.P. Fitzpatrick *Mac Nuada*.

The young Lord steps away, his eyes full of fury. He

grabs his panting escort by the arm and literally drags her toward the exit. The Fae woman looks over her shoulder at Declan and me, her face twisted with hatred. "This isn't over between us, Parker," she calls out.

"Wanna' bet on that, Crabtree?" I mutter loud enough for several people standing near us to hear. I point a thumb at my chest and then towards her. "You and me, girl. It's happening!" Then I grab for my husband's hand as I watch those two evil snakes slither out the door.

WISDOM 4

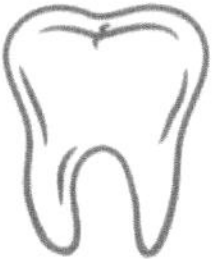

Tattle Tales

AFTER SUFFERING the circus in the ballroom, one would have thought the Universe would have freed me from also having to deal with that adolescent jackass, Connor McDougal *Badh*. I had hoped the kid would have had the wherewithal to slink out the door behind his weasel-of-a-brother, if not out of embarrassment, then at least out of some sense of House and family loyalty. This, however, turns out not to be the case. My clueless, would-be suitor intends on first taking full advantage of the lavish buffet my in-laws have provided for their guests and thus was one of the first people to arrive in the dining room.

His teen-age appetite gives me a brief reprieve as I watch the kid make several trips to the buffet. Eventually, he stuffs the last bite of a custard pastry in his mouth, wipes it with the sleeve of his shirt, and heads towards where Declan and I are sitting. I consider making a run for the restroom but figure the kid is faster on his feet than a slow-moving, postpartum-tooth-fairy-mama, so instead I quickly develop a series of subject-changing topics I can use to avoid the awkward "suitor story."

I can tell by the look on my *Mo Shiorghra's* face that he's not entirely pleased to have his meal interrupted by yet another member of House *Badh.* Still, having been trained in court protocol all his life, Declan is easily able to keep a tight rein on his personal feelings and doesn't outwardly growl at the boy as the kid touches his forehead in respectful greeting. "I am sorry ta' interrupt yar' meal, ma' Lord, but I missed the earlier opportunity ta' congratulate ya' on yar' return home and the birth of yar' son and heir." I witness Connor give me a sideways glance, one I return, which causes him to blush a deep shade of pink.

Of course, my husband, who never misses a damn thing, sees it as well and that freakin' one eyebrow of his goes up in query. "I am most grateful far' yar' kind words, Master Collin. 'Tis good ta' see ya' have reached yar' manhood. No doubt yar' a favorite among the young lasses of *I Idir.*"

The Tax Man's comment on the boy's love life is perhaps the worst one he can make in this particular situation, and I wonder if perhaps I'm not holding my mental shield tight enough. The kid turns an even darker shade of red and shifts from one foot to another in obvious nervousness. He hesitates and opens his mouth to speak while my own mouth suddenly goes dry. "As to my…faux pas regarding yar' Lady, ma' Lord, I hope you will understand that ma' intentions were of the most noble kind.

T'was nothing more than a simple misunderstandin'," the boy stammers.

Now both eyebrows are up and his Lordship's lips are pressed in a thin line. "I'm afraid ya' have me at a disadvantage, young Connor. What is this 'faux pas' ya' speak of?"

The kid grimaces and replies, "Perhaps this is a story best told by yar' own lovely Lady, ma' Lord."

"That's a good idea, Connor. I'll be sure to catch his Lordship up when we're..." I agree.

The Tax Man doesn't let me finish my sentence. He smiles, but I'm pretty sure it's not an expression of mirth, all the while raising a hand to shut me down. "Humor me, Rosalinda. I'd much prefer if House *Badh's* youngest son be the one to tell this tale." Yeah. It's never a good sign when hubby uses my full name to address me.

Declan pulls out the empty chair on the other side of him and motions to the kid that he should sit. My husband's Otherworld brogue is now so heavy, I have to listen extra carefully to understand all the words. "Cam' sattle' yarself', boy, and tal' me all about this so-called "faux pas" passin' between yar'self and ma' Lady."

I can't help but feel sorry for the kid whose face has gone two shades lighter. I can tell he'd like nothing more than to high-tail it out of this room, but snubbing a direct invite of hospitality from Lord *Mac Nuada* in his own home would be no small rudeness. In truth, even I'd like to use the little bit of magic I possess to put myself and Dylan somewhere else. Anywhere but here.

Young Master Collin sits stone-faced and silent until my husband leans over and looks him straight in the eye.

"Don' keep me in suspense any longer, lad. Do tell me yar' story."

Stuttering, the kid throws me directly under the bus. "I'mmmmm vera' surprisedddd yar' own Lady has not already informed yar' Lordship of this...this embarrassing incident. I would have thought she would have relayed the story much sooner than this."

The Tax Man doesn't even look at me. "T'was a very busy time far' ma' Lady. Ma' own return so close ta' our son's birth surely required all har' attention. No doubt this "faux pas" ya' speak of entirely slipped har' good mind. 'Tis vera' good ya' are here ta' tell me yarself'."

As a counter mechanism to his nervousness, the boy pulls a napkin from the table and begins twisting it around his hand. "I hope your Lordship will see the humor in this...miscommunication. In truth, 'tis a most amusing tale."

Mac Nuada half smiled. "I do love a humorous narrative. Best ya' just get on with it, ma' man."

"Well, you see, yar' Lordship...the rumors around all of *I Idir* were that ya' had...uhmmm...made the full sacrifice far' the glory of The Crown. Yar' probable death was distressing news, of course. But the source of this information was quite...knowledgeable, and so we believed it as told. As such, I...I thought that...in the interest of both of our houses...with yar' Lady already proven to be fertile and without a mate... I should put forth ma' interest in handfastin' her as soon as she was delivered of child. I wanted to be considered first among any other suitors."

I'm not completely sure what Declan actually thought the boy was going to tell him, but clearly, this was not the tale he expected. A flash of confusion crosses his face before he asks with disbelief apparent in every syllable leaving his mouth, "Wait…ya' came all the way ta' ma' home in the Mundane world? While I was fightin' far' ma' vera' life against the feckin' North Koreans…ta' ask ma' *Mo Shiorghra* ta' be yar' mate…even though she was so near ta' bringin' ma' son inta' the Universe?"

Master Collin appears to shrink in his chair. Unable to look up at Declan, he murmurs to the floor below him. "We thought ya' dead, ma' Lord. Yar' own Lord *Athair* believed it as well. T'was his idea far' me ta' ask after the Lady Rosalinda. Lord *Nuada* insisted this arrangement would be beneficial ta' both Houses, though he was insistent that yar' son be raised at *Dun Siorai* as House *Nuada's* new heir. My own *athair* thought it was a satisfactory joining for a third son of House *Badh*. 'Tis the vera' reason he gave his permission far' me ta' travel ta' the Mundane world on ma' own. He and Lord *Nuada* discussed the terms of the new handfasting contract in great detail before I left."

As the years go by, I swear I will never forget the look on my beloved's face at Collin McDougal's revelation. It was a mixture of shock, hurt and utter incredulity…there for only the briefest moment and then replaced once again by that smile that held no warmth. "But as ya' ken' see, Master *Badh*…I am vera' much alive… so ma' mate has no need of another," Declan answers. "And this, young Collin, is a vera' fortunate thing far' ya', as the Lady Rosalinda is a mighty fierce and insatiable lover. She would have undoubtedly shred ya' ta' ribbons durin' yar' vera' first tumble."

Not expecting this bizarre response about my supposed sexual prowess, the kid looks up in confusion and embarrassment, stumbling over his words and not daring a look at the wanton Lady Rosalinda he might have had, but didn't. "And we all give thanks that the Universe saw fit ta' return ya' ta' our fold, ma' Lord. Blessed be!" he replied in a voice that cracks. Sensing an open opportunity for escape, Collin stands up. "And now, Lord and Lady *Mac Nuada,* I shall take ma' leave. I am sure ma' dear family wonders what keeps me away from Raven's Hollow." He again salutes my husband with a respectful forehead gesture and then practically runs out of the dining room, tripping over the leg of an errant chair and nearly landing on his ass, not even slowing down to answer the shout-outs from some of his cronies.

I know better than to try and discuss such a private matter with his Lordship in such a public place. We do our best to put on complacent and cheerful faces for the rest of the day, though I fully expect to eventually face the music and explain why I hadn't told my One and Only much earlier about the whole, ridiculous debacle with Collin McDougal *Badh.*

Later that evening, when we do return to our quarters and Declan still hasn't brought up the topic, I decide to go ahead and mention it myself. I settle in the rocker to nurse Dylan before bed, then quietly ask, "Do you want to talk about it?"

Sitting across from me, he blandly returns my question with one of his own. "Talk about what, Lass?"

I sigh. I hate when he's like this; non-commutative, punishing me with silence. "You know damn well what I mean. The story that the *Badh* kid spilled at dinner. About his handfast proposal."

He shook his head. "No. I am not in the mood to discuss it right now, Rosalinda. I'd much prefer to sit har' in peace…watchin' ma' cherished wife feed ma' *stor* (darling) son. There's time enough ta' explain ta' me in the morrow why ma' One and Only would keep such a monumental incident like that from her devoted *Mo Shiorghra*."

Yup. No doubt about it. The Tax Man is definitely not happy with me.

WISDOM 5

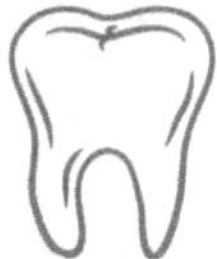

Wings

"I ᴋᴇɴ' not fathom it, Love. 'Tis of no sense at all! Why would ma' *athair* wish ta' find ya' a new husband if both ya' and ma' *mathair* told him I was still alive?" The Tax Man switches hands, doing a second repetition of one-armed push-ups while bare-ass naked. Obviously, my husband does not fight fair.

What I want to say to him is, *"He did it because your father is a narcissistic, self-serving bastard with no compassion or empathy for anyone but himself."* What I actually say is far more diplomatic. "I don't know, Sweetie. Perhaps you should ask him that question yourself?"

Finished with his push-ups, Declan pads over to the oversized door between the bedroom and bath where he's installed a make-shift pull up bar. With all the good parts facing toward the bathroom, he begins the next step in his daily routine. I watch the muscles in his arms and back, as well as the ones in his perfect ass, tighten and release as he raises and lowers himself up and down. Hot damn. "Ya' don' understand how it sits ba'twain' a Lord and his heir, Rosie Lass," he grunts. "He is ma' Liege Lord and his word rules. Once I completed The Ritual, I was no longer just his offspring. I became his *'lamh claiomh'*...his 'sword arm,' sworn to action as he sees fit."

"I get that you have responsibilities to your House, Declan, but aren't you still allowed to be your own man? And how is it that you became Duncan's Liege Lord?" I ask. "I know he's your cousin, but he's certainly not your son. How is the position the same? I know for a fact he didn't participate in that crazy Ritual thing."

Lord *Mac Nuada* lowers himself to the ground and grabs a towel to wipe the sweat from his body, making sure to drag the whole process out so that I could get a good eye full. Cheater. Wrapping the towel around his waist, he plops in the chair across the table from me. "When I was in ma' late twenties," he explains, "and still hadn't found ma' *Mo Shiorghra*, ma' *athair* made a big deal of ordering me to find another to act as ma' *'lamh claiomh.'* The task was both embarrassing and difficult for me, as it made it seem as if ma' own sire, like most of *I Idir*, didn't believe the Universe would ever lead me ta' ma' intended mate. When I asked ma' cousin ta' accept the position until the time came that I produced a son of ma' own, he instantly agreed. I was much relieved. Duncan has always known that he will need ta' relinquish the position when my own son reaches manhood. T'was a very generous sacrifice on his part, as he will lose Ruling Class status when that day comes."

We both look at our son sleeping in his heirloom

cradle, though I have no doubt the two of us have completely different emotions regarding the day he speaks of. I find the magical ritual House heirs must undertake at age fourteen to be emotionally cruel and barbaric, and the possibility that my own son might surely have to face it has weighed heavily on my mind since the moment of his conception. My husband, on the other hand, views the hundred years old tradition as a sacred responsibility, one that will define Dylan as the man he will someday become. I see some difficult discussions over this topic in our future.

"Once ma' own *athair* decided I needed a *'lamh claiomh'* until I produced a son old enough to partake of The Ritual," Declan continued, "the other House Lords followed suit. They all began seeking out trusted "seconds" for their own heirs. The Crown was strongly supportive of the trend. It kept the heirs from personally fighting among themselves, which would have undoubtedly led to petty feuds amongst their Ruling Council fathers. Now, all the heirs routinely have temporary 'sword arms.'"

This isn't a topic I want to start my day with, so I bring the subject back on point. "I get that it's hard for you to talk things over with your father, Declan. But truthfully, he was not particularly supportive of me while you were in North Korea. He was extremely angry over my calling The Morrigan to intercede in what your mother said was definitely a House problem, but I felt I didn't have a choice. His Lordship was in an all-fire hurry to cart my ass off to *Dun Siorai* despite my pleas to stay in the Mundane world and have Robyn deliver my baby in the hospital. If it hadn't been for Her Majesty...or Lady

Nuada...I'm not sure he would have cared one bit about my feelings on the subject." I pause, knowing full well that I am treading on thin ice as the "newcomer" to the family. "Please don't take this the wrong way, Sweetie, but his Lordship can be somewhat of a bully."

The Tax Man doesn't answer, instead nabbing a biscuit from the breakfast tray and slathering it with marmalade jam. He takes a bite and chews it completely before responding, as if he needs the extra time to formulate an appropriate response. "I sympathize that it might be difficult far' ya' ta' adapt ta' Otherworld culture, Lass, especially as ya' have spent almost yar' entire life living as a Mundane. But *Sidhe* men are...well...far more...masculine...in their psyches than human males. 'Tis just a fact of nature. My *athair* spent most of his life here in the Otherworld. He didna' travel ta' the Mundane world far' his education as I did, and thus his views were shaped entirely by Fae culture and tradition. He is behaving as he should...as Lord of House *Nuada.* It is not entirely fair ta' judge him by an entirely different set of rules you yar'self do not fully understand."

His words catch me totally off guard. In all the time I've known Declan Fitzpatrick, which, granted, isn't a terribly long time, I've never heard my *Mo Shiorghra* utter such a ridiculously...well...misogynistic statement. For my husband to excuse his father's narcissistic, abusive behavior as a result of my "misunderstanding" masculine Fae culture completely blows my mind. I blink a few times and take a few deep breaths in lieu of dumping the entire jam pot in his towel-covered lap. "I see," I say with more than a hint of sarcasm. "I am most grateful for your

Lordship wisely pointing out these facts to poor female me."

Apparently, the modern "husband mindset" of the Tax Man kicks in and he realizes I'm pissed. He changes his tactic, letting the towel nonchalantly drop from his hips. "I think I will head to the shower." Smiling sweetly, he adds, "Since our wee Dylan still sleeps, perhaps ma' Lady would care ta' join me?"

His blatant pandering doesn't help my nasty mood. "Your Lady would not," I say. "The baby will be up any minute now and he'll want to be fed. I don't need to be losing his breakfast in the shower." And because I'm feeling especially 'unheard,' I add, "Besides…I've grown tired of all this high-school style necking. It just leaves me frustrated."

The Tax Man's smile drops. I've obviously gone and hurt his feelings. It's not his fault we can't be intimate. It's too soon after Dylan's birth and my lady parts are not in tip-top working order. However, even if I were "good to go," so to say, his off-putting lecture about Fae masculinity was about as sexy as a major root canal. "As you wish, Lass," he says as he trots off to the bathroom without another word.

I'm not wrong about my morning schedule. Dylan wakes up less than five minutes later, howling to be fed his second breakfast. He's not quite finished nursing when his father returns to our bedroom, dressed in full leather riding gear, his still-short hair wet from the shower. Declan hadn't announced his plans for the day, so I'm required to ask. "Are you riding this morning?"

"Aye, Love. There are some horses in Avalon I am

interested in purchasing. 'Tis a long ride so I thought I'd get an early start."

"I see." This horse stuff is news to me. I have no choice but to wonder if it's in response to our disagreement this morning. His way of avoiding any further discussion on a touchy subject.

He slips on his riding boots before asking, "Da' ya' need me ta' stay here, Lass? If there's some other task ya' wish me to attend ta', I could go ta' Avalon another day."

"No. It's fine. If you have things to do, you should do them. Dylan and I will hang out here."

"Perhaps the two of ya' two could come along if ya'd like. By carriage of course," my husband offers.

I look out the nearest window at the gray, drab March sky, dark clouds off to the east foretelling of rain later in the day. Traveling for hours with a demanding newborn in the confines of a drafty, damp carriage over rough terrain is not a tempting offer. "Thanks for the invitation, Sweetie, but I think the two of us are going to pass. Your *mathair* is looking forward to visiting with Dylan today, and I promised Cook I'd pass along some of our favorite recipes so she could add them to the menu."

"I understand, *Mo Stor* (My Darling). 'Tis not a particularly lovely spring day." He kisses the top of our son's fuzzy red-haired head, then leans over to kiss me on the lips. Despite my annoyance at his earlier comments, I feel a familiar flush of desire. That's just how it is between us. It's been this way since the first time he kissed me. "I expect it will be a lengthy round trip there and back, plus the time I spend in Avalon, so do not worry if I am late in returning."

Not worrying isn't even possible. Since North Korea, I fret whenever the Tax Man leaves my side. I don't say as much. It won't help anything by bringing up the obvious. We're both trying to move past that awful experience. "Da' ya' wish far' me ta'bring ya' something back, ma' Love," he asks. "The city market in Avalon is famous far' its selection of fine wine and *milseoga seaclaide* (chocolate desserts)."

I grasp his hand and hold it to my heart. "Just bring yourself back in one piece, Tax Man. That's all Dylan and I need."

He kisses me a second time, holding his lips to mine longer than normal. "Aye, *Lonad mo Chroi* (Center of my Heart). *Le sciathain ar mo chosa* (With wings on my feet)."

WISDOM 6

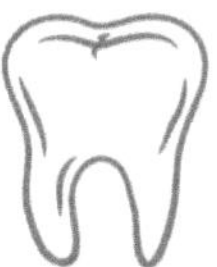

Those Damn Scones

I WATCH Declan ride away from a window that overlooks the south end of *Dun Siorai's* huge holdings. When I first visited my husband's ancestral home, before our handfast, I viewed his personal quarters, so far from the center of everything and everyone, as a planned "slight" from parents who looked unfavorably on their only son. Now, living here, I understand what this collection of spacious rooms actually is. They are far enough away from the daily hustle and bustle necessary to run such a large estate, giving its inhabitants the feeling of living in an oasis of peaceful solitude. As an added benefit, the location offers a spectacular view of the countryside from any one of its multiple arched windows and is an excellent vantage point to monitor the comings and goings of any visitors to *Dun Siorai*.

I wait until Dylan falls asleep before attempting to take my own shower, dragging his cradle closer to the bath-

room so I can hear him if he awakens. I barely undress
and turn on the water when my baby boy lets me know in
no uncertain terms that he was only interested in a very
short nap. Tossing on a robe, I rock him for nearly an
hour until he's far enough under to put back in the cradle,
and then take the quickest shower possible, opting to
braid my hair wet rather than taking the time to let it air
dry. This means it will look a tangled, weird mess when I
unbraid it before bed, but spare minutes to myself are
such a luxury that I do what I have to do to finish dressing
before the baby's next feeding.

I am already nearly an hour later than I said I'd be
when I made arrangements to meet Lady *Siobhan* in the
solar parlor. New mom's luck holding out, I'm able to
transfer the sleeping baby from cradle to pram without
waking him, thus making the long walk to the center of
the house a much quieter experience.

As expected, my husband's *mathair* is tapping her foot
over my late arrival. "The tea has gone cold waiting on
you, Rosalinda. I was required to ask Master Hobart to
arrange for a new tray. Whatever has kept you?"

I consider throwing Declan under the bus, blaming
him for taking up so much time in the bathroom this
morning, but I doubt she'd consider it a reasonable
excuse. I try honesty instead. "I'm sorry, Lady *Mathair*.
Dylan required more of my time than usual this morning.
I was late getting dressed."

Dragon Mama no longer flinches when I call her
"mother." Our time together waiting for Declan's safe
return from North Korea and Dylan's birth has changed
the dynamic of our relationship. That's not to say that

Lady *Siobhan* has lost any of her razor-sharp edge. She still has quite the bite and her sarcasm has no boundaries. But the two of us have gained enough insight over those miserable six weeks that we have now developed a more mutually respectful attitude toward the roles we play in my husband's life. I am thrilled for my Tax Man. Although he and his mother are not lovingly close, they are at least not at each other's throats, and the energy between them is not nearly as volatile as it once was.

"I still do not understand why you refuse to take on a nanny for my *aingeal milis* (sweet angel). It's unseemly in your role as Lady *Mac Nuada* not to take advantage of the traditions allowed to you by your position," my mother-in-law scolds. "We here in the Otherworld don't take to the idea that a new mother must be a slave to her own child, especially one with the resources you have at your disposal," my mother-in-law says.

"I don't wish to have anyone else caring for my son, Lady *Mathair*. I'm perfectly capable of seeing to his own needs."

She gives that shared-trait single eyebrow arch and I wonder if someday Dylan will give me that same look. "And if you go back to your life in the Mundane world, Rosalinda? Will you return to your work as a caregiver of teeth as you did before?"

"Not if, Lady Siobhan…WHEN we go back to our lives in Salem. And yes to your second question. I plan on returning to my dental practice," I say.

"Then it stands to reason that you will require someone to care for my grandson, does it not?"

She's got me there. I will need to consider daycare for

Dylan when my family leave is up. Unfortunately, with all that has happened leading up to his birth, childcare discussions were put on hold. "You're correct. I'll need someone to care for the baby when Declan and I are at work. I suppose my husband could work from home a few days a week, and I'm off on Wednesdays, but we'll probably need someone to fill in for the odd days neither of us are available."

Lady *Siobhan* laughed. "You are expecting *Deaglean* to care for the infant? At the very same time he plies his trade?"

"Of course," I say. "Most fathers today help with childcare. It's very common in the Mundane world."

"No wonder your world is the mess it is. You Mundanes are constantly fighting the natural order of things. Tell me, little mama...how many of your son's nappies has my *Deaglean* changed since his birth?"

I try not to get defensive. That kind of stance doesn't work with the Dragon Mama, but the truth is, she's got me on this one too. "Why ask if you already know the answer, Lady *Mathair*. I'm sure that somehow you are aware that Declan hasn't actually taken care of any of Dylan's day to day needs. However, in my husband's defense, he has his own healing, physically, magically and spiritually, to deal with in the aftermath of his vicious treatment by the North Koreans. I'm sure once he feels up to it, he'll cheerfully pitch right in."

With a sardonic smile she adds, "Of course. You can ask him about it when he returns from his unencumbered day in Avalon."

I'm guessing from my body language that Dragon

Mama knows she might have gone just a bit too far. I'm also pretty sure she doesn't wish to ruin the tenuous cease-fire between the two of us either. "Come…let us not ruin the day with our different philosophies, Lady Rosalinda," she says. "Though I am asking that you do me this one favor, at least while you are making *Dun Siorai* your home, of meeting with some of the candidates I've assembled as a possible nanny for my grandson. Already the staff is spreading gossip throughout *I Idir* over your stalwart adherence to Mundane ways. I request that you don't make matters worse by denying this one point. You are Lady *Mac Nuada*. You are expected to live up to the title, for my son's sake, if not for your own."

Personally, I don't give a rat's ass over what the "staff" thinks. In fact, I'm going to go as far as believing that the people who help keep *Dun Siorai* running prefer dealing with Declan and me over the Lord and Lady of the House. However, I've worked very hard to get to this level of congeniality with my husband's *mathair*, and this isn't a sword I relish dying on. At least not today when I'm already battling my husband over his father's selfish behavior. I'm not actually promising anything by agreeing to interview her candidates. My plan is to drag the decision out until it's been decided we can return to Salem. Once home, I can figure out my own daycare issues without any interference from my in-laws. "As you wish, Lady *Mathair*. I'm willing to at least meet with your suggestions of potential nannies. Perhaps it wouldn't be a bad thing to have some help with Dylan."

Lady *Siobhan* gives me a self-satisfied smile, which truthfully, reminds me of the Tax Man when he believes he's won an argument. "Excellent decision, Rosalinda. I knew I could trust you to see the sense of my suggestion. I have total faith you will come to understand how things are done when one is a citizen of *I Idir.*"

I have no intention of living full-time in the Fae Otherworld, at least not for a long, long time. Since falling in love with the Tax Man, I've become more open-minded about my Fae heritage, but I still call Salem, Massachusetts, in the Mundane world, my home. Until Declan is named Lord of House *Nuada,* a possibility so far into the future that I don't even lose sleep over it, he and I are free to live as we choose. I can throw Dragon Mama this bone and live happily with myself.

Quiet for far too long, my son begins to fuss in his carriage. I don't even put my cup into the saucer before his grandmother has him in her arms, cooing and soothing him like...well...a grandmother should. If any good has come out of Declan's kidnapping, it's the metamorphosis of *Siobhan* Fitzpatrick, a woman so different from the bitter, hopeless figure I witnessed standing on *Carraig an Bhroin.* If Lady *Nuada* once struggled with her role as a mother, she now excels in her position as *mhamo* (grandma).

Dylan's granny settles herself in a rocker in the solar parlor before addressing me. "I'm sure you'd enjoy some personal time, Rosalinda. I don't mind watching my *uan beag* (little lamb) while you attend to other things."

I figure I have another hour or so before my son needs to nurse. It would be much easier to meet with the cook without trying to sooth Dylan at the same time. I take Lady *Siobhan* up on her offer without hesitation. "I do need to speak with Cook about some dishes we'd like to see added to our menu. If you wouldn't mind keeping Dylan while I see to that, I'd be grateful," I ask.

"Of course. Do what you need to do. Take all the time you need. My sweet boy and I will be just fine."

I give her a curtsy and then make my way to the huge kitchen area at the other end of the house. I feel a tad guilty about the giddiness I feel over my freedom. This is the first time since Dylan was born that I haven't been only a few feet away from him, and the lightness of personal space is so invigorating I practically skip through the halls.

"Cook," as everyone calls her, is a Fae Brownie and a member of House *Bwca*. Much of what the Mundane world has written about the Fae population of the Other-world is pure nonsense, and, as a whole, downright degrading. I could go on and on about the ridiculous notions most humans hold over their superior place in the Universe, but I won't, since my "free time" is limited and there's so much I want to do in this gifted hour. Cook's people hail from the northern part of *I Idir*, and like many of the members of Hose *Bwca*, she excels in the domestic arts. Her culinary talents are thought to be in direct competition with that of Cabler Dos, the head chef at *Crann Bethadh*. I personally have never been to The Morrigan's home here in the Otherworld, but I can attest to the fact that House *Nuada's* "Cook" surely knows her way around the kitchen.

This dreary morning, I find her in the middle of kneading dough as part of the planned evening meal. She stops when she catches sight of me, and wipes her hands on her long apron while she drops a short curtsy. "Good Morrow, Lady *Mac*. Welcome to my *cistine* (kitchen). I look forward to yar instructin' me on some of his Lordship's favorite Mundane dishes. Our *Mac Nuada* has always been a hearty eater, he has."

I find her comment odd, since the Declan I know has always seemed rather picky and overly health-conscious to me, but I assume she's been feeding him a lot longer than I have. "I appreciate your willingness to add some of these things to your normal menu, Mistress, but I don't want to cause you extra work."

"'Tis no trouble at all, Lady *Mac*. I am curious to the ways of the Mundane world. I've been told that they have food one can cook in minutes without usin' any magic."

I determine that Cook is probably referring to using a microwave oven, a topic that would require more time to explain than I currently have. "They do have means to do that, Mistress, but none of the recipes I want to share use that particular appliance."

"I am much relieved to hear that, my Lady. I am too old to be tryin' new human magic." She gestures to a fancier chair with a brocade cushion, unlike anything else in the kitchen and obviously brought in special for me to sit upon. "Please make yourself comfortable, Lady *Mac Nuada*. I am all set far' yar' trainin."

We spend the next half hour going over some entrees that are not normally part of Otherworld cuisine. The Fae woman's face lights up in curiosity and delight over my description of thin crust pizza. "And this be something his Lordship especially craves?" she asks. It's no secret that Cook dotes on my Tax Man. We discuss the types of Otherworld cheese that might work in lieu of classic Mundane mozzarella and I guess "*I Idir* pizza" is likely to make its way to a dinner table in the very near future.

"I am anxious to try these new things, dear Lady. Is there anythin' else ya think Lord *Mac* might like?" she asks.

"The only other thing I can think of that might be a nice surprise would be some blueberry-lemon scones for tea time," I say. "I have an excellent recipe I can share." I smile at the memory of the basket of those home-made scones that were the catalyst for the Tax Man and I first connecting.

Cook crinkles her forehead in concern. "Blueberries?" she asks.

"Yes. I think you call them *smeara gorma* here in *I Idir?*" I add, proud of my growing mastery of the Otherworld Gaelic spoken here.

The Fae woman slips off her stool and wanders over to the larder, bringing back a basket of berries with her. "Ya' don' mean these fruits, do ya', Lady *Mac?*"

They definitely look like the blueberries we have in the Mundane world. I pick one up and taste it to be sure. Yup. They taste the same as well. "Yes. These are them. I make a scone studded with these berries with just a hint of citrus flavor. They're quite delicious. His Lordship is a big fan," I explain.

"I'm afraid ya' must be mistaken, dear Lady. Lord *Mac Nuada* ken' no' eat *smeara gorma*. His lips and eyes swell somethin' terrible if he dares ta'eat a single one. It's been like that since he was a boy. I only keep these berries around for Lord *Nuada.* He favors a venison sauce that requires them."

This revelation comes as a complete shock to me. "Are you sure, Mistress?"

"Aye, my Lady. Everyone who works in this kitchen knows to keep *smeara gorma* far away from Lord *Mac.*"

WISDOM 7

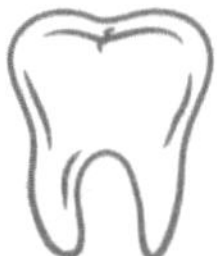

Liar, Liar...Pants on Fire

THE THOUGHT that Declan bold-faced lied to me about eating the scones I made for him that first week we met upsets me more than it should. I know it's a silly thing to worry about nearly ten months later, especially as we've come so far in our relationship since that initial encounter. Still, up until this moment, I had been under the impression that my husband didn't lie. Ever. And to find out that this belief about him might not be true was somewhat disturbing, to say the least.

I need to ponder how I wish to handle this sticky discussion with my Tax Man when he returns from Avalon, and so with a bit of time to spare before I head back to the solar parlor to feed Dylan, I take the long way back through the formal gardens that surround the west side of the estate. Since it's still early spring, the various fauna and foliage that make up the lush grounds are still quite bare, but I know by April's end this spot will be awash with a symphony of color and scent.

The garden appears deserted, so when something furry crosses my path into the hedges that back up to *Dun Siorai's* woods, I jump and let out a small shriek. The mysterious animal is followed by a very dirty boy of about seven or eight in hot pursuit. Seeing me, he comes to an abrupt stop, removes his tattered cap, and gives me a quick bow. "A thousand pardons, ma' Lady. I am hart' sarry' ta' startle ya'. Didja' happin' ta' see ma doggo come through this way?"

"Is your dog ginger colored? About this high?" I ask as I hold my hand about a foot off the ground.

"Aye. That be him," the boy says.

"Then as far as I can tell, he ran through those hedges and high-tailed it into the woods."

Before I can say anything else, I hear a gruff male voice coming from the same direction as the errant dog and boy. "When I git' ma' hands on ya', I'm gonna peel the skin right off ya' both and nail it ta' ma' cart!"

The boy's eyes go wide. "I must be gone, bonny Lady. I'd be mast' grateful if ya' dinna' mention seeing me or ma' doggo ta' the Tinker Man." Then he was off, filthy bare feet barely touching the ground as he scampered off in search of the animal.

It's only a few moments later when said "Tinker Man" makes his appearance in the garden, a wicked looking knife in his right hand. Seeing he's not alone, the startled workman immediately stops and slides the knife back in the sheath attached to his belt before removing his cap and bowing as protocol directs. "Many pardons, Lady *Mac Nuada*. I hope I dinna' give yar' hart' a fright."

"No, Master Tinker. I heard your yelling so I knew someone was coming this way. However, I am concerned about who you might be chasing with a knife of that size in your hand."

The tinker turns a deep shade of red. "Truth be, ma' Lady, I am in search of a pair of dirty thieves...one possessin' four legs, the other one walkin' on two. They done' made off with me best leather strop. Would ya' perhaps have seen them go by har'?"

I now had a better understanding of what was going on, but it irked me that a grown man would chase after a small boy and defenseless animal with a large knife. "No. I'm afraid I haven't seen anyone come this way," I lie. "They must be a fearsome pair if you need to hunt them down with such a formidable weapon."

Master Tinker turns his face, unable to lie directly to mine. "Aye, Lady *Mac*. A vera' fearsome pair."

"Perhaps you should describe them to me, kind Sir, so that I may relay to my husband that there are thieves wandering *Dun Siorai*."

It was the grown man's turn to go wide eyed. "I'm sure that won' be necessary, dear Lady. No need to worry his Lordship with ma' troubles. T'was only a leather strop, after all. Not worth yar' good husband's time."

I smile, all sweetness and refinement. "That is a relief, Master Tinker. My husband is very particular about honesty and fair play being the pillars of House *Nuada*." *Most of the time, I think as I recall Declan's lie about the scones.*

Anxious to be out of my range of attention, the tinker

gives another bow and hightails it back in the direction he came from. Once I know the man is safely gone, I wander through the hedges where I noted the boy and dog went. "You can come out now. The tinker's gone," I shout.

It takes a few minutes, but eventually the boy shyly strolls out, the dog at his side with the missing strop between his teeth. "Me and *Seamus* are vera grateful to ya', nice Lady. I dinna' wish ta' be skinned. *Seamus* neither."

I bend down and scratch the dog's head. I guess him to be a terrier of sorts, with a darling masked muzzle and a carrot shaped tail now in the throes of full wagging. "You're most welcome, young man. I assume that *Seamus* is your dog's name?" I ask.

"Aye, nice Lady. He's a fine young laddie, donna' ya' think?"

"I agree. He's a handsome pup. Although I suggest you train him not to steal other people's things. It's bound to get him into real trouble someday."

"He donna' mean anything by it, Lady. He's just a wee babe cuttin' some new teeth. He gots a mighty taste for soft leather, he does. I 'spect he'll grow out of it at some point."

"And you?" I question the boy. "Who might you be?"

"They call me *Buaf*. It means "toad" in Mundane English in case ya' were wonderin'."

"Pleased to make your acquaintance, Master *Buaf*." Personally, I think it's an awful burden to name a small child after such an unattractive creature. It's bound to cause him some grief when he's older. "My name is Rosie. Do you live near here?"

The boy points to the large house behind him. "Oh, I live there. At *Dun Siorai*."

"You do? Well, what a coincidence. I live there too."

"Truth be?" the boy questioned. "I ain't seen ya around befar'. Are ya' a guest of Lord and Lady *Nuada*?"

"You could say that," I laugh.

"'Tis good to know ya' Lady Rosie. Me and *Seamus* hope to meet up with ya' agin', but now we must be gettin' back to the big house. Cook will tan ma' backside far' bein' gone so long."

"If Cook scolds you, just tell her you were busy 'helping' Lady Rosie. Hopefully, that should spare you some grief."

With a tip of his hat, the boy gives me a huge grin, allowing me to see the dreadful state of his teeth. The dentist in me shudders. Still, despite the dirt and grime, the boy has a handsome little face with unusual gray eyes and fiery, copper colored hair. I think perhaps I'll do some research and locate his parents. If he lives at *Dun Siorai,* chances are good his parents are staff members who were afforded residency under its roof. Maybe there was something I could do to improve the state of my new found friend, especially those horribly neglected teeth.

WISDOM 8

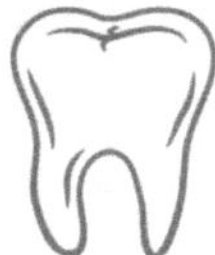

The Tax Man Tells His Tale

IT TAKES two days before I decide how I best want to handle the "blueberry scone controversy." Truthfully, I thought I was being rather clever in my method, one that offered Declan the chance to bring it up on his own rather than me having to tell the tale which would put him directly on the defensive. I ask Cook to bake a small batch of four scones as part of our morning breakfast tray. The poor woman was beside herself, fretting that she would surely lose her position if she sent anything containing blueberries to Lord *Mac Nuada*. I swear to her that I absolutely would never, ever let my beloved *Mo Shiorghra* eat the forbidden fruit, and that I would take full responsibility for requesting these scones. Not wishing to upset the newest member of the household, Cook agrees to do as I ask.

When our breakfast tray arrives, my husband is still in the shower after his morning run, so I put everything out and wait patiently for him to finish and dress. I almost chicken out twice before he joins me, and even consider hiding the damned things in the pockets of my gown rather than dredging up old issues. However, the larger part of me is dying of curiosity to know what possible reasons the Tax Man would have had to lie to me about something as silly as a food allergy.

As he usually is after a morning run, Declan comes to the breakfast table relaxed and cheerful, making me more than a little guilty as he kisses both Dylan and I "good morning" before taking his customary seat. In too deep to turn back now, I smile sweetly and say, "I have a surprise for you, Sweetie. Do you recall that I told you I met with Cook the other day about including some of my own recipes to our meals?"

"Aye," he says as he pours tea into my cup and then his own. "I am vera' much lookin' forward to a havin' a taste of home. Cook is a kind soul to do that far' us."

My mouth goes dry, but in for a penny, in for a pound, I uncover the basket containing the scones. "Remember how I made these for you after I spilled the coffee in your lap, Declan? And then how you insisted on returning the basket to me? I think I knew I was in love with you right then and there! I thought having them again would be a nice walk down memory lane."

His body language goes tense while his mental shield slams firmly into place. He doesn't take the basket from my hand so I place it back down on the table in front of him. "My memory seems ta' be a bit different than yar' own. As I recall, Lass, ya' weren't all that pleased ta' see me at yar' front door. In fact, ya' fiercely scolded me for returnin' yar' basket and then threw me out of yar' house," my husband relates.

"I know, Sweetie. I already said I was sorry about that. I was really feeling awful that night. Plus, I was mortified over you seeing me at my absolute worst and then hearing me vomit like I did." Being the evil bitch I am, I push the basket closer to him. "But today we can laugh over the whole incident, right?" I reach in and pull out a single scone and hold it up. "I propose a scone toast...to good times and good memories."

I watch as he gingerly picks up the biscuit, careful to avoid touching any obvious blueberries, and then raises it up as I had done. It's unbelievable to me that he'd let it go this far without coming clean over his dishonesty. "Aye... ta' the most wondrous time in ma' life and the Lass who is at the heart of it." Then I watch in absolute horror as he brings the scone to his lips.

I don't even stop to think. I reach out and slap the scone out of his hand, perhaps a tad too hard, because the damn thing flies out of his grasp and ends up across the room. "Seriously, Tax Man...were you really going to eat those blueberries just to avoid admitting that you lied to me? Make yourself sick over it?"

Part of me is relieved when he laughs. I suppose it's better than him getting all cranky about it. On the other hand, he's still not apologized for being less than honest so early in our relationship. "I am glad that ya' didna' make me actually bite into it, Rosie Love. I was wonderin' if ya' were gonna take this prank that far," he says.

"It's not a damn prank, Declan. When Cook mentioned you were allergic to blueberries, the realization that you lied to me about eating the scones I made especially for you hurt my feelings."

He holds up a hand. "To be clear, Love, I never lied ta' ya' about that. If you carefully recall the entire incident, I never once said that I had actually eaten them. As ya' never asked, I was never required to answer."

"Bullshit," I counter, feeling less guilty and more aggravated. "I specifically recall a certain email in which you said that you normally don't eat 'junk food' but that you took a chance and regretted it now because you believed I had poisoned you. Sounds like 'a whopper' to me, Mr. Tax Man!"

"I suppose ya' could look at it like that, Love, but if I told ya' how nervous I was about cockin' it all up with ya', would ya' forgive me?" he asks.

"I'm supposed to believe that Salem's most notorious playboy was ever lacking confidence with the ladies?" I reply. A flicker of hurt crosses his face, and I regret being so casually flippant. If anyone was "cockin" something up, it was me at this moment.

My *Mo Shiorghra* takes my hand into his across the table. I squeeze it in return because now I just feel shitty. "I will tell you this one more time, Rosie, and I hope ya'll' finally understand the truth of it. I know it will be difficult far' ya' ta' fully understand, not havin' never gone through anything like this, and I'm well aware of how ya' feel about The Ritual custom, but 'tis part of who I am. I also know ya' will think I am exaggeratin' when I say that I knew ya' were ma' 'chosen' the moment ya' walked into yar' office on that first day I met ya'. I felt this over- whelmin' sense of ma' emotions...ma feelins'...suddenly unlocked after all those damn years. It was vera', vera' intense and I was admittedly flustered. It was like I'd never spoken ta' a woman before in ma' entire life. You spillin' that coffee on me saved me from makin' even more of an ass of myself than I already was doin'."

"You didn't make an ass of yourself. I was already smitten with you …tongue-tied and wholly out of place," I counter.

"And mar' beautiful to ma' eyes than ya' ken' ever imagine, Love. I practically ran out of the feckin' office so I could breathe again. I didn't know what ta' do. I dinna' know a single thing about ya' except that I was crazy, over the moon far' a woman I had spent less than five minutes with! I spent hours googling everything I could find about Dr. Rosie Parker. I'm sure if ya' would have known about that ya' would have thought me some creepy stalker, but I was desperate."

"Oh, Declan…" It's all I can muster. I've heard parts of this story before but with our hands connected like this I can actually feel everything he's feeling as he tells me his story. I'm the one overwhelmed now.

"Then," he continues, "when Eleanor related how ya'd come to the office ta' see me, I just about fired her on the spot for not lettin' me know ya' were there, even though I'd been the one who expressly told har 'not ta' disturb ma' conference call. I never in a million years expected ya' ta' come ta' me. She gave me the basket with the scones and I knew I dinna' dare eat a single one, so I just kept them, admirin' 'em, until they got all hard and moldy and I had to throw them out. Returnin' the basket was just ma' way of seein' ya' again…seein' where ya' lived…and ta' double-check that what I had felt in yar' office was the same a few days later. And I did. Feel the same, I mean. I wanted ta' tell ya' how I felt but ya' clearly dinna' seem ta' care far' me and when ya' sent me away, I was so angry with ma'self' for ruinin' it all…"

"It wasn't you, Declan. I looked terrible…messy and sick. I didn't want you to see me like that," I say with a deep ache in my throat. "I didn't mean to make you feel bad. I was just…unsure of everything. I couldn't imagine that someone like you would want someone like me…"

"Then we were both in the same bad way, Rosie, ma' Love. But when I saw yar' name on the list the Black Knight gave me of tooth fairies I needed ta' investigate…I knew. Knew it then an thar' that this was proof the Universe was movin' us together. I never thought you were a traitor, Lass. I saw the Black Knight's orders to protect ya' as ma' chance ta' work at makin' ya' feel more comfortable 'round me. It was a strange path, but I trusted that the Universe would have its way. I am forever glad that I did."

My voice is almost squeaky now, unshed tears burning at the back of my throat at the most romantic profession of love any woman could ask for. "I heard you," I finally admit, months later, "…that afternoon in my loft when you were working on my taxes. I was bringing up the tea tray and I heard you talking to yourself. You called me 'Sweet Rosie Lass.' I nearly dropped the tray when I heard that. It made me so happy."

"Then I bless the Universe for lettin' ya' hear it, Love. It makes the memory of a difficult day sweeter to ma' thoughts." He reaches for my other hand, just as our son begins his morning symphony of wails. "I am truly sorry for bein' less than honest with ya, ma' Sweet Rosie Lass. I truly thought if I told ya' I was allergic ta' yar' blueberry scones ya' might be too hurt…or too embarrassed…ta' ever take a chance on seein' me again. I wasn't willin' to risk it."

"I'm glad you didn't tell me, Tax Man. Because you're right. I probably would have been really, really embarrassed. I would have taken it as a sign that we weren't meant to be together and would have completely avoided you from then on. I shudder to think about it." I let go of my husband's hands and rise from the table to rescue my son from his cradle. I pause, suddenly getting philosophical over the events of this morning. "You know, Sweetie…it's funny how we often miss the really important signs, the ones staring us right in the face, for others that don't matter in the least."

That prophetic statement would come to mind many times over the course of my life.

WISDOM 9

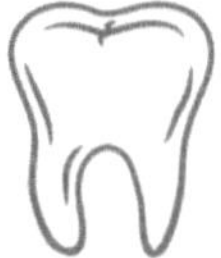

Daddy Duty

I DAWDLE GETTING DRESSED, enjoying the solitude and knowing the Tax Man is attending to our son. His *mathair's* insinuation the other day that Lord *Mac Nuada* didn't expect to share in Dylan's care rubs my Mundane self the wrong way. Thus, I make a point of taking longer with my toiletry than usual this morning in the hopes that my hubby will be required to change at least one diaper. In truth, he hasn't once offered to take on the chore. Then again, I've jumped in to handle it myself at every given opportunity, so perhaps I am somewhat to blame for his delay in pitching in. With that in mind, I work the lavender oil conditioner through my long hair knowing perfectly well it needs to sit on my head for at least fifteen minutes.

His Lordship is agreeable, if a tad surprised, that I ask him to stick around this morning so that I could shower and dress without dragging the cradle behind me.

Normally, once he's finished his early rising routine, Declan is immediately out and about, handling the myriad of things he's planned for his day. As today is Tuesday, I'm aware that he has scheduled a meeting with Rory Dell regarding his Mundane business holdings. I'm also aware that Rory doesn't cross over until at least 6:00AM Salem time, which calculates to 11:00AM the next day here in the Otherworld, meaning he has nothing especially pressing to do before then, so I have little guilt over keeping him here in our quarters.

By the time I leave the peaceful solitude of the bathroom, I can tell *Mac Nuada* is tapping his foot in anticipation of turning our wee Dylan back over to me. The baby is complaining loudly, and noting the way my fastidious husband is wrinkling up his handsome nose, I guess that our baby boy needs a diaper change.

"'Tis good yar' finished, Lass. From the smell of things, I think our *coinin beag milis* (sweet little rabbit) needs a cleaner bottom." He attempts to hand the baby back to me.

I put both hands up. "If you knew he needed a change, why didn't you just go ahead and change him?" I ask.

He looks at me as if I've suddenly grown three heads. "Me?" he questions. Then he awkwardly forces out a laugh, the baby still in limbo between us. The Tax Man isn't kidding. His Baby Lordship is pretty ripe. "I'm hopin' that yar' just tryin' to tease me, Lass. I ken' not' imagine that ya' really mean far' me ta' change his dirty nappy."

"Why wouldn't I?" I ask. "You're his father. Plus, we brought Mundane disposable diapers with us...at least the ones that arrived undamaged. I find it difficult to believe that a man who can speak twenty-seven Mundane languages and only the goddess knows how many Otherworldly ones, who can run multiple lists of numbers in his head while humming a tune, and vanquish just about anyone in *chaturanga* (an early form of chess), is unable to figure out a pre-folded diaper with self-stick tabs!"

The chin comes out, the eyebrow goes up, and a stand-off has undoubtedly begun. "Is this the penance far' me bein' less than honest about yar' scones, Lass?"

It's exactly the wrong thing to say. "I can't believe you just said that, Declan Phineas Fitzpatrick! Do you truly believe that taking care of our son is some kind of punishment? Or is this your way of "lording" it over me? A not-so-thinly-veiled-statement that the care of our child is somehow below your title?" Okay. I'll concede my last comment was a little below the belt. I know without a doubt that my Tax Man tries especially hard not to wear his "station" on his sleeve, and accusing him of doing just that will prick his conscience.

"I would hope that ma' own *Mo Shiorghra* would know me well enough to realize the title does no' make the man. If this means that much ta' ya', Rosalinda, then I will attend ta' wee Dylan's messy bottom ma'self, though I am askin' that ya' at least remain near in case I run into any trouble," his Daddy Lordship says.

I ignore my husband's use of my full name. "Absolutely, Sweetie," I say, careful not to sound as if I'm gloating. "I'll be right here next to you."

Declan carries the baby over to the low dresser we've adapted as a changing table. "Ya' and I will figure this out together, *fear beag mo chroi* (little man of my heart). I will have yar' word, Master Dylan, that ya' will not piss on yar' *daidi's* (daddy's) favorite tunic."

Although I brought a small amount of Mundane baby clothes with me from Salem, I've found the Otherworldly, gown-style infant wear to be far more convenient than struggling a squirmy infant into one-piece sleepers. No snaps or leg holes makes it easier to flip the gown up and take care of business. As the Tax Man proceeds, we both get a whiff of what awaits, and I hear him unconsciously gag. I'm half-tempted to just give in and take over, but I know if I do, I will have lost this golden opportunity forever. "You're doing great, Sweetie. Try to fold all the poop inside, then you can just sort of roll it back-up and reseal it with the sticky tabs."

My husband turns to me, eyes watering, while he tries to speak without holding his breath. "Is it always this… messy?"

I shrug. "He's a nursing infant…so pretty much. Be thankful we're not using the cloth nappies your *mathair* suggested. They leak all over."

Before his Jr. Lordship can comment, there's a sharp rapping sound at one of our windows. Like always, it startles me and makes me jump. "'Tis most likely a raven-gram. Will ya' take possession of the message, Love?" Declan murmurs between clenched teeth.

I hesitate. I detest those beady-eyed, black-feathered, gossip-mongers. The thought of getting close enough to one of them to retrieve the scrolled parchment from its pointy, clawed beak makes me queasy. Plus, there's a definite possibility that the evil bird will get a good look at Declan struggling with Dylan's diaper and gleefully spread what he sees all over *I Idir*. Although I don't agree with the Fae's unenlightened views on gender roles, I'll be damned if I'll give that ugly, cawing, tattle-tale more dirt to spread about my husband. "I'm sorry, Sweetie. But you know how I feel about the ravens. Maybe you should go get the message yourself."

Like a man receiving a stay of execution, the Tax Man tries to keep the look of relief off his face. "If that's what ya' wish, Love, then I will see to it. Ya' will have to take over ma' job with the wee rabbit," he says, as he hands me the wet washcloth he's about to use on Dylan's bottom.

"I understand, Tax Man. But this doesn't mean there won't be a next time."

He doesn't respond, in a hurry to attend to the raven who's begun another round of tapping at the window, more insistent than the previous pounding. When Declan opens the glass, the raven hops onto the inside windowsill. Out of the corner of my eye, I see the green and gold ribbons tied around the scrawny legs of the bird, and my heart beats a tad faster in my chest. Green and gold are the colors of House Morrigan. The message is no doubt from Her Majesty, and I wonder what new chaos is in our future.

Lord *Mac Nuada* unrolls the scroll and reads it without speaking. His face gives nothing away, but his body language and mental state is relaxed, so whatever news the damn bird has brought, it isn't causing my husband any concern. He speaks directly to the bird, "My Lady is attendin' to our son. She will send a response with one of our own ravens shortly."

The message-bearer turns its shiny, black head toward

me, as if to verify that Declan is telling the truth, then flies off with a flutter of its wings, still leaving me in the dark over the scroll's contents. "Send a response to what?" I ask. My voice is higher than normal, an outward sign of my concern. From experience, I've learned that raven-grams rarely bring tidings of good cheer.

"It seems ya' been invited to *Crann Bethadh* for afternoon tea with the Lady Dear Heart, Lass. She specifically states that ya' should bring our son along with ya', as she looks forward to meeting the newest member of House *Nuada*. When ya' finish up with Dylan, we will have ta' compose the proper response and send it off as soon as possible."

Proper response? Do I have any other choice but to graciously agree? It doesn't seem likely one can send regrets to an 'invitation' offered by a member of the Royal family.

WISDOM 10

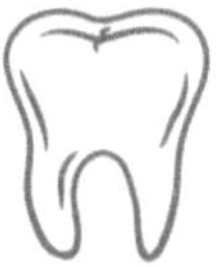

The *Scathach*

THE REST of the day leading up to my invitation to *Crann Bethadh* is spent "preparing" for it. Apparently, getting an invitation to the Seat of *I Idir* is a big hairy deal, one requiring a whole cache of protocol requirements; a gracious reply, the correct attire, an appropriate hostess gift, an acceptable means of transportation, and a temporary "nanny" for Dylan, which I'm told is highly expected.

"You didn't really plan on changing dirty nappies in front of the *Banphrionsa*, did you Rosalinda?" the Dragon Mama scolds. "It's not like I haven't already explained to you, in great detail, what your station requires of you."

"And what am I supposed to do if he's hungry? Not feed him?" I ask.

"Nursing one's infant in the presence of other females is perfectly acceptable. But the focus of your visit should be limited to lighthearted conversation with the Lady Dear Heart. Under no circumstances are you to discuss anything…political…or any topic having to do with the governing of *I Idir*. And it goes without saying that any 'family issues,' yours or hers, are entirely off limits. Am I making myself clear, Lady *Mac Nuada*?"

"Clear as glass, Lady *Mathair*," not bothering to hide my sarcasm.

She gives me a frosty look, then changes the topic to the hostess gift she's selected for me to bring; an ebony trinket box with an image of a raven head carved into the lid, a genuine green sapphire in place for its eye. I don't find it particularly attractive, but then what do I know about gifts for Fae princesses? I recall the beautiful hand knit baby blanket that Lady Dear Heart sent when Dylan was born, and decide it will be what I wrap my son in for this visit so that I can tell Her Highness just how much her token meant to me. I wish I had something I've personally made to give her in return, but remembering to pack craft supplies beyond a small bag of my miniature needlework was not a high priority when we left home.

The worst part of this whole experience is having both my husband and his *mathair* discuss my apparel as if I were a mannequin without an opinion. When it comes to their personal appearance, it's hard to say which of the two of them is the fussiest…or do I dare to say…vain? Granted, both my husband and my mother-in-law always look like they've just stepped out of a fashion shoot, whether it's one in the Mundane world or here across the Veil. Everything about them says "put together," whether they're off to buy horses in Avalon or meeting with other Ruling House ladies to play card games. Fashion has never been my forte, and so I stand there like a useless lump of clay and let the two of them "mold" me into someone ready to have tea at *Crann Bethadh*.

My "fashion team" has decided on understated, daytime elegance. My fitted and lined chemise is made of finely woven linen in a winter white, with molded bra-like cups and mother of pearl buttons completely down the front and worn without a corset to allow for easier nursing. This is paired with a striking tartan plaid skirt in house colors that fits directly under my bust line, as I still have no waist so soon after giving birth. My hair's been braided up in some complicated Celtic pattern, held in place with a simple gold comb, and Lady *Siobhan* clasps an elegant gold chain with a walnut-sized garnet around my neck. I wear my handfast ring along with the simple gold band from my Mundane wedding as I always do, despite my mother-in-law's complaints that the blue stones clash with all the maroon and gold of the rest of the ensemble. I couldn't take the rings off even if I wanted to, which I don't, and I draw the line at wearing gloves to hide them.

Even as I board the carriage ordered to take me the three miles to *Crann Bethadh*, my husband and his mother bombard me with a series of "dos and don'ts" to the point of ad nauseam, while the temporary nanny, a pale, silver-haired female, Elven-born of pixie descent and dressed in leather breeches and tunic, holds the bassinet-style basket with my son on her lap. By the time the enclosed hackney pulls away, I'm ready for the whole afternoon to be done and over with.

Truthfully, bouncing around in the carriage does nothing for my sore lady parts, and I'm relieved when we finally pull up to the driveway. Dylan has slept the whole way there, which is not a good thing. It means that as soon as he wakes, he's going to be calling out to be fed. "Try not to wake him, if at all possible," I instruct the nanny. "I would like to at least get a chance to greet the *Banphrionsa* before I have to whip out a boob."

The pixie puts a hand over her mouth to hide her grin, the first normal reaction I've seen from her since we left. "Yes, ma' Lady. 'Tis best to let sleeping babies lie far' as long as ya' can. The wee new ones like his little Lordship have the appetite of a wolfhound."

Her odd comparison makes me laugh, though she's not wrong. I swear I spend most of the day with our son latched onto my boobs. "Have you ever been to *Crann Bethadh* before?" I question the nanny.

"Aye, Lady *Mac Nuada*. Many times. I sometimes nanny far' the Lady Dear Heart when the Lady Fury is not available."

"Lady Fury?"

"Aye, Ma'am. She has been the youngest *Banphrionsa's* nanny since right after her birth. Her given name is Fiona, though only those closest to her would dare call her such. I suggest using her title whenever possible."

I wrack my brain over the Otherworldly history I'm aware of. "Is she like...a real Fury?"

"That she is, ma' Lady."

"And she works as a nanny?" I ask, not quite comprehending what I know about The Furies with child care. It's a bizarre contradiction to have one of the deadliest warriors in the Otherworld rocking babies to sleep. "Isn't that a bit...unusual," I say, attempting to sound more diplomatic than I feel on the subject.

"Not if you consider who the child is, Lady *Mac*. The Lady Fury is the young *Banphrionsa's* bodyguard as well. All of the great Houses hire nannies who can equally protect as well as care for their precious infants, especially if they are the House's planned heir. As you are aware, Her Majesty has named the youngest *Banphrionsa*, the Princess Mairead, as the heir to the Throne of *I Idir*. It makes perfect sense that she would be under the watchful eye of Lady Fury."

The idea of a baby or a child needing protection of that sort shocks me, but then I recall that this pixie woman just mentioned that she sometimes "filled in" as Mairead's "nanny." "I'm sorry…I'm not sure anyone told me your name, Mistress?"

"I am called *Birgit* ma' Lady. I am great-granddaughter to Magda," the pixie revealed.

"Wait…as in Lord *Mac Nuada's* 'Magda?' His childhood *Buime* (nurse/nanny)?"

"That be the same one, dear Lady. I am tenth genera-tion *scathach*," the woman replied, unable to keep the obvious pride out of her voice. "Duly trained and marked," she adds, pushing up the sleeve of her tunic to reveal an elaborate series of inked symbols, two of which I recognize as the *Dara* and the *Ailm*, Celtic marks of courage and strength. I scramble to try and place the English translation for *scathach*, guessing that it must be similar to a Fury if *Birgit* can substitute as protection for the *Banphrionsa*. I try not to sound like a complete idiot. "So does that mean that your great grandmother Magda was also a *scathach?*"

"Of course, dear Lady! 'Tis a role passed down from

mother to eldest daughter, not unlike yar' own tooth fairy heritage."

Strangely enough, I don't give her mention of my tooth fairy roots a single embarrassed thought, as I'm far too busy wondering and worrying why my Tax Man needed a childhood "bodyguard," and why one was sent with us today.

WISDOM 11

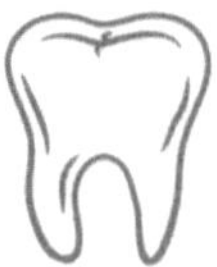

Not in Kansas Anymore, Toto

ALTHOUGH I'VE SEEN the Seat of *I Idir* at least a hundred times from afar, this is the first time I've ever been this close to the giant oak tree The Morrigan calls home. Yes. An oak tree. I'm not speaking of your Mundane style oak tree that grows to an average size of sixty or seventy feet. *Crann Bethadh*, The Celtic Tree of Life, stands over 160 feet tall and is nearly 90 feet wide, with a root system that drops twelve feet into the ground. The inside of the tree contains 143 rooms of varying size, not including a few subterranean spaces tucked away in the root system.

I can understand that it's a difficult concept to wrap your head around. From the outside, *Crann Bethadh* looks like any other living oak tree, complete with bark and branches, and sporting parachute-style leaves and bowling ball-sized acorns that drop every autumn. However, the inside of the tree serves as the ruling domain for one of the largest kingdoms in the Otherworld, much as the White House is home to the United States President and Buckingham Palace is the residence of the British monarchy. Not only seeing it up this close, but actually being invited inside, shows just how crazy my life has become since the day the Tax Man entered it.

The three of us are met at the main entrance by both valet and security staff. *Birgit* has her sleeve rolled up so that the ink marking her as Dylan's *Scathach* is easily seen by the Queen's Troll Guard. I've also never seen a troll up this close before, as they are not native to this part of the Otherworld. The small group that lives here in *I Idir* are asylees from *Asgard*, all serving as personal guards to the Queen and the Royal House. They are small, not particularly attractive, very, very fierce, and, l am told, totally devoted to The Morrigan and her House.

We are escorted to the main entrance where we are met by another group of trolls and an attractive *Sidhe* woman. She drops a curtsy and says, "Welcome to *Crann Bethadh*, Lady *Mac Nuada*. The Lady Dear Heart is expecting you. My name is *Aoibheann*. I am the head of the household staff. If you would please follow me, I'll take you directly to the Family Quarters."

I try not to gawk as I'm led through halls of polished oak, artwork and decor of various mediums on gilt tables, consoles and the walls themselves. Though it is still early spring, floral pieces are everywhere in abundance. I must not be shielding very well, because *Aoibheann* smiles at me and remarks, "Her Majesty is partial to flowers year 'round. We have a special greenhouse on the grounds specifically to attend to the House's floral needs."

I hope the heat I feel crawl up my neck isn't too obvious, and I put more strength into my mental shield. "They are incredibly beautiful, *Aoibheann*. Please give my regards to your…horticulturalists."

The housekeeper smiles pleasantly at me. "I will surely pass your compliment along to them, Lady *Mac Nuada*. It pleases them to know that others take note of their efforts."

Aoibheann leads us to what appears to be an elevator, which all things considered, seems strangely Mundane, located as it is inside…well… a tree. Despite there being no buttons to push or flashing LED signs to track off the floors, I feel the chamber rise upward. I assume it's moving via mental magic and goofy me has the uncontrollable urge to say, "Hell's bells, Toto…I have a feeling we're not in Kansas anymore," but I don't because I figure no one in this particular group will get the *Wizard of Oz* reference anyway.

The elevator doors open and we step into another hallway of polished wood with more artwork, these all having ravens as their main subject matter. I deduce that we must be in the section of the fortress that acts as living quarters for The Morrigan's inner circle. Dylan begins to fuss in his carrier basket and I inwardly groan. He's due for a feeding, and like his Mama, patience doesn't seem to be one of his virtues. No doubt I'll have to feed him sooner than later. I'm hoping as a mother herself, the *Banphrionsa* will be understanding of the necessity of my need to nurse my baby as soon as the formalities of a greeting are over.

The corridors twist and turn in every direction and by now I have no idea how to get back to the elevator. At the end of one particularly wide hallway, are a set of intricately carved doors with more ravens and Celtic symbols, equipped with large iron handles. *Aoibheann* knocks and then enters without waiting for a response. She drops a curtsy and both *Birgit* and I follow suit. The *Banphrionsa* is standing at the window looking out, and when she sees me, she rushes over, breaking protocol by throwing herself into my arms. "Rosie Fitzpatrick! It's so good to see you! I'm thrilled you could come on such short notice. I wanted to invite you sooner, but Himself insisted you needed time to 'acclimate' yourself to life in *I Idir*."

I return the hug which feels totally genuine to me. "I am most honored by the invitation, Your Highness. Thank you."

The princess pulls away and smiling, grasps my hands. "Unless Herself is in the room, there's no need for any of that protocol nonsense with me, Rosie. My friends and family call me 'Maureen'...or 'Mo' for short. I'm hoping you will as well."

An image of Mo, Curly and Larry of The Three Stooges suddenly pops into my head and I quickly shove it away. Still, the thought of referring to The Morrigan's great grand-daughter...the *Banphrionsa* of *I Idir* as "Mo" is out of the question, so I go with "Maureen." "That's very sweet of you. Thank you...Maureen."

She leans over to admire my son, who now has gone red-faced and wailing. "And this little guy with the loud opinion must be wee Dylan." She looks at me. "May I?"

I assume she's asking permission to pick my son up. "Absolutely," I respond.

The princess leans over and picks up Dylan even as he continues to fuss. "Well, aren't you just the most handsome little lad!" She eyes him critically. "I hope you aren't offended, Rosie, but I think he's the spitting image of his daddy."

I laugh. "No offense taken, Your Hi... Maureen. I get that a lot. He does heavily resemble his father."

Still with Dylan in her arms, the *Banphrionsa* adds, "I can sympathize. Except for the red hair, my *Mairead* is one hundred percent her father's daughter. I suppose you can never tell what the genetic roll of the dice will bring. Out of seven siblings, only my brother Kevin and I inherited any Fae DNA. Same parents and all. Go figure," she says, her Boston accent sounding like a touch of home here in the Otherworld.

Dylan is now flinging his hands and howling, a sure sign the boy is ready for nursing. "It seems his little Lordship is intent on being fed." Addressing the housekeeper, the princess says, "*Aoibheann*, why don't you take *Birgit* to the nursery so she can visit with Lady Fury and *Mairead*. Once Lady *Mac Nuada* has finished nursing the baby, we'll have our tea and they can all join us."

"I will do just that, Your Highness. Please let me know when you are ready for tea service." *Aoibheann* and *Birgit* both drop a curtsy before exiting, leaving me alone with Dylan and the Lady Dear Heart.

The princess leads me to a comfortable looking rocker with a footstool near the window. "I've found this to be the most comfortable chair for nursing, Rosie." She signals that I should take a seat and then hands me my son. "You go ahead and feed him. If you're uncomfortable with me being here, I can go into the bedroom until you finish."

I certainly don't want to make a nuisance of myself by asking the *Banphrionsa* to wait in another room. Besides, I'm guessing with her own daughter being less than a year old, she's probably still nursing as well. "I have no problems with you staying, Maureen. It was nice of you to ask, though."

Her Highness, Princess of House Morrigan, plops herself in very un-lady-like fashion into a chair next to me. "I'm so glad I can stay and visit with you, Rosie. I swear I'm going crazy these past few weeks, shut away like a prisoner. Completely bored to tears. Ted's almost never here, my brother is busy with church stuff, and truthfully, I'm really looking forward to some good old-fashioned girl-friend talk with someone from back home."

WISDOM 12

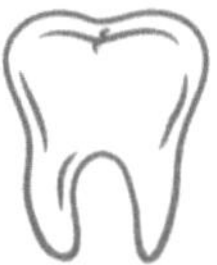

Baby Talk

THE IDEA that the *Banphrionsa* of *I Idir* considers the Mundane world her "home" is surprising enough, but the suggestion that she and I are "girlfriends" completely throws me off my game. We've met on a number of occasions, the most recent being when she accompanied the Black Knight to our home to make me aware that Declan had gone missing in North Korea. And she was, of course, in attendance at both our handfasting and our Mundane wedding. Today, however, is the first time she and I are meeting one on one, in a social setting, without our husbands. I'm not sure how I expected this afternoon would go but I can say with certainty that I didn't expect her to be so…well…informal.

While I nurse Dylan, the Lady Dear Heart regales me with funny stories about her large Irish family, who other than her older *Sidhe* brother, know nothing about her Fae connections or that their great grandmother is the Celtic goddess of war and destruction. "Ted has shared with me that you have an older sister who knows all about the Otherworld." The *Banphrionsa* sighs and adds, "It must be wonderful not to hide such a monumental reality from your family. I always feel bad lying to them about almost everything."

I can't imagine having to lie to my beloved sister about such an important aspect of my life. Fortunately, that decision was taken out of our hands at a very early age, my mother insisting that she was not going to live a lie. Petitioning the Throne for permission to reveal her heritage to her spouse and children, she received authorization to do so with the sacred promise that none of us would ever breach the need for absolute secrecy. Using the history of our own hometown of Salem as an example of how people react to things they don't understand, my mother made sure Claire and I both comprehended the necessity of keeping the secret of our family heritage to ourselves. "That must be difficult...you not being able to share any of this," I wave my free hand around the room, "with the people you love."

"It's not only difficult," the Princess confesses, "it's lonely as hell. I don't have a lot of close friends either, for the same reason. It's not much fun having to watch every word you utter. Thank goodness for Roxie. I don't know what I'd do without her. She's been part of this whole magical journey from the start. Do you know the Lady Roxanne?"

I think back to the awful night of my bachelorette

party when the "Lady Roxanne" was in her other role as "Deputy Spinelli." It's not a story I want to share with the *Banphrionsa*. "We met only once…for a few brief minutes," I offer. "She was in uniform at the time." I change the subject before my hostess can ask me about it. "She's a ward of Her Majesty, is she not?"

"Yes, and that's one 'bat-shit-crazy' story in itself, though maybe you should ask your husband to tell you about it someday. I'm not supposed to 'discuss' it…if you get my drift," she says with an exaggerated wink. It's her turn to change the subject. "How 'bout you Rosie? Are you getting used to being exiled here in LaLa Land?"

I laugh at her term. The Otherworld can seem a bit over the top, especially, I suppose, when you're stuck living in a giant tree like she is. "I'm taking it one day at a time. Truthfully, I admit to being more comfortable in the Mundane world, but I'm so very grateful to have my husband back safe and sound and our son born healthy that I try to ignore the negatives, lest the Universe prove to me just how bad 'bad' can be."

"Amen to that, Lady *Mac*," the *Banphrionsa* says. "It was a scary time. We all were worried about Fitz, especially my husband. Ted thinks very highly of Lord *Mac Nuada*, you know. He took it personally when Fitz ended up captured. Thank heavens Herself intervened. In truth, she rarely interferes in events such as these for fear that she'll be accused of playing 'favorites' within the Ruling Council. My grandmother must hold your Lord in high regard if she was willing to break her own rules."

The hair on my arm stands up as my mother-in-law's

words about The Morrigan always having an ulterior motive come back to haunt me. This is most assuredly not the place to be having such thoughts. I brush them away, and once again, tighten my shields. "I'm afraid I'll never be able to show Her Majesty the depth of my gratitude for bringing Declan back to me, and in time for our son's birth, no less. It meant the world to me."

The Morrigan's great granddaughter laughed. "Well don't you worry, Rosie Fitzpatrick! Herself will most definitely let you know when and how you can show your appreciation. She always finds a way to get a return on her infrequent good deeds."

Her flippancy regarding The Morrigan shocks me, though I suppose like in every family, the *Banphrionsa* knows her ancestor better than most. Dylan has finished his nursing and has dozed off, so I cover up and place him back in his carrier. Noting this, the Lady Dear Heart asks, "Are you up for some tea, Rosie? I'll have the staff bring in the tray."

"Tea sounds wonderful, Maureen. Thank you." Remembering the gift, I dig into my tote and retrieve the wrapped token Declan's *mathair* selected for me to bring. "I brought something for you. From House *Nuada*," I say as I offer her the box.

"A gift wasn't necessary, Rosie. I'm just thrilled to have your company. As I said, it's quite dull around here. But I appreciate you thinking of me." The Princess unwraps the token and holds it up. "It's beautiful. Thank you so much."

I can tell she's being polite. Looking around the room we're sitting in, I note that the Black Knight's Lady prefers soft colors, floral prints and lots of lace, and my gifted dark ebony trinket box stands out like a sore thumb. "I have to be honest, Maureen. The Lady *Siobhan* selected your gift. It wouldn't have been my first choice either."

This makes my new-found confidant giggle. "No worries, my friend. We do have a thing for ravens around here, though personally I've never been much of a bird fan. Herself will probably scold me for telling you so."

"Whoa…do you think she heard you? Like for real?" I asked, my apprehension rising.

Maureen shrugs. "No doubt. There's nothing at *Crann Bethadh* that she isn't aware of. I'm pretty sure she can get past just about any mental shield, though Ted claims he can keep her out of his head. I'm not sure if he really can or she only lets him think that he can. Hard to say. Either way, you have to assume that if you think or say anything here in this giant fortress, she knows about it."

I give an involuntary shudder, and in return hear the slightest ghost of a laugh in my head, like the tinkling of small bells. What did I expect? I willingly invited The Morrigan into my head in order to save my husband's life. Undoubtedly, she now has open access to all my thoughts, especially here at *Crann Bethadh*.

Before I can dwell on that horrific thought, a door opens on the far side of the room and we are joined by *Birgit* and a tall, attractive woman with an exceptionally athletic build who I'm guessing is the Lady Fury. In her arms she's carrying a very squirmy baby girl that I recognize by her unusual teal-colored eyes as being the youngest *Banphrionsa*. Princess *Mairead* puts her arms out and fusses to be returned to her mother.

"She's in rare form today, my Lady," the Fury says. "Our girl is just about ready to pull her ears off from the sides of her head in order to shed those magical ear studs."

"If she's in one of those moods, then there's not a chance in hell I'm allowing that," the baby's mother responds.

I must have an expression of complete confusion, because as Maureen tucks the baby firmly into her lap, she explains, "Mairead's magical abilities have matured far faster than the rest of her. She was causing so much havoc, Herself put those ear studs in to dampen my daughter's use of magic until she learns to better control it. They're made of brass and set with stones that interrupt her magical energy. She's only allowed to have them out to 'experiment' if Herself or her paternal grandfather, the Lord Merlin, are here to manage whatever she conjures up. I once had a herd of zebras in the nursery at my daughter's beckoning, so I'm not kidding when I say she can be a handful."

"Isn't she less than a year old?" I ask, wondering how an infant could possibly produce magical zebras.

"Fae babies mature much faster than human babies," the Lady Dear Heart explains, "and Mairead...well... because of her...uhmm...unique heritage...there's no specific guidelines as to the track of her development. We're all just taking it as it comes, but it does cause some issues when I'm with the rest of my family. My daughter's abilities are hard to explain." The baby fussed and wiggled in her mother's lap. "She wants me to put her down, but I'm pretty sure she's going to head straight toward your

Dylan. She's absolutely fascinated by other children. Are you comfortable with that?"

I really wasn't comfortable. The littlest Raven wasn't your typical baby, and my own Dylan had finally just dozed off. But how could I ever say that out loud and not sound both ridiculous and overprotective? I assume that with two trained "bodyguard" nannies in the room things couldn't get terribly out of hand, right? "It's fine," I lie.

The Lady Dear Heart places the baby on the floor on her tummy, and as predicted, the little princess pushes up on her knees and crawls across the polished wooden floor toward my son's basket. She sits staring at him for a full two minutes before taking her chubby hand and patting the ginger-colored fuzz on the top of his head while giving all of us the most glorious of smiles. It's downright adorable and I scold myself for being such a worry wart Mama. Then, without warning, Princess Mairead begins babbling at Dylan, loudly enough to wake my sleeping son. I expect for him to open his eyes and begin a serenade of infant wailing, but instead he's suddenly wide awake, staring directly at the little *Banphrionsa* while he begins to excitedly blow raspberry type bubbles at her as if he were attempting to speak, which in all circumstances is completely impossible because my son is only a few weeks old.

All four of us appear stunned at the interaction going on between the two infants. "Do you think she's actually communicating with him?" Lady Dear Heart asks.

"It sure looks as they are," the Lady Fury comments.

I shake my head. "Seriously, I don't think that's even

possible. Exchange of communication is way beyond either of their developmental range."

"I'm sure you're right, Rosie. It's just simple infant play," Lady Dear Heart agrees, though the expression on her face doesn't match the comforting words. "They couldn't possibly be having a meaningful conversation, right? That would just be…well…too difficult to believe… even for Fae babies."

WISDOM 13

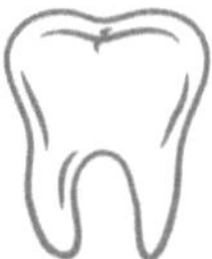

Command Performance

IN THE BACK of my mind, I always knew it was too good to last. During these past few comfortable weeks, I never had a single doubt that, at some point, life within the walls of *Dun Siorai* would eventually revert back to the dysfunctional mess I remember from my earlier visits. Considering all the personalities involved, it was simply inevitable.

Other than that horrid forced event "celebrating" Declan's safe return and our son's birth, we've had little to no contact with my husband's *athair*. His Lordship seemed to be going out of his way to ignore us, and truthfully, it was genuine blessing, as it was obvious from the moment we arrived at *Dun Siorai* that Callum Fitzpatrick *Nuada* still harbored a deep grudge against me for thwarting his plans regarding Dylan's birth. After my husband learned the awful truth regarding his father's insistence that he was dead at the hands of the North

Koreans, the two of us have avoided discussing the old goat's bizarre behavior or the reasons Lord *Nuada* believed his only son and heir was dead.

Thus, up until now, my little family of three had been able to peacefully cocoon in our private wing within *Dun Siorai,* taking our meals alone in our quarters, spending plenty of uninterrupted time together, and coming and going as we pleased. That's not to say that we were isolated. My son's *seanmhathair* (grandmother) came to visit him often, spending an hour or two cuddling and cooing our sweet boy while my husband scratched his head in utter confusion. Even Declan's sisters occasionally came by to see the baby, fawning over *Nuada's* newest heir with excited, proud smiles and more than a little sense of envy. Though four of the five of them had found mates, none of the unions had, as of yet, produced any offspring, so Dylan became a hopeful substitute for their mother-hood dreams. It was all together striking to me how different the ladies of *Dun Siorai* were in both personality and spirit when they were not in the shadow of House *Nuada's* Lord. I understand that my view of the man is undoubtedly colored by our troubled history, but it's hard to deny the changes in his daughters' behavior when he wasn't around.

It's for that very reason that my heart freezes in my chest when Lord *Nuada's* valet, *Corvot,* arrives at our door with a message for Declan from his father. My husband is already in a less than stellar mood regarding the slower than expected healing of his magical energy along with the latest bad business news from Rory Dell about fluctu-ations in the US Mundane stock market. An unexpected missive from his *athair* doesn't improve his attitude. The manservant lingers in the doorway, I assume to take back an answer to his Master. The Tax Man makes a face, somewhere between a frown and a grimace, then pockets the paper. "Tell his Lordship that it will be as he wishes."

I wait for *Corvot* to leave before asking, "What now?"

Declan tenses up his shoulders and sighs, as if gearing up to battle over a mandate I won't like. "His Lordship wants the entire family at the table for the evening meal tonight…Dylan included."

Being made to suffer through a meal with Lord Pain-In-The-Ass is bad enough, but according to Otherworldly tradition, I know for a fact that the meal won't even begin until after sundown, which coincides with my infant son's scheduled bedtime. "For Pete's sake, Declan, you know that Dylan nurses, has his bath, and goes down by 8:00pm. Changing that schedule means he'll be up and down all night."

"I understand 'tis not the best of circumstances, Lass, but I ken' no see a way to decline this invitation."

I can't help but snort. "Oh…this is no invitation, Tax Man. This is a summons by the 'great and mighty Lord *Nuada*.' An invitation would have come directly from the man himself, the same man who has gone out of his way to ignore us. You know yourself that he hasn't come to see the baby once since that awful party."

"And how is that a bad thin', Rosie? I am grateful he's let us be as long as he has. Perhaps if we just do as he asks, he'll ignore us for a few more weeks." He tosses the parchment note on the table, takes Dylan from my arms and flops into the padded rocker I use for nursing.

Our son looks up at his father's face and waves chubby fists, his matching green eyes open wide in what I swear is contemplation. "Won't he be surprised when you don't offer him a boob," I tease. "He seems to know that's his chair for snacking."

"Then my wee *mac* (son) will be most disappointed that I've no lady's *cluidin* (nipple) ta' share," he laughs. The Tax Man and his son stare at each other for a remarkably long time, and my husband is the first to look away. "Most days I still ken' no' believe he's far' real, Love. That he is truly flesh of ma' flesh and bone of ma' bone, and I that I have a *teaghlach* (family) of ma' own. I surely don' deserve such treasure. I want ta' be a batter' husband and father than ma' own has shown himself ta' be. I know 'tis wrong for an heir to speak so about his Liege Lord, but ma' *athair* is a…difficult man ta understand."

Personally, I think the word "difficult" is an under-statement, but I let it slide. "No worries there, Sweetie. You're nothing like his Lordship." I catch his look and quickly add, "I mean that in a good way. You're far more evenly tempered, considerate and well…less confronta-tional…then your father. I don't mean to be disrespectful toward his Lordship, but you have to admit he can be rather…volatile."

I mean it as a compliment but by the disgruntled look aimed right at me, I'm guessing it wasn't taken as such. "Ya' think I am weak, Lass? 'Tis not a vera good trait far' someone destined ta' be Lord of House *Nuada*. A Rulin' Lord must be above the pull of flighty emotions," he grumbles.

"You know perfectly well that's not what I mean," I say,

not liking the way this discussion about family dinner is going.

"Then ya' should be clear on what ya' do mean, Lass, lest I misunderstand ya."

I'm suddenly on the defensive, though I'm not entirely sure why. No doubt there's something else at play here. "All I'm saying, Declan, is that your *athair* acts before ever thinking things out," I add. "He never stops to consider whether the words leaving his mouth are appropriate for the situation, or how his actions might affect those around him." Behind me, three crystal wine goblets on a tray explode without warning. Startled, I jump at the unexpected noise. "Shit! Did you do that?"

He shrugs. "Aye."

"Why?" I ask.

Another annoying shrug. "I suppose so that ma' own *Mo Shiorghra* might never think me too feckin' predictable."

In my head, I hear a silky voice like a smooth, winding ribbon running through my thoughts. *Patience and understanding, little tooth fairy mathair. This be no short and easy road for either of you."* I know who the voice belongs to and it alarms me. It's the first time I've heard The Morrigan in my head since I'd given her permission to enter my mind in order to save Declan's life. Despite the tension of the moment, and the overwhelming emotions of that monumental day, I fully understood the ramifications of my decisions and I wasn't going to now lie to myself that I did not. Especially when I know that given the same odds, I'd do it all over again. I smile at my husband. "Predictable? You, Tax Man? Never," I say with what I hope sounds like adoring wifely conviction. "Though I'm surprised the breaking glass didn't startle the baby."

My son's whole attention is solely focused on his father's face as he nests quietly in Declan's arms. It's moments like this one that I regret the loss of electronics here in the Otherworld. Had we'd been home in Salem, I would have had my cell phone out, forever digitally capturing this sweet moment between father and son. As it is, I try to imprint the image on my brain instead.

"*Mo bhuachaill milis* (my sweet boy) knows he is safe in his *athair's* arms." The Tax Man looks up at me, and I can read the uncertainty and worry in his aura. "I would hope his *mathair alainn* (beautiful mother) feels the same."

The truth behind this conversation suddenly becomes clear to me, whether by my own bond with him, or a magical push from the Raven goddess in my head. My *Mo Shiorghra's* confidence in his ability to defend his family or his House has been shaken to the core by his North Korean capture. It shouldn't come as a surprise. Since being rescued, my husband's sleep is often plagued by night terrors in which he thrashes and fights a dream-induced enemy. The first few "morning afters," I'd suggested he might want to talk about it, get it off his chest, which he adamantly refused. When it continued, I mentioned that perhaps he might want to talk to Robyn about dealing with what was obviously PTSD. This little piece of offered advice got me seven hours of stony silence. All those horrendous memories of what he'd endured in captivity, coupled with the very slow progress of his magical abilities and general physical healing, make my usually self-assured Tax Man snappy and skittish.

I drag a chair over to the nursing rocker and sit myself next to my husband and son. Taking his free hand in mine, I squeeze it and lean over to kiss his stubbly cheek, a result of his decision not to shave for the past few days. "There's nowhere I feel safer than with you, Lord *Mac Nuada*...or no place I'd rather be. We're a family...the three of us. Now and always."

Together, the two of us come up with a strategic plan on how to handle the awkward timing of tonight's "family meal." The method involves me nursing Dylan right before we leave our quarters for dinner, then arranging for *Birgit t*o be close at hand outside the formal dining room, so that when our baby boy begins fussing, which I can absolutely guarantee he will do shortly before 8:00 PM, his new nanny can take him back to our rooms, feed him a short bottle, bathe him and prepare him for bed with the hope that he can wait for another longer feeding until I return from dinner.

I hadn't been sold on the idea that our baby needed either a nanny or a bodyguard. *Dun Siorai* was guarded like the "Eternal Fortress" it's named as, and Dylan and I rarely left the estate's secure grounds. With no other distractions, I'm perfectly capable of caring for my son 24/7 so the necessity of having full-time "help" seems silly. However, the young woman herself was easy to like; efficient, caring and always careful not to step on my toes. And if she could handle a sword or a knife better than most Fae men, why should I hold that against her. Plus, I'd be lying if I said I didn't enjoy a few stolen hours to myself. As of yet, we hadn't set up anything "full-time," but *Birgit* has been a regular visitor to our quarters since that original trip to *Crann Bethadh,* tending to Dylan when Declan and I have other places to be.

It's a mild spring night with a brilliant full moon and the Tax Man is unusually restless, so we take the longer, outdoor garden path to *Dun Siorai's* formal dining room on the far west end of the estate. As it's near the end of March, the garden's greens are covered in tight buds in anticipation of both April's sun and abundant rain, and the newly overturned soil smells rich and dark. Our son is peacefully bundled up in his carriage as his father pushes him along, and I breathe a sigh of contentment at this stolen moment of calm before the storm waiting inside.

The garden is empty this time of the day, thus we are more than a little surprised when a small shaggy dog comes running up the path barking furiously at us, startling my husband and causing him to pull the large knife he carries from his boot. I recognize the pup and put a hand out to delay him. "Stop, Declan. I know that dog. He's friendly. I think his name is *Seamus.*" The dog hears his name and looks up at me, tilting his head in question. "Is that your name, boy?" I ask the dog. "What are you doing out here in the garden? And where's your young Master?"

The pup barks in response and begins heading down a side path. When we don't follow, he retraces his steps back to us and again barks at me. "I think he wants us to follow him. The dog belongs to the kitchen boy. Maybe something's wrong. We should follow the dog and make sure," I say.

The Tax Man looks down at the carriage and makes a face, and I know that he's debating the security issues with the baby and I present. "Seriously, Sweetie," I interject, "this is *Dun Siorai*. No one who doesn't belong here is getting inside its walls."

Apparently, the Tax Man agrees and pushes the carriage in the direction of the dog's path, though I note that he tucks the wickedly sharp knife in his tunic belt where it's easier to access and not back in his boot. *Seamus* leads us deeper toward the far edge of the garden where the formal landscaping meets the dense woods surrounding the estate. The pup eventually comes to a stop just past the tree line. Lord *Mac* leaves Dylan and I where the stone path ends. "I will see what is makin' the wee *madra* (dog) so frantic. I want ya' and Dylan ta' wait here." He looks at me with fierce intensity. "If ya' need ta', da' ya' think ya' ken' move the *bairn* and yourself inside the house on a moment's notice?"

It's after sundown and my limited magic is stronger here in the Otherworld than back home, so I nod my agreement. "Yes. I can do that," I say.

"Good garl'," the Tax Man says with more grimness than I believe the situation calls for. It's a sign over just how cautious my husband's gotten since his capture. "I will let ya' know if I want ya' ta' grab Dylan and disappear. I expect ya' ta' obey me immediately, Rosie. No hesitation. Just go. Do I have yar' word ya'll do as I ask?"

With the hope of lightening the mood, I snap him a sharp salute. "Aye, aye, Sir!"

He makes a cranky Declan face. "I am no in the mood far' teasin', Lass."

I sigh. "Yes, Sweetie. I promise that if you tell me to, I will grab Dylan and disappear. No questions or hesitation."

"That's all I'm askin'," he says. Then, he kisses me and turns to follow the dog inside the darkened woods.

WISDOM 14

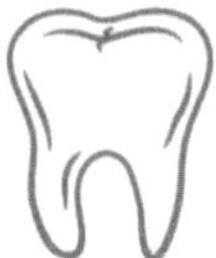

A Hole Mess of Questions

IT's hard to determine how long I stand at the edge of the garden waiting for Declan to return. Time has a way of altering itself when you are in a holding pattern of anxiety. In addition, Dylan is getting fussy, so I assume he's either hungry, wet, or both, and I'm pretty sure we're going to be late to this command performance dinner. Very late. I break down and send my husband a mental message. *"Are you alright? What's going on? It seems like you've been gone a long time."*

It takes a minute or two, but eventually he answers me. *"I am fine, but the situation has taken longer than expected ta' resolve. I shall return ta' ya' in a few minutes."*

His communication tells me nothing, so I roll Dylan's carriage back and forth with excessive energy as my son's displeasure at being tightly swaddled increases. Finally, I see two figures and a dog wander out from the tree line. When they reach the end of the garden path, I recognize the smaller figure in the brightness of the moon light. "*Buaf,* is that you?"

"Aye, my Lady. Tis' I. His Lordship has rescued ma' sorry self."

I look up at Declan whose clothes are stained with mud and extremely wrinkled. "The *buachaill* (boy) had somehow fallen in a deep hole and could not escape." He lifts the boy's left arm and shows me the child's very swollen wrist. The Tax Man's aura is an angry shade of red, though I can't tell exactly what has him so riled up.

"That looks badly swollen, *Buaf?* How did you end up in that hole?" I ask. "I'm guessing the fall is how you sprained that wrist?"

The child looks up at me with wide eyes, then looks down at his dirty bare feet. It's then I notice that he has a sixth toe on his left foot, something I didn't catch the first time we met. An odd little genetic quirk from someone in his Otherworldly line, and, more than likely, one he likely gets teased about. The poor kid has sure gotten off to a rough start in life. I scold myself for not following up on my earlier plan to find his people and offer some assistance without damaging their *Sidhe* pride.

My *Mo Shiorghra* answers for the boy. I can hear the ring of anger in his voice, though I'm finding it difficult to believe Declan would hold any hostility over what seems an unfortunate accident. "Young Master *Buaf* claims that he stumbled inta' the hole while he and the *madra* were huntin' *coinini* (rabbits). Apparently, they did not see the deep pit in the darkness of the woods."

I catch the Tax Man's eye and guess he thinks the boy is lying, but even then, his anger seems out of proportion over what appears to be a freak accident. If anything, I've always found Declan to have a soft spot for kids. A kernel of concern forms in my gut over these changes in my husband's personality since his rescue, so I try to run interference in the child's defense. "Is that true, *Buaf*? Was this just a simple accident?"

The boy doesn't look me in the eye. "Aye, Lady *Mac*. Me and *Seamus* had our eyes peeled far' *coinini*. I dinna' see the hole until t'was too late."

"And your wrist? It got injured in the fall?" I question.

"Aye, my Lady. I suppose I musta' fallen hard on it," the boy mumbles under his breath, still looking down at his feet.

"Well, it needs some ice on it to take down the swelling, then a wrap to immobilize it until you can heal it up yourself."

The child doesn't answer me. Instead, I hear my husband mutter a string of obscenities in my head that makes me cringe. The Tax Man I know and love would never get this hostile over a child's misfortune. I try my best to diffuse the tense situation. "No doubt we're already late for dinner, my Lord, and now I'm pretty sure that Dylan needs changing. He stinks to high heaven. How about I take the baby and *Buaf* back to our quarters. I'll freshen up Dylan, do a little first aid on that sprained wrist and meet up with you in the dining room. I'm sure you can come up with some excuse as to my tardiness."

I note that my husband has his jaw and his chin set in a classic expression of annoyed stubbornness. "I will also need ta' be changin' ma' attire befar' I ken' meet with ma' *athair* and *mathair*. I will take our son back ta' our rooms and call far' *Birgit* to attend to him there. I want ya' ta' take the boy ta' Cook. Tell her Lord *Mac* wants the boy's wrist looked after and wrapped. Then, he is ta' have access ta' a bath and some clean clothes, and the *madra* is ta' be given shelter in the main stable. Be sure Cook knows I inten' ta' personally check that ma' orders have been followed. I will meet ya' in the hallway outside the dining room in thirty minutes and we will greet Lord and Lady *Nuada* together."

I'm about to question Declan as to why he just can't use magic to change his clothes, but then I notice the sheen of sweat on his forehead despite the cool evening temperatures. It dawns on me that he's probably used whatever magical energy he could muster up to rescue the boy from the hole. Nodding my agreement, I say, "That is a most astute plan, my Lord," careful to use his given title in front of staff members. "I will meet you in the hallway in one half hour."

Declan turns the baby carriage around and begins to return to our little corner of *Dun Siorai*. I put an arm around the injured boy's shoulders and head off in the direction of the kitchen. I hear Declan in my head, *"See that the boy is also given some damn boots for his feet. There's no feckin' reason that anyone on this estate should have ta' do without basic necessities. And, far' the love of all the goddesses, Lass...see if ya' can get the boy to tell ya' how he really ended up in that hole."*

* * *

Cook almost jumps out of her skin when I suddenly appear in her kitchen, *Buaf* in tow. "Lady *Mac Nuada!* Whatever are ya' doing' here in the kitchen? Ya' should already be in the dinin' room. We're supposed ta' be servin' the first course in a matter of minutes." She notes the boy's filthier than normal appearance. "This little *ollpheist* (monster) hasn't caused ya' any *mischiall* (mischief), has he?" The round woman leans over to grab the child's ear, but I step in front of her to prevent it. "He's done no such thing, Mistress. He's actually the victim of a nasty accident. Somehow the boy fell into a large hole at the edge of the woods near the garden. I believe he's badly sprained his wrist and is in need of some first aid."

The woman wipes her hands in her apron in a wringing motion, embarrassed, I assume, over the fact that I stopped her from manhandling the boy. "That's most unfortunate, ma' Lady. We'll see ta' it that the boy doesn't bother yar' evening any further."

My annoyance at her complete lack of compassion for the unfortunate child makes me sound bitchier than I usually am with *Dun Siorai's* staff. "I'm afraid my Lord *Mac Nuada's* orders are a bit more specific than that, Mistress...orders my Lord expects promptly and fully executed." I proceed to list all the things Declan wants done, including arranging shelter for *Seamus* the dog. Her lips are set in a grim line, and I get the distinct impression she is not pleased too have more duties added to her plate by House *Nuada's* heir and his busybody wife, but she doesn't offer a single verbal comment.

"Please let Lord *Mac* know that I will see to all his requests, ma' Lady. He has ma' word."

"Thank you, Mistress. I'll surely let him know, but don't be surprised if his Lordship checks on their completion himself. "

"Aye, Ma'am," Cook says. "Lord *Mac* is known to follow through on his orders…much like his sire."

I don't particularly care for the woman comparing Declan to his pig-headed father, but of course, I can't express my true feelings either, so I only nod in agreement before leaving to meet my husband in the hallway. I take two steps, then suddenly think of something and turn around to add, "And Mistress…I want ice on that boy's wrist immediately. No waiting until after dinner is served."

✳ ✳ ✳

The Tax Man is already waiting when I finally reach *Dun Siorai's* formal dining room in the west end of the house. "That was quick. Is everything settled with Dylan?" I ask.

"Aye. *Birgit* was waiting for me when I reached our quarters. Our wee boy quieted right down when she picked him up. I find that young woman ta' be quite impressive. I dunno' why ya' keep puttin' off acceptin' har' employment full-time, Love. She is ma' *Buime's* own granddaughter. I have not a single doubt she'll care for Dylan like he was har' vera' own."

With all the chaos this evening has already dumped in our laps, I don't want to have this important family discussion standing in the hallway. "I didn't say a firm 'no' to the possibility, Sweetie. I just need a little more time to wrap my head around the idea of having 24/7 full-time help. Especially help that carries a deadly knife strapped to her thigh."

"I would think knowin' that Dylan was well attended in yar' absence would make returnin' to yar' practice much easier when the time comes. I know it would make me mar' secure knowin' our son was in excellent hands when we both were away from the house."

"Wait. You would have *Birgit* come with us to Salem?"

"Of course. She would undoubtedly expect a full contract for as long as our son needed her. 'Tis the way it is done. I realize it would take some gettin use ta'... havin' someone else in the house all the time…but in ma' mind, the advantages outweigh any problems."

I'd never even considered that the woman would accompany us back to our normal life in the Mundane world. What my husband was now suggesting was a much bigger decision than just having the pleasant *Sidhe scathach* babysit our son while we temporarily hid out in *I Idir*. Did Declan really believe our son needed a full-time bodyguard in both worlds? In typical Rosie fashion, I put off having a discussion I anticipate will be a difficult one. "You make a lot of good points, Sweetie. Let's table this conversation for a time when we're not in such a public place. I always feel the walls have ears at *Dun Siorai*."

Declan nods his agreement and puts his arm through mine. "Before we face dinner with ma' family, I wanted ta' ask if ya' were able ta' get the boy ta' reveal any more details as ta' how he ended up in that feckin' hole?"

"No. I tried to get him to open up about it, but he said his wrist hurt too much to talk, so I didn't want to press him." I put a hand on my husband's chest to keep him from opening the door to the dining room. "Why are you so sure *Buaf* is lying to you about what actually happened?"

The Tax Man speaks to my head instead. *"As ya' said yourself, Lass, the walls of ma' ancestral home have ears. We'll speak on this later tonight when we are alone."*

WISDOM 15

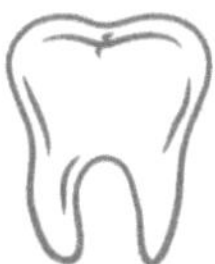

Family Fun Time

TEN PAIRS of eyes turn and watch my husband and I enter the dining room. None of them held even the tiniest sign of relief or cheer over our late arrival. "Good evening, happy family," Declan announces, and I wonder if anyone else catches the distinct note of sarcasm in his voice.

"You're late, *Mac Nuada*. There are no excuses for tardiness. And where is my new grandson? I thought I made it perfectly clear I wanted the entire family present for the formal evening meal," his Lordship growls.

I curtsy, and Declan bows in adherence to Otherworldly protocol, but forgoes the usual hand over the heart greeting between sire and heir. "My apologies on both accounts, ma' Lord. T'was an evening for *Lugh* to vex us with unseen circumstances."

"'Tis no *leithsceal ceart* (proper excuse) for an heir of House *Nuada*. And still you have not yet explained why my grandson is not here in attendance," Declan's *athair* replies.

I open my mouth to expound on Lord *Nuada's* question, but my husband cuts me off. Though he's tightly shielding his emotions and thoughts, I can tell by the way he has his jaw set that he's in full "cranky Declan" mode. "Ma' son will be joining us shortly. T'was discovered on route that our wee Master Dylan required a complete change of clothes before he could take part in this loving family celebration. His nanny will bring him along when this has been accomplished."

"I do not like having my orders disregarded, *Mac Nuada*," his Lordship complains.

The Tax Man gives his father another curt bow before adding, "I am sorry, ma' Lord. I have as yet been unable ta' teach ma' son ta' *cac* (shit) when it is convenient far' his lordly *seanathair* (grandfather). Perhaps when he is older, I can properly instruct him in this lesson."

There's an audible gasp from the far end of the table, which I assume comes from one of Declan's sisters. His siblings and their spouses all look thoroughly shocked at their brother's boldness, all big eyes and pale faces. Dragon Mama, on the other hand, doesn't work too hard to hide the smirk resting on her attractive face. I'm not stupid enough to try and mediate between two *Tuatha De Danann* males in the middle of a lordly pissing match, so I just squeeze Declan's hand; mouth shut, shield up.

"You go too far, *Mac Nuada*. Son or no son, I am your Liege Lord and you would do well ta' remember that," Declan's *athair* warns. "As yar' sire, I am sympathetic ta' the injuries ya' suffered at the hands of the North Kore-ans, though we both know the sacrifices ya' made far' The Crown do little ta' benefit House *Nuada*. I will only forgive blatant disrespect and disobedience far' so long. Ya' will find that hiding under the wing of the Raven Queen is not ta' yar' advantage."

The tension in the room ratchets up by several degrees. According to the laws of *I Idir*, Lord *Nuada* words border on treason. There are only two other people in this room that are aware that I gave The Morrigan access to my thoughts in order to save my *Mo Shiorghra*. Declan's father isn't one of them. I feel a wave of panic bubble up over the idea that I am acting as a conduit between what's being said in this room and Her Royal Highness.

Lady *Siobhan* must feel the same. She clears her throat and then rings the small bell by her plate, causing the side doors of the dining room to open and let in the waitstaff with the first course. The Tax Man and I take our seats at the only empty spots at the table, on either side of his Lordship. I would have very much preferred to sit next to my husband rather than across from him, but at this point, I just want the whole evening over with ASAP. Dragon Mama sits to her son's left, while I take my place next to Declan's middle sister, *Caoimhe*, who, among the four women, is the most mild-tempered.

The first course is a nod to the early harvest of the growing season. A bright green *anraith* (soup) of what appears to be leeks, peas and, according to my amateur chef's palate, a light touch of fresh watercress. Even for the Otherworldly types, dinner is late and everyone actively tucks into their soup, glad to finally be eating as well as being freed from forced conversation.

His Lordship takes a few spoons, then makes a face and pushes the bowl away. Ignoring both Declan and me, he addresses *Sean,* husband to the Tax Man's oldest sister, *Saoirse.* "So, how will House *Nuada* fare in the *Epona* races come *Beltane, mac is sine* (oldest son)?"

Lord Pain-in-the-Ass's use of "oldest son" in regards to *Sean* is meant as a dig to my husband, who out ranks his sister's spouse in both title and age. It annoys me to no end, but Declan ignores the insult, engaged in quiet conversation with his *mathair,* of all people, while obviously enjoying the soup his father pushed away in disparagement. Have I mentioned before what a dysfunctional mess the Fitzpatricks are?

His Lordship asking *Saoirse's* husband about the House's equine team is no show of favor. Everyone in the family, myself included, is aware that *Sean* is the least accomplished rider in the group, besides me, of course, who had never ridden a horse in her life until a few weeks before my handfast. Unfortunately for the poor man, who is a botanist with academic leanings and a matching reserved demeanor, he'd gone and handfasted a girl from a family of *Sidhe* who all could probably sit a horse before they were even weaned. The handsome scholar not only has very little skill in the saddle, he genuinely seems terrified of the overly large, high-tempered Fae stallions.

Sean flushes a light pink and stammers out his reply. "Your stable undoubtedly is one of the best in *I Idir,* my Lord. I would venture to guess your *Beltane* team will bring House *Nuada* the honors it deserves."

"Spoken like someone who doesn't know a stallion from a gelding," Lord *Nuada* mutters, "or anything about havin' and usin' a set of balls, for that matter." Turning his vitriolic attention to his eldest daughter, he added, "As is proved by the fact that my *Saoirse* still has no babe in her belly even after four years of mating."

Declan's oldest sister has never been overly kind to me, but my heart still breaks for her. I see how she looks at Dylan with such longing and wistfulness. It's clear she harbors a deep desire for children of her own, and her father pouring salt in those infertility wounds is beyond cruel. My Tax Man must guess I'm about to open my mouth and say exactly those words because he gives my thigh a squeeze under the table and instead draws his *athair's* attention towards himself. "I am hopin' ya' won't make all of us men pull out our cocks far' comparison, ma' Lord, though I remain mar' than confident in the size of ma' *bod mor* (large penis). Suffice ta' say, ma' lady wife will tell ya' that she has no complaints."

I almost choke on my soup, and I don't have to look up from my bowl to know that everyone at the table is staring at my husband in complete horror. I feel the shock radiating from every chair around the table. From the corner of my eye, I can also see that his Lordship has gone all red in the face and is amazingly at a loss for words. It's actually Lady *Siobhan* who comments. "Really, *Deaglean!* This is the family dinner table. I won't stand for such vulgarity."

"I apologize, Lady *Mathair*. I plead a sudden loss of good judgment," my husband says as he dabs at his mouth with his napkin, an air of complete boredom hanging about him.

I have no idea what is going on here, or what the hell has gotten into my normally staid husband. All the mental messages I try and send him are met with a solid shield preventing me, or anyone else for that matter, from gaining access. His locking me out of his head like this is a big red flag. Though I've known from day one of meeting Lord and Lady Fitzpatrick that House Nuada did not hold to traditional family dynamics, what's happening here this evening goes beyond "dysfunctional."

Lord *Nuada* rises from the table, and I begin to worry in earnest that he's going to make some type of physical advance on my husband. Declan must feel the same, because I feel him tense up across from me. At the same moment, the main door to the dining room opens to admit *Birgit* pushing Dylan into the room in his carriage. Upon the arrival of his grandson, Lord *Nuada* gives his only son a look that could kill but sits back down in his chair. "Bring the *bairn* ta' me," he orders the nanny.

I note that the *scathach* looks to my husband first, and apparently finding something signaling an affirmative answer in his mask-like expression, hands our son to his grandfather. Lord *Nuada* takes Dylan into his arms in the manner of a man who has fathered six living children and is no stranger to infants. There's no hesitation on his part, no fear that he's holding the baby incorrectly. He appears to examine our son, unwrapping the blanket he's been swaddled in, then counting fingers and toes, and tracing the Fae curve of his tiny ears with a finger. His Lordship is surprisingly gentle, something I wouldn't have expected from his gruff demeanor and imposing stature. "Aye...we ken' put away any doubt on whether he is yar' son, *Mac Nuada*. He looks exactly as you did when ya' slid all bloody from yar' own *mathair*."

And just like that, any warm, fuzzy feelings I have regarding my son's paternal grandfather evaporate in the aftermath of his deeply insulting comment. My face feels hot and I don't dare look up at my husband whose anger I can feel floating from across the table. There's no doubt in my mind that the Tax Man is not himself this evening. In all the time I've known him, he's held the best poker face I'd ever seen, a hallmark of "super spy" status. Tonight, every emotion is plainly written upon his person.

"I find yar' comment insultin', ma' Lord," his heir growls. "Ya' disparage ma' beloved *Mo Shiorghra* while insinuatin' that I am weak enough ta' be cuckolded. 'Tis rude and uncalled for."

Dylan's *seanathair* (grandfather) tucks the blankets back around the baby and returns him to the care of *Birgit*, grinning at his ability to so easily rile up my husband. He adds with no small measure of sarcasm, "Yar' far' too thin-skinned, *Mac Nuada*. I was just engagin' in a wee bit of *ag spochadh* (teasing). My grandson is a fine wee laddie. He will make House *Nuada* proud someday, though I must say yar' own behavior tonight is alarmin' ta' me. What has ya' so *leimneach* (jumpy) tonight? Is that why ya've gone and hired a *scathach* far' yar' son? Da' ya' think someone will attempt ta' steal yar' *bairn* from his cradle?"

Something about Lord *Nuada's* statement makes all the hair on my arms stand straight up. *Birgit* must sense my uneasiness as well, because she rolls Dylan's carriage to the other side of the room, leaving space between our son and my husband's family, positioning them both closer to the door. And in that single moment, I decide right there and then to make the young nanny bodyguard a full-time member of our little family.

WISDOM 16

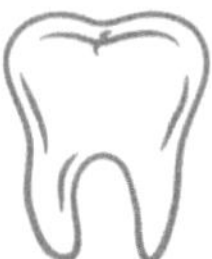

Getting The Family Business

FOR THE NEXT TWENTY MINUTES, conversation lags as everyone focuses on their meal; a roasted leg of lamb, new potatoes, and some type of leafy green vegetable that reminds me of a cross between Mundane spinach and Swiss chard. Thankfully, the rest of tonight's menu must appeal to his Lordship, who has stopped his barrage of intimidation in order to attack his plate like a starving inmate. Sadly, the calm peace of quiet chewing is short lived. After inhaling his food, Declan's father pushes the plate away, folds his arms across his full belly, and shifts in his chair to address my husband. "I have need of ya' far' the next few days, *Mac Nuada*."

The Tax Man stops eating, his fork mid-air while he answers. "In what manner, ma' Lord?"

"I have holdings in *Asgard* that need immediate attention. I require ya' to ride out on the morrow with a plan to stay in the area for a minimum of three ta' four days. We can discuss the details in ma' study after dinner."

I catch the Tax Man's eye as he looks to me and then to his father. His Lordship apparently notes the look as well. "I am sure yar' lady wife can do without yar' attention far' a few days, *Mac Nuada*," my father-in-law states. "Rumors around the Council say she's the *Banphrionsa's* newest pet. No doubt our Lady Rosalinda will be kept busy on The Throne's leash. Besides, as long as ya' are hidin' out here at *Dun Siorai*, ya' shud' be willin' ta' take on the responsibilities that come with yar' title."

As of late, I've been rethinking my earlier decision in awarding Dragon Mama the title of "most messed-up parent." I've come to the recent realization that The Tax Man's father has her beat, hands down. His Lordship just happens to be more subtly underhanded in the way he goes about his bullying. Lord Callum Fitzpatrick *Nuada* makes it seem as if his communication holds no venom, but there's always a mean-spirited angle or cutting insinuation hidden among the bland words. Without a doubt, he has to know his remark about Declan "hiding out at *Dun Siorai*" would deeply wound his son's masculine pride, yet he goes ahead and works in the taunt along with his request.

My husband puts down his fork, all attention now directed towards his *athair*. "I'm not 'hidin' out' as ya' imply, ma' Lord. I'd like nothing better than ta' join ma' team in trackin' down those Mundane bastards," he says in a low tone that registers his anger. "The decision far' me ta' remain here while I recuperate rests with the Black Knight... at Her Majesty's command, of course. In addition, ma' Lady is no one's pet, and any time spent at *Crann Bethadh* is of har' own choice. Lastly, as ta' yar' request of ma' time, I didna' realize that House *Nuada* still had holdins' in *Asgard*. Hasn't business trade with that kingdom been discouraged since *Odin's* refusal to sign the unified treaty against Mundane expansion into the Otherworld?"

"Mine was not a request, *Mac Nuada.* I am yar' Liege Lord. If I demand ya' ta' go ta' *Asgard* then go ya' shall. Take yar' own man along if ya' feel the need far' back-up. It matters not ta' me if ya' want the company or not, but as far' as me doin' business in the *Asgard* kingdom, House *Nuada* does not take its orders from the Raven Queen, especially where our treasury is concerned. It continues ta' gall me ta' no end that Herself put the life of ma' heir at risk in the pursuit of her self-involved vendetta against the Mundanes. I am not even sure I ma'self agree with that damn treaty of hers. It may be that it would be entirely more advantageous to all the Houses of *I Idir* to each negotiate our own workable compromises with the Mundane governments instead of lettin' The Throne make all the decisions far' us.

My mother-in-law and I both stop chewing at the same time, fully aware that in the eyes of The Crown, his Lordship's words are treason, and that I am, most likely, still an open pipeline directly to Her Majesty's ear. Lady *Siobhan* jumps into the conversation. "Discussions regarding House financial business at the family dinner table has always been forbidden, my Lord. 'Tis your own rule, as I recall. I suggest you and *Deaglean* take this debate to your study after we have finished our dinner.

Dessert has yet to be served and 'tis your favorite tonight…*piog biabhoige* (rhubarb pie) with fresh clotted cream."

Lord *Nuada* merely grunts. "Yar' Lady *Mathair* is correct, *Mac Nuada*. 'Tis a conversation better left between the two of us. We will talk after dinner."

I barely take the last mouthful of my dessert when Dylan begins to fuss in earnest. He's past due to be nursed so I use the opportunity to excuse myself from the table and head back to our quarters, leaving Declan to deal with his father. On the long walk back, I broach the subject of a full-time position with *Birgit*. The silver-haired *scathach* offers a rare genuine smile, seemingly pleased at the offer.

"It would be an honor, ma' Lady. My grandmother will be beyond pleased that I have been asked to care for the son of her beloved *Mac Nuada*. I am sure you are aware that she holds a special place in her *croi* (heart) for his Lordship. She calls him *leanbh a anam* (child of her soul). I can begin my tenure immediately. I assume Lord *Mac* will see to the formalities?"

"Formalities?" I question.

"Aye, ma' Lady. Tradition requires a contract and a ceremony. 'Tis the way it's always been."

I don't have a clue as to what either of those things involve, but I suppose the Tax Man will. "I'm sure his Lordship will know exactly what's required, *Birgit*. We're absolutely committed to keeping the necessary traditions." I think back to dinner, and a concern crosses my mind. "Can you still care for Dylan while we see to the formalities?"

"Of course, my Lady. I will stay with Master Dylan in the nursery until provisions can be made for the formalities. The wee laddie and I will be the best of roommates."

I try not to show how relieved I am at the thought that my son's nanny, a trained Fae assassin bodyguard, will be at his side day and night. The events of this evening have left me with a lingering feeling of unease, and if Declan abides with his father's orders to go to *Asgard*, I'm glad to know that there will be another pair of watchful eyes on my son at all times.

It's late by the time my *Mo Shiorghra* returns to our quarters. I've long finished nursing Dylan, and the baby and Birgit have settled down for the night in his nursery, while I, myself, have washed up and changed into my night clothes. I sense his aura even before he walks into our bedroom, the restlessness and discontent hanging about him like an ill-fitting shadow. "I'm sorry far' keepin' ya up, Lass," Declan apologizes. "I am later than I planned ta' be." He looks at the empty cradle next to our bed. "Our wee 'Pay-not' is settled in the nursery tonight?"

"Yes. Surprisingly, he fell right to sleep despite all the extra...excitement." I leave an extra-long pause before adding yet another issue to the Tax Man's mental plate. "*Birgit* is with him. I asked her to be Dylan's permanent *scathach*. I hope you don't mind that I didn't check with you first?"

My husband settles himself into his favorite chair, an extra wide, well-worn leather piece, and pulls off his boots. Leaning back, he pats his lap in suggestion that I should join him, and I'm grateful that almost all of my postpartum soreness has faded. I make myself comfortable across his knees, putting my arms around his neck, breathing in the woodsy scent of him I know and love. He answers my nuzzling by sliding a hand underneath my nightgown and resting it on my bare hip. It's been a long time since we've been able to cuddle like this, just the two of us, alone, and for a tiny while, we just rest in the pleasure of our closeness.

The Tax Man's hand wanders while he speaks, making it hard to concentrate on the matters at hand. "The decision to employ a nanny for our 'Pay-not' has always rested with ya', ma' Love. I never wanted ya' to think that I didn't find ya' more than capable of carin' for our son. But I would be lyin' if I said I wasn't pleased with yar' decision. Havin' Magda's own granddaughter tendin' our wee boy feels right ta' me."

I return my *Mo Shiorghra's* handsy attention by running my fingers through his finally-growing-back hair, and tracing the curve of his pointed ear which I know from personal experience drives him absolutely crazy. From my intimate seat on his lap, I can tell it still has that same effect, and when the logical, medically trained part of my brain murmurs *"no, no no...still too soon,"* I want to swat it away like some annoying, buzzing fly. Still, the last thing I need here in *I Idir* are lady-part complications, or the look Doc Brannigan would give me for jumping the gun before he'd given the thumbs up. I put my hands back around my husband's neck and try not to wiggle in his lap. "Let's be honest here, Tax Man. We both know *Birgit* is no ordinary nanny, but I do feel better knowing she's at Dylan's side, even if it does seem ridiculous that our child requires an armed bodyguard."

"There is nothin' wrong with a sense of security, Lass. My *Buime* (nurse/nanny) means the world ta' me. I want that far' my son even though he has two lovin' parents. A child can't be loved too much."

"*Birgit* mentioned some kind of contract and a ceremony. I would guess you know what she means?"

"Aye. 'Tis an ancient tradition, and worthy of her title and trainin.' It is no small feat ta' wear the ink that she does. Becomin' a *scathach* requires special skills that most *Sidhe* will never master. I will handle the details, though it will have to wait until I return from *Asgard*," my husband explains.

"So, you're going after all?" I ask, not hiding my disappointment over Lord *Nuada* getting his way.

The Tax Man sighs, his voice registering his weariness over the events of the past evening. "It is just easier to go along with ma' *athair* than trying to dissuade him from any course of action that he has settled upon. Plus, I need to go and see for myself what kind of trouble his Lordship has involved our House in. His words against The Throne worry me, especially with yar' open connection to The Morrigan. We can never be sure if and when she is privy to your thoughts. It is a difficult situation that requires constant awareness."

"I'm sorry that I put us in this 'trick bag,' Sweetie, but

truthfully, I'd do it all over again if it meant getting you home. Maybe someday the spell will fade."

My husband pulls his hand out from under my nightgown, and I try not to pout. We both know tonight's intimacy isn't going anywhere further. Instead, he places both hands on my cheeks and brings my mouth to his own to kiss me in top-notch Tax Man fashion. Pulling away first, he grins and asks, "Do ya' still think ma' kisses are better than a freezer full of meat, Sweet Rosie Lass?"

My mind instantly goes back to our first night together; Himself teasing me about choosing him over Jimmy, the butcher's son. The memories of the night that followed, the hours in which our bond was sealed with the magical transfer of his ink on my shoulder, do nothing to douse the heat of the moment. This time, I'm the one to initiate the kiss, and when we finally come up for air, I reply, "Poor Jimmy never stood a chance against you, Tax Man." Then, for good measure, I run my finger over the very sensitive tip of his ear again.

WISDOM 17

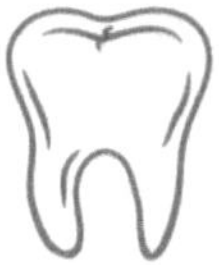

Coffee Break

NEEDLESS TO SAY, I am not a happy camper regarding my husband's decision to travel to *Asgard* as his *athair* demands, only this time when he prepares to leave, I don't give him the regrettable "cold shoulder" in the same way I did when he left for North Korea. I learned my guilty lesson the hard way over that mistake. This time, when he walks out the door to face goddess-knows- what, the Tax Man will have no doubts he's taking my whole heart with him.

I can tell that Duncan is as nervous about this trip as I am. This is their first adventure together since Declan's return from Korea, and I have little doubt that my husband's cousin is reliving all the traumatic events of that previous outing. I don't have to read his mind to understand that Duncan is carrying his own boat load of guilt over that failed mission; the way he keeps shifting from foot to foot and fidgeting with the leather baldric anchoring his sword to his back speaks volumes regarding his overall nervousness.

Heading toward the door, the Tax Man stops and picks Dylan up from his cradle. "Ya' be a good laddie far' yar' lovely *mathair*, ma wee *mac binn* (sweet son). *Daidi* (Daddy) will bring ya home somethin' special from *Asgard*." He kisses our son on the top of his head and hands him back to *Birgit*. Then turning to me, Declan envelops me into a tight hug. "I will not be gone long, Love. A day or two at most."

I try not to think that this is exactly the same thing he said to me before leaving for North Korea. I must not be shielding very well because I hear him in my head. *"I will be fine, Love. I give ya' ma' word. 'Tis nothing like the last trip."* Switching back to oral communication he adds, "Shall I bring ya' somthin' back as well, sweet lady? *Asgard* is known far' their fine silk thread. I know how much ya enjoy your wee needlework."

"Your lady only wants her husband back. ASAP. In one piece," I counter.

Despite an audience, my husband kisses me with enough gusto to curl my toes. "So ya' don't forget me while I'm gone," he explains with a grin, then motions to Duncan as the two of them take their leave.

I spend the rest of the morning rearranging Dylan's nursery simply because I have nothing else to do and my anxiety level is over the top. *Birgit* must sense my nervous energy and the need to keep busy, so she says nothing about me taking over her job. Instead, she offers to take the baby to visit with his grandmother, a ploy to give me some personal space that I recognize and appreciate. Now

I can curse my father-in-law in both English and the Otherworld old language to my heart's content in complete and utter privacy.

Less than an hour into the job and surrounded by stacks of random baby paraphernalia, I hear a tapping noise on the window of our parlor which can only be one thing. I detest raven grams, the Otherworldly method of formal communication. To begin with, I've never been much of a "bird person," never having the slightest urge to keep any of the feathered creatures as pets. However, the messenger ravens of the Otherworld are in an "icky" category all by themselves. If at all possible, I usually let Declan handle the retrieval of raven-grams, but since he's not here, the job falls to me. I know from experience the damned thing won't go away until it hands off its directive.

Pulling myself from my baby kingdom, I trek through our quarters to the parlor at the west end of the suite of rooms. I open the glass and the wretched, sharp-beaked, beady-eyed courier hops onto the inside ledge. It tilts its oily, little head in my direction and gives me the usual once-over while waiting for me to retrieve the message. I note the green and gold ribbons, a clue that the message is coming from *Crann Bethadh*, the royal seat, and my stomach tightens. I haven't quite gotten comfortable with the idea of having any type of relationship with the royal family, though once I recognize the handwriting and the casual demeanor of the message, I relax. The note is from the *Banphrionsa*, the Lady Dear Heart, aka "Maureen," inviting me to attend *I Idir's Ostara* faire as her guest in the hopes that I'll help make "an Otherworldly snooze fest a bit less boring."

Ostara is a Fae holiday welcoming the early return of spring, a celebration of balance, rebirth and fertility. It was not an observance we kept in my childhood home. My dad's Christian beliefs strongly focused on the Easter celebration instead. It wasn't until I was an adult and actively delving into my Fae spiritual nature that I realized how many of our family's Easter "traditions," the bunnies, eggs and bulb plants, were also part of the *Ostara* rituals. It had been years and years since I'd attended any kind of faire in my Otherworldly home, the last time being a *Beltane* bazaar when I was a little girl of eight. It was also the same day I met Mel for the first time and the memory of that moment lightens my heart.

A pleasant spring day out with the light-hearted princess of *I Idir* seems like the perfect cure for my anxiety and homesickness, so I grab paper and pen and compose a return note for the bird to deliver, one accepting the Princess's gracious invitation. Then, leaving the nursery a mess, I hurry off to speak with Lady *Nuada* on the protocol regarding the proper attire for a day at the faire as a member of the royal inner circle.

* * *

Despite the truce between Dragon Mama and myself, forged at the birth of my son, I can still count on Lady *Siobhan* to rain on my parade. As my beloved husband would say, "No zay-bra' altogether changes its stripes, Lass." While rocking Dylan in the solar parlor, she pauses in her singing to him to scold me on my presumed imperfections. "Did your *mathair* perhaps drop you on your head, silly girl?" she asks as she coos at her grandson. "Or do you just ignore my advice out of sheer, pig-headed stubbornness? How many times have I warned you about being too eager to be part of the royal court? It will no doubt be your downfall."

She says this all while wearing a smug little expression on her face over the idea that a daughter of House *Nuada* has caught the interest of the royal family. Social ladder climbing is how the game is played in the Otherworld on a level a hundred times greater than anything in the Mundane world. The *Sidhe* structure their entire existence around power, wealth and reputation. Climbing on the backs of other people to get ahead socially and financially is considered a desirable talent and not an immoral character flaw.

"I happen to enjoy the *Banphrionsa's* company, Lady *Mathair.*" I stress the overly-familiar title of "mother." I've never been invited to use this more familiar moniker, but do so because I know it sometimes annoys her, a clue that the Fae snarky-ness of the Otherworld is rubbing off on me as I spend more and more time here. "We have a lot in common. We were both raised in the Mundane world, we both have fated mates, and we are both new mothers."

Dylan starts to fuss and his grandmother expertly drapes him over her left shoulder while patting and rubbing his back, all without missing a word in the conversation. "That is all fine for passing interludes, Rosalinda. But you must never forget that the *Banphrionsa* is the Morrigan's own. The blood of the ancient ones runs in her veins and I venture to imagine that her magical skills supersede that of most of the souls in this kingdom. You, on the other hand, are the daughter of a tooth fairy and a human with magical talent that is far less than your own son will exhibit in just a few short months. Do not believe for a moment that you are a true player in a game you do not even understand the rules of."

I should be used to Dragon Mama's sharp tongue by now, but in my current mood, her cruel words cut deep. My face crumples and I blink back the tears that burn at the corners of my eyes. I don't want to give my mother-in-law the satisfaction of knowing she got to me, but I'm tired of having my feelings hurt on a daily basis. Lady *Siobhan* must realize how much her words have affected me because she sighs dramatically, then signals *Birgit* to take Dylan from her arms. Ever the professional, the *scathach* retrieves the baby and discreetly leaves the room.

Declan's mother points to the chair across from her, and I find myself following her directive despite the overwhelming desire to flee to our quarters and have myself a really good pity party. Instead, I plop into the chair in a very unladylike manner and cross my arms over my chest in what I hope looks like defiance. The Lady studies me for a moment while I work to ignore that familiar singularly raised eyebrow. Goddesses help me if Dylan has that same genetic quirk. "I'm relieved to see that you have enough grit not to dissolve into a puddle of feminine tears over my harsh words. It is a hopeful sign," she says, "if you intend to someday be Lady *Nuada*."

"I have no desire to be Lady of House *Nuada,* so you can stop worrying about my damn 'grit' as you call it," I reply with obvious terseness. "Declan and I are going back to our lives in Salem as soon as possible. You all can keep your back-stabbing, body-climbing, bullshit to yourselves. My *Mo Shiorghra* and I don't need or want any of what the Ruling Council has to offer. We'll build our family and live our lives as we see fit."

Two steaming mugs appear on the table between us that smells surprisingly like Mundane dark roast coffee, a beverage widely shunned by the *Sidhe* population. My Lady *Mathair* nods. "Aye. It is as you suspect...'tis that wretched Mundane coffee swill I grew accustomed to drinking while exiled in the Mundane world. I need your word, Rosalinda, that you will not breathe a word of this to anyone. I could never show my face in the streets of *I Idir* if it was made public knowledge that Lady *Nuada* secretly imbibes *laib Mundane salach* (filthy Mundane mud)."

I can't help but crack a smile. One...because my hoity-toity mother-in-law has gotten herself addicted to my perfectly Mundane Gevalia French dark roast...and two... because I see this as her way of opening the discourse between us by sharing her own secret with me. Wrapping my hands around the second mug, I take a sip of home and reply, "You have my word, Lady *Mathair*. I won't tell a soul that you're obsessed with Mundane coffee."

She gives a nod, an acknowledgement that she is putting us on equal footing. "I know you think me harsh. Cruel even. But what I say to you I would say to my own daughters if they had somehow been interesting enough to catch the attention of The Throne. You will walk a dangerous path when it becomes common knowledge that you have been welcomed into the very private and tight royal circle. And it WILL become known once you are seen accompanying the *Banphrionsa* to an event as public as the *Ostara* faire. In agreeing to this outing, you are willingly exposing yourself to the public eye...to ridicule and speculation along with any elevated social status and admiration you might garnish. There are those who will be envious of your connections to The Raven's Crown and see you as a threat. You must forever be conscious of the fact that in this capacity, you represent not only your mate, but House *Nuada* as well. I want you to understand all of this in advance, Rosalinda, lest you find yourself in over your naive little head."

I snort and get the stink eye in response. "I'm sorry, Lady *Mathair*, but I think you're making a big deal over nothing. I genuinely like the *Banphrionsa*...on a personal level. She reminds me of home, and she's fun to be with. She's not at all like you'd expect royalty to be. Not stuffy or showy at all. I enjoy her company. Besides, I already sent a raven-gram accepting her invitation. I am to be picked up shortly before noon.

Now both eyebrows are raised and Lady *Nuada* looks at me over the rim of her coffee mug. "After everything I've just told you, the blunt warnings I've honestly laid out, you still intend to go forward with this very public display?"

I can't raise my eyebrows like my husband or his mother, but I can stick out my little tooth fairy chin with the best of them. "I'm no shrinking violet, Lady *Siobhan*. People can stare and gossip all they want. I've received plenty of that same type of treatment in my life. I WANT to go to the *Ostara* faire as part of the royal court. I've already gone and accepted the *Banphrionsa's* personal invitation and I don't intend to back-out at the last minute."

She smiles at me and puts her mug down on the table. "I was hoping you'd say that, girl." Rising from her chair she adds, "Follow me. We have only two hours to make you into an acceptable companion to the *Banphrionsa* of *I Idir.*"

WISDOM 18

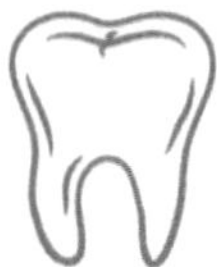

Faire Weathered Friends

IT TAKES every bit of those two hours to deck me out in Otherworldly high fashion with lots of magic thrown around in order to finish on time. My Lady *Mathair* found nothing to her liking in my own wardrobe, and because I am shorter, rounder and abundantly more-bosomy than either she or any of her daughters, my apparel has to be quickly created to suit my postpartum figure. In addition, because I am attending the faire as Lady *Mac Nuada*, I am required by protocol to dress in the House colors of maroon and gold, shades that, for the most part, aren't particularly flattering to my coloring.

Admiring the finished product in the full-length cheval mirror, I understand perfectly where my Tax Man gets his top-notch fashion sense. My gown is simply stunning. Somehow, Lady Siobhan has found a shade of gold so light it almost looks like a creamy ivory instead. The fabric itself is a chiffon-type silk, layered from the waist down and cinched with a maroon corset that gives me an hourglass figure and pushes my generous boobs up and out. The top layer of fabric is embroidered with trailing vines in a soft, spring green and rose buds in the same maroon color as my corset, while the bodice and sleeves are worked in traditional Celtic *Sidhe* knotwork.

My unruly curls are neatly braided and wound at the back of my head in a complicated pattern, with garnet-tipped hair pins stuck in random spots to catch the light. Around my neck, I wear my husband's handfast gift, the lovely garnet and gold topaz choker set in a knotted, hand-wrought platinum setting. I touch the gems at my throat, wishing that my Tax Man were here to see me in all this finery. I'm not the kind of girl who is obsessed with the trappings of fashion, normally happier in my comfortable, wash and wear clothing. But today, even I realize I look especially awesome.

Lady *Nuada* and her personal maids step back and admire their work, walking full around me to check all angles. Even *Birgit*, who I've never seen wear a dress, is grinning at my appearance. With a sigh, Declan's mother comments, "I do wish you had a longer, slimmer neck, Rosalinda. Still, your finished appearance is satisfactory for the events of the afternoon."

Leave it to Dragon Mama to suck the joy out of a moment. "Gee, thanks, Lady *Mathair*. You do have a way with words," I retort.

The staff ladies look at each other in shock over my bold response to their Lady's verbiage, while *Birgit* suddenly gets busy with Dylan in order to hide the shadow of a smile that's playing on her face. My mother-in-law gives me a scathing look, but adds, "Do not expect me to coo at you, Lady *Mac Nuada*. You are not a child to be coddled. Obviously, you have working eyes in your head. You can see for yourself that you look every bit a daughter of *Danu* (Celtic goddess of motherhood and fertility). Do not let the eyes of others decide your worth."

* * *

I meet the royal carriage in *Dun Siorai's* courtyard, a borrowed, lightweight, wool wrap with ermine trim thrown over my arm, as my gifted silver fox cape is much too warm for March's milder temperatures. I am accompanied by only two of House *Nuada's* security men, selected by my mother-in-law herself, as traveling with a larger retinue might be construed as a sign I don't trust the abilities of *Crann Bethadh's* Troll Guard.

There is an unusual large gathering of staff flitting about outdoors, most likely looking to catch a glimpse of the royal carriage and its celebrity occupant. I see *Buaf's* dirty, little face and that of his canine companion peeking through the hedges that line the brick-paved lane leading up to the front entrance. I remind myself to check on the boy when I return to see if my husband's directives have been followed.

The stately black carriage with its recognizable Raven crest and matching set of midnight-black Fae stallions stops a few feet in front of me. I'm a bit surprised to see the Lord Warrior, the legendary *Cu Chulainn*, consort to the Queen, following behind the coach on his own horse. He almost always is seen only at the Queen's side. I momentarily catch the big man's eye, causing him to smile and wink at me, which always makes me blush a deep pink color. A footman steps down to open the carriage door and lend me a hand inside. As I step up, I have a perfect view of the kitchen boy jumping up and down and waving me a joyous goodbye while his mischief-making pup is busy digging up the newly planted pansies.

The Princess of *I Idir* greets me warmly with a hug and a kiss to the cheek, though the sight of her takes my breath away. She's dressed all in silk the color of spring leaves, her red curls bundled up and hanging loose around her face and shoulders, a jeweled circlet crown made of rose gold and set with a line of perfect, forest-green emeralds resting on her forehead. The *Banphrionsa*'s face is a younger copy of The Raven Queen's, and though I've seen her on several other occasions, both here in *I Idir* as well as in the Mundane world, this afternoon she looks one hundred percent Otherworldly, an ancient goddess walking about in modern times.

"I'm so happy you could come with us today, Rosie," she says, dropping any premise of formality. "I wasn't sure you'd be able to get away with the baby's feeding schedule and all."

"I'm so very honored to be invited, Lady Dear Heart."

"Oh pooh," she replies, "please call me Maureen when we're alone like this. That protocol nonsense gets on my nerves. I just have to remember to mind all my P's and Q's when I'm with my grandmother or in a public setting where I'm representing Herself. I assume you going out like this on your own is okay with Fitz," she asks, using Declan's nickname among friends. "I know from personal experience how pissy fated mates get when they don't know where we're at."

Listening to her refer to The Black Knight as being "pissy" makes me giggle. "Declan is away on business until tomorrow, but I'm sure he won't mind. All of *Dun Siorai* knows where I'm at, and Lady *Nuada* sent along two of our House's own 'shadows.' I expect there's nothing to worry about," I say. "Seriously, what could possibly happen wandering around a local holiday faire with a pack of security at our back."

The *Ostara* faire is held in the town square of *I Idir's* capital city of *Nead an Fhithigh,* or "The Raven's Nest" as it is known in English. It is named such because it's the closest urban area to *Crann Bethadh* and the seat of *I Idir's* Throne. I'm actually quite familiar with the quaint, bustling town. Near the town square is the *Ficail Chisteain* (Tooth Treasury) where I am required to drop the teeth I collect as a member of the Tooth Fairy Corps, and if I remember correctly, there is a little shop that sells the best Otherworldly chocolates two blocks west of that building.

This is also the same place where I attended the very few Fae celebrations my mom deemed to bring me to as a child. In the very center of the square is a large fountain depicting what is, without a doubt, a statue of The Morrigan in full battle attire, the mighty *Caladbolg* upright in her left hand, surrounded by the heads of her dying enemies which bizarrely spout water from their gaping mouths into the waiting pool below. My logical, Mundane adult mind shudders at the bloodthirsty aspect of that memorial, but as a half Fae child, I found the fountain strangely comforting, a reminder that The Morrigan was always there in defense of her people.

The carriage rolls to a stop in front of a reviewing stand, and the footman appears at the door to first assist the *Banphrionsa* in alighting the vehicle, and then me. I had erroneously believed that there would be a few more people in the Princess's company today, but it appears it's only going to be the two of us along with the Lord Warrior which makes me suddenly feel very self-conscious. I'm led to a chair on the stage, while the Lady Dear Heart stands behind a large podium bearing a carved image of a winged bird I assume is meant to be a raven. The *Banphrionsa* is surrounded by a small army of fierce and decidedly unfriendly-looking trolls that traditionally serve as guard to the Royal House, with The Lord Warrior standing directly behind her, an imposing figure with thick, muscled arms clasped firmly behind his back, a wicked sized dagger strapped to his tree-trunk thigh.

I'm a little overwhelmed by the show of force at what is purported to be a peaceful festive gathering. It's hard to imagine anyone being stupid enough to take a shot at harming the Princess. Just the thought of what her mate would do to anyone who might try is scary enough. Add to that the idea of having the wrath of The Morrigan hanging over your head, as well as the hellish retribution from the man standing directly behind her, who I'm told considers the *Banphrionsa* his "goddaughter."

There is so much to take in that I don't know where to look first. Instead, I paste a look of pleasant interest on my face as the Lady Dear Heart speaks to the assembled crowd. She addresses the cheering multitude in the old language while I envy her flawless accent and relaxed body posture that speaks of the confidence she has in her royal role. Despite months of tutoring, my Otherworldly Gaelic still sounds choppy and awkward, and I usually end up speaking English whenever it's possible, a cop-out which certainly hasn't helped my mastery of the language.

As expected, the *Ostara* faire is well attended, with all types of Fae from every part of *I Idir* converging on the kingdom's capital. After months of being cooped-up inside, the chance to be outdoors in the sunshine, visit with old friends and neighbors, and replenish winter's empty larders, the faire is always a big draw. Today's especially mild weather has brought more folk out than usual, and no doubt the merchants are rubbing their palms together in anticipation of the day's hefty earnings. In the distance, I notice a small stall with a wide banner advertising *"Errai Leathair Min - Is Fearr Sa Riocht* (Fine Leather Goods-Best in The Kingdom)" Just a few days before, the Tax Man had complained that his favorite tunic belt had become too worn in the spot where his scabbard rests and would sadly have to be replaced. It might be a sweet gesture for me to find a new substitute if I can discover something that would meet my husband's finicky tastes. I note the location of the shop and make a mental plan to stop there later in the day and check their offerings.

At the podium, the Lady Dear Heart is nearing the end of her welcome speech, thanking the people in the name of Her Majesty for their loyal support. I discreetly scan the faces in the happy, cheering crowd. After years of living in the Mundane world, it still amazes me to see green and blue skin tones, unusual facial features, and non-human physical forms. It reminds me of just how much the Mundane population has gotten wrong about the Fae, and, remarkably, how much they've actually gotten correct in their varied myths and fairytales.

I witness a *Sidhe* male toting a laughing mer-toddler with tiny gills on his neck and a wave of melancholy rushes over me as I regret not being here, in this moment, with my *Mo Shiorghra* and our son for Dylan's first *Ostara* celebration. I can picture it clear as day; Declan walking beside the baby's carriage as I push it along, "the very important daddy" proud as a peacock, showing off his first-born son to every well-wisher, a big 'ole grin gracing his handsome face. The imaginary visual makes me smile. I sigh and turn my head. That's when I see her, standing off to the far left of the stage, arms crossed, staring straight at me with a deep scowl on her face. The very last person I want to see on what I hoped would be a pleasant day; the one and only Marcy Kilcrabtree.

WISDOM 19

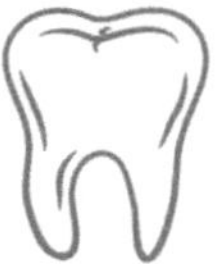

Pretty as a Picture

I LOOK AWAY from the crowd and down at my feet, while a feeling of anxiety rises from my stomach, into my chest, and finally takes hold of my mind. In my panic, I apparently am not shielding very well as the Lord Warrior and a few members of the Troll Guard glance over their shoulder at me with questioning looks. I give a vague wave and they eventually turn their focus back to the *Banphrionsa*. When I finally find enough courage to look back up in that same spot, Marcy Kilcrabtree is gone and I wonder if maybe I had just imagined the whole thing.

If my imagining that I saw that wretched woman here at the faire is just a reaction to my overall jumpiness, my physical reaction to it apparently is not. I hear my husband in my head, far away and sounding like he's in a tunnel. *"Are ya' alright, Love? I suddenly felt yar' heart racing! What's got ya' so worked up?"*

"I'm fine," I mentally reply. *"I'm at the Ostara faire in The*

Raven's Nest. Lady Dear Heart's invited me to attend as her guest. I thought Marcy Kilcrabtree was here but I was mistaken. Believing I saw her here caught me off guard is all."

There's a substantial pause before I hear his reply, and I wonder if the Tax Man is surprised by the turn of events, annoyed by them, or both. *"I hope ya' have taken proper security with ya, Lass."*

"Yes, I have two of House Nuada's men with me, plus the Royal Troll Guard that always accompanies the Banphrionsa. The Lord Warrior is here as well, though I'm not sure why. It seems overkill for a holiday festival."

"These are troublin' times, Rosie Lass. 'Tis best to be vigilant. Is Dylan with ya?"

"No. He's back at Dun Siora with Birgit."

In the same manner he can feel my emotions, I can feel his as well. Lord *Mac Nuada* is a mix of apprehension, regret at not being with me, and just a tiny smidgeon of pride over what I'm guessing is the fact that his *Mo Shiorghra* is being publicly included in the royal inner circle. It's not the kind of thing Rosie Parker gives a hoot about, but I'm not going to change my new husband's attitude regarding his *Sidhe* roots or what he considers his family obligations. *"I am heartfal' sorry that I canna' be with ya today, Love. Had I known about the invitation ahead of time, I would have refused ma' athair's request."*

"It's not your fault, Sweetie. The invitation came by raven-gram only this morning. I didn't know myself. Your mathair and I had to scramble to find an appropriate gown in time, though I do wish you could see me...I do believe you'd find me... quite fetching," I tease.

I hear him laugh on the other end and the sound of it

makes me immediately feel better. There's been far too few moments of lightness in the past few months. *"Ya' cad' be wearin' an ole' feedbag and I'd forever find ya' fetchin', ma' Love, though I would vera' much like to see ya' in yar' faire finery. The lovely sight of ya' would surely be a remedy ta' ma' sour mood"* There's a short pause, and then he adds, *"Perhaps there is a way I still ken' see if ya' ken' find a full-length mirror in one of the merchant stalls. I'm sure among the tailors and the seamstresses ya' will be able ta' find such a thing. When ya' do find it, let me know. I believe if we both concentrate hard enough, maybe ya' ken' pass the image on ta' me."*

The idea delights me and I can't help smiling, though I hope I don't look like an idiot sitting up on the stage grinning like a clown. *"Sounds like a plan, Tax Man. I'll look for a mirror as I make my rounds. I assume I'll have to move along with the Banphrionsa's entourage, but I'm sure she'll stop if I ask. You know she's really a down to earth person despite her title. Can you believe she actually said to me that the Black Knight can be 'pissy' when he doesn't know where she is at all times. I'd never use that term in reference to the Queen's Hand of Justice."*

The Tax Man laughs again. *"Well...she isn't much wrong, Lass. The man does not like surprises of any kind. Now, I best pay attention to where my harse' is steppin'. The roads leading to Asgard are woefully in need of attention. Let me know if and when ya' find a mirror, Love."*

"I will, Sweetie. Please be safe. I hate when we're apart," The words lie heavy on my mind with a sense of deep apprehension that I've been unable to rid myself of since the North Korea mission.

"Aye, sweet Rosie, you be safe as well. Stay close to the royal

entourage. Ya'll be plenty protected there. Buy yar'self anything ya' wish and charge it ta' ma' account. I want ya' ta' have a pleasant outing."

"I'll do just that. Of course...with that option I just might have to hire someone to carry all my purchases to the carriage," I joke.

"Yar' every wish is mine ta' fufill, darlin'. I love ya', Mrs. Fitzpatrick."

I can feel the knot forming in my throat, that awful ache of missing him. *"I love you too, Mr. Fitzpatrick. Tomorrow can't come fast enough for me. I hate sleeping alone."*

Lost in my mental conversation, I'm startled when the entire group begins to leave the stage. I drop my mental connection to Declan and rise quickly as the Lord Warrior and the Troll Guard pause to let me step in behind the *Banphrionsa*. Flustered at being caught not paying attention, I don't stop to lift the hem of my gown which has puddled underneath my chair. This causes the edge of it to catch on a rough spot on the leg of the chair rendering a small tear when I stand. One of the armored trolls steps out of formation to unhook the fabric from the chair leg as I try not to die of embarrassment, hoping that Lady *Siobhan* doesn't read me the riot act over the damage to my gown when I return to *Dun Siorai*. Then, just as suddenly, the tear vanishes. I'm confused until I catch the eye of the Lord Warrior who just smiles and offers me his arm down the stairs of the raised platform. This is, of course, the Fae Otherworld where magic is the answer to most of life's daily problems.

The group regathers in front of the stage where the Princess is mobbed by people pushing tokens towards her as well as myself; bouquets of flowers, baskets of colored eggs, early spring vegetables, and rabbit figurines made out of every conceivable material. I follow Lady Dear Heart's lead, smiling and thanking each recipient for their gift as I pass them off to waiting staff. Some people ask after my husband and son, and I answer their interest with a grateful heart even if my use of their language is mediocre at best.

This royal meet-and-greet takes much longer than I think any of us had anticipated, but the princess refuses to leave anyone out. By the time we accept the last greeting and gift, I can tell by the sun's position in the sky that it is mid to late afternoon. Breakfast is a forgotten memory and my mouth is parched from constant chit-chat. The Lord Warrior recommends that we settle somewhere for a respite of food and drink, but his goddaughter nixes his suggestion. "I have strict instructions from Herself to visit every stall and make a single purchase from each of them whether I have any use or desire for whatever they're selling," the Lady Dear Heart explains. "Herself doesn't want it rumored *Crann Bethadh* showed favoritism to one vendor over another."

"'Tis my Queen's way," *Cu Chulainn* admitts. "She desires ta' be fair above all things, though I donna' believe that she expects ya' or Lady Rosalinda ta' faint from hunger or thirst. I have no doubt that both of yar' mates would hold me fully responsible should their ladies suffer any ill effects over today's events. Is there a way we can somehow compromise, Beloved Niece?"

"I don't mean to be difficult, *Uncail Cullain*," Dear Heart replies, the casual familiarity between them fascinating to me. It's not what I'd expect of the royal family. "It's just I don't relish a scolding from Herself over not following the directives she's specifically laid out for me. It has to be after 2:00 PM and there's a large number of vendors here. I worry we won't get to them all before dark." The *Banphrionsa* turns to me. "I'm so sorry, Rosie. I should have warned you this would end up being a command performance. You must be regretting accepting my invitation."

"Not at all. I'm having fun," I reply. "This is all new to me, and I'm excited to be part of it. Besides, as much as I love my son, it's good for me to have some grown-up time to myself. I'm up for whatever happens today."

The Morrigan's granddaughter gives me another hug. "You're the best, Rosie Fitzpatrick! If I have to be stuck hiding out here in *I Idir* I'm glad to have found a friend like you."

"Aye. Lord *Mac Nuada* is indeed blessed in his chosen *Mo Shiorghra*. His Lady is as sweet as she is lovely," the Lord Warrior adds.

Their words make me blush, and for the first time in all my trips here to the Fae Otherworld, I feel like this place could actually be "home." "You're all too kind," I stammer, my emotions bubbling up. "I feel equally lucky that this is the path the Universe has laid out before me."

"Speaking of paths," Lady Dear Heart says, "we should probably get going on the one in front of us today. I suggest we start with the food stalls on the right side so we can grab something to eat and drink as we move along. How does that sound to everyone?" she asks, including all our security staff in the question, and I think to myself that there's a lot to like about *I Idir's* half-human Fae princess.

* * *

I would be lying if I said that by the time we reached the last few vendor stalls on the right side of the faire grounds I wasn't completely exhausted. It had to be nearly 5:00 PM, and I was beginning to feel the effects of not nursing Dylan since late this morning. I knew I'd left *Birgit* with enough prepared bottles of breast milk to cover his feedings while I was gone. My baby boy doesn't care much for the rubber-like nipples that were a poor substitute for his mother, but he'd take them if he were hungry enough. What I hadn't counted on was the very uncomfortable, too-full feeling I was now experiencing along with the fear that I might start leaking at any given moment. In this light-colored chiffon dress, the tell-tale stains would be hard to miss.

I wasn't the only one showing the wear and tear of a long day. The *Banphrionsa's* bouncy curls were beginning to go limp, and I could see by the way she rocked from foot to foot that she was tired of standing. Even the robust *"Uncail Cullain"* needed to cover a discreet yawn, and the pages in charge of carrying our purchases looked ready to drop. When we finally got to the stall advertising the fine leather goods near the end of the line, it dawned on me that I had entirely forgotten about finding a mirror and attempting to send Declan an image of me in my *Ostara* gown. All the dressmakers had been on the other side of the faire grounds and I myself didn't relish the idea of walking all the way back. I also figured that my dutiful security detail would like it even less. But struck with a bad case of wifely guilt, I attempted to excuse myself and trudge back to find a full-length mirror.

"Is there something I can get far' ya' instead, Lady *Mac Nuada*," the Lord Warrior offers. "Truth be told, ya' look a wee bit *tuirseach* (tired)...bein' a new *mathair* and all."

I feel silly explaining why I have to go back, but the legend isn't wrong. I'm running on empty, and my boobs are sore as hell. I sheepishly explain to him what I want to do. The big guy gives me a smile full of merriment. "I ken' not blame his young Lordship far' wantin' a look-see at his beautiful Lady wife, so newly handfasted as ya' both are. The desire between fated mates is a blazin' fire." Embarrassment colors my face, which makes the man laugh out loud. "Ya' don't need a mirror, sweet Lady. I ken' send yar' Lord the same vision I see in front of me own face. Now go ahead and give yar' husband a lover's smile...aye...just like that."

I figure I'll never live this one down, but for my Tax Man, the mortification is worth it. It isn't long before I hear my *Mo Shiorghra* in my head. His words make me much too warm and don't do anything to help the ache in my breasts. His words come out in the old language which they often do in the midst of our intimacy. "*Is maith an rud go bhfuil me anseo, a phiscin mhilis, ar eagla go ngoidfinn thu taobh thair de cheann de na stallai sin agus go dtogfaidh me mo chuid ama leat...direach ansin le daoine ag eisteacht.* ('Tis a good thing I am here, sweet kitten, lest I steal ya' off behind one of those stalls and take ma' time with ya'...right there with folks listenin')"

The Lord Warrior is still standing there, grinning like a fool at me while I hope like hell he can't actually hear the words the Tax Man is sending me. Feeling trapped and wholly embarrassed, I smile at the legend and slip into the leather shop to find a gift for my husband.

Taking notice that I am a member of the royal entourage, the owner comes over to wait on me himself. I explain what I'm looking for, and he leads me to the far corner of the stall where he has his finest work on display. My eyes immediately go to the belt that has musical notes worked into traditional Celtic knotwork patterns, done so subtly that one almost misses them. It's a remarkable piece with a price tag to match, but once I hold it in my hands, I know nothing else can match up. I buy the belt, smiling as I picture Declan's face as I give him this gorgeous piece of wearable art. Filled with the joy that comes with the finding of a perfect treasure, I happily turn to leave only to come face to face with Marcy Kilcrabtree.

WISDOM 20

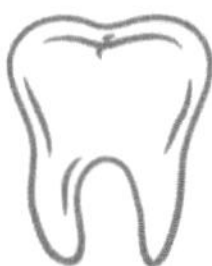

Chick Fight

"LADY *MAC NUADA*...FANCY finding you here...off your leash and on your own," the witch says, standing so close I can smell her perfume, an overpowering mix of jasmine and vanilla.

I attempt to walk past her, hoping to ignore her completely and rejoin the royal entourage outside, but the Kilcrabtree woman moves in tandem, preventing me from passing in the tight confines of the leather stall. "Please take yourself out of my way, Cadet," I ask calmly, knowing perfectly well that using her low-ranking, Tooth Fairy Corps title won't help the situation.

Her face immediately registers the anger I expect over the perceived slur. She snarls back at me. "As you are fully aware, Parker, I'm no longer assigned to the Corps. I am a member of the Black Knight's 'personal' team...or have you forgotten?"

"Is that so?" I reply with feigned innocence. "I had heard…otherwise."

For a mere second, the woman's face registers a flash of concern. "Heard from who, *Mac Nuada?* Who's spreading outright lies about me?"

Truth be told, I've heard no such thing. In fact, since that awful 'welcome home' party earlier in the month, Declan and I have carefully avoided even mentioning Marcy's name, lest the Universe hear us and put her in our path again. But the Fae love gossip more than any other pastime, and "having the goods on someone" means having the upper hand. I detest Marcy Kilcrabtree with a depth I've never before experienced in my life. What she put my beloved Tax Man through, the risks she took with my family's future, still leaves me anxious and makes me willing to take chances with the Universe's rubber-banding karma, something I usually avoid.   Smiling sweetly with no warmth in my tone I add, "Oh you know how it is, Marcy, dear. People talk. You can never tell what news you'll pick up in…general conversation. Now if you'll excuse me, I musn't keep the *Banphrionsa* waiting any longer."

If from that innocent comment the wretched girl somehow thinks that I'm inferring that I might have heard something said about her within the royal circle, well it's just too damn bad. I quickly step to the right, but Kilcrabtree anticipates the move and beats me to it, still blocking my exit. The green hooded cloak she's wearing swings open and I note the large pendant hanging around her neck. It's hard to miss with its gleaming obscenely large, dark red center stone handsomely set in an intricate woven Celtic setting. It's a stunning and obviously expensive piece, and, if I had to guess, a gift from the obnoxious Lord *Mac Badh*, though the blood-colored stone is an odd lover's token, as traditionally, House *Badh* favors emeralds as their signature gem. Plus, as his House heir, the young Lord would be held, like my husband, to the prohibitive dictates of The Ritual. A horrible thought crosses my mind. Could Marcy Kilcrabtree possibly be *Mac Badh's Mo Shiorghra*? I shove that idea from my head. The Universe couldn' be so cruel…could it?

The weasel woman catches my interest in her jewelry and smiles, the lack of goodwill in her facial expression as obvious as mine. "Quite a stunner, is it not?" Marcy runs a hand down the chain and pets the gem as if it were a cherished pet. It's a creepy gesture and I give an involuntary shudder. "You see, Parker," she says, again using my maiden name as if it's some kind of insult, which to my mind, it certainly is not, "you're not the only one who can sport the family jewels," Kilcrabtree boasts.

It's a weird ass comment that confuses me. Is she referring to the term "family jewels" in the crude, slang way, obscenely referring to *Mac Badh's* testicles? Or is she just bragging that she too is handfasting an heir to the Ruling Council? Either answer is stomach-turning and makes me in even a bigger hurry to get the hell out of Dodge and go back to *Dun Siorai* to feed my baby. "Whatever, Marcy. Just get the hell out of my way and let me pass before I call someone to personally move you," I threaten.

She doesn't move out of the way, and in fact takes a few steps forward until we're practically nose to nose.

"You stand there so damn smug, Parker. Thinking you got it made, allowing yourself to become the Raven's little pet. I'll let you in on a little gossip of my own…watch your back, Fido. There's a real good chance you leashed yourself to the wrong Master."

In my head, I hear the tinkling of little bells, which is a sure fire sign The Morrigan is listening in. This is all going down badly, and I now wholeheartedly regret my decision to stray from the safe and secure confines of my husband's ancestral home. "What you're saying, Cadet, is paramount to treason. What makes you think I won't immediately go outside and report your exact words to the Lord Warrior and the Troll Guard?"

What the witch doesn't know is that it's far too late for that. My threat is meaningless. Her Majesty has already heard the damning words straight from the horse's mouth. The hate in the woman's eyes flares like gasoline on a campfire. "I know for a fact you'll keep your mouth shut, Fido," she mutters, "because you love your baby, and we both know that babies are such fragile little things… always at the mercy of a multitude of terrible accidents and life ending diseases."

It was the worst threat the bitch could have ever made. I lose control of my very last sense of decorum. I narrow my eyes, bending my head toward her so now our noses are actually physically touching. "If you come anywhere near my son, you lying, evil bitch, I'll feckin' take you out myself. I'll use my damn bare hands to squeeze the very last breath from your scrawny little chicken neck," I growl, loud enough for everyone around us to hear. Then, I give her a hard push to the chest with both hands. She's not expecting any physical confrontation, so she's not prepared for my sudden attack. Marcy Kilcrabtree loses her balance and stumbles backwards into a table holding a collection of saddlebags which tumble with thud to the floor around her. In the melee, the sleeve of my gown catches on a rough part of the hanging pendant's setting, and as she falls backward, the chain snaps, leaving the necklace dangling from the threads of my sleeve. I pull at the gem, and in my haste, make another ragged tear in my gown. Disgusted, I toss the cursed thing at Marcy's feet and stomp out of the leather store without a single word.

In the aftermath of my unfortunate encounter, the Lord Warrior decides the best course of action is to bundle both the *Banphrionsa* and myself back into the carriage and head home to our respective residences. I do my best to apologize for my wholly improper behavior. The Princess and the Lord Warrior keep reassuring that they sympathize with me over the whole situation and reiterate that it was Marcy Kilcrabtree herself who broke all kinds of rules and protocol regarding behavior towards a guest of The Crown. I understand that their words are meant as a kindness to me, but I fully know that my bad decisions in confronting the woman in such a public, physical manner will reflect poorly on House *Nuada*. I fully expect my in-laws to read me the riot act when I return to *Dun Siorai,* and it's only a matter of time before Declan hears of it as well. As I've already said, gossip is the life blood of the kingdom.

The princess offers to accompany me inside to help explain my innocence in the whole fiasco while smoothing things over with Declan's parents. It's a lovely gesture, but one I know better than to accept. Toting home the *Banphrionsa* of *I Idir* without giving Lady *Nuada* proper notice will not win me any brownie points, nor will it help my cause. I graciously decline the offer and with a final apology, Declan's ill-fated new belt in my hand, I trudge through the estate's main entrance.

* * *

Every *Ostara* goddess in the Celtic pantheon must be looking out for poor me with pity on this particularly lousy day. No one is waiting for me in the grand foyer, and the staff is going about their normal business without giving me knowing looks out of the corner of their eyes. I take that to mean that news of my brawl at the faire hasn't yet reached *Dun Siorai*, so I hustle off to our quarters which thankfully are in a more remote area of the estate.

Birgit and Dylan are waiting for me, the latter loudly expressing his demand to be fed. Apologizing for the baby's fussing, the nanny explains, "Our wee Lordy no likes the rubber nipple, ma' Lady. He be makin' his feelings known for the better part of an hour despite me tryin' all the tricks ta' fool him inta' takin' the bottle. I swear even *Lugh* (Celtic trickster god) would be stymied ta' enchant the youngest *Mac Nuada*. The *bairn* wants no one but his dear *mathair*."

"I'm so sorry, *Birgit*. I never expected to be this long," I say, as I take my son from the nanny's arms and settle myself in my favorite nursing chair. My son instantly stops his crying, looking up at me with eyes the color of spring leaves, a match to those of his *athair*. "*Na deora nios mo, a cheann beag. Ta Mamai anseo le do dhinnear* (No more tears, little one. Mama is here with your dinner)," I murmur in the old language, bad accent and all. Slipping the bodice of the gown down from my shoulders, Dylan nuzzles up against my bare skin. And for the next hour, I forget about Marcy Kilcrabtree. Forget about facing my in-laws. Forget about the aching homesickness that lies in my heart. Instead, I close my eyes and dwell in this special moment with my son.

WISDOM 21

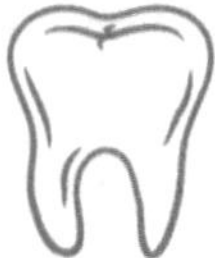

Cooking Up a Mystery

THE EVENING after my return from the *Ostara* faire is surprisingly quiet. *Birgit* and I have dinner by ourselves in our quarters, uninterrupted by any unwanted guests or a summons from my angered in-laws. Over our meal, I pour out the whole story to my son's *scathach*, who vows on her life that she will allow no one to harm my son. Knowing she sleeps at Dylan's side, armed with goddess knows what type of weapons, is a bit disconcerting, but I'll admit I rest easier having her with us, especially with Declan still not home.

By midnight, when I still as of yet haven't been rounded up for a severe scolding by Lord or Lady *Nuada*, I turn out the lights and attempt to sleep, though my mind keeps replaying the events of the day. I consider reaching out to Declan but eventually decide against it. He's expected home tomorrow afternoon. I determine a face to face *"mea culpa"* is probably the better way to go in this situation.

By morning, unrested and tired of waiting for the other shoe to drop, I make plans to beat my in- laws to the punch by seeking them out before they come looking for me. Weighing my options, I determine that Dragon Mama is the lesser of two evils and more likely to feel my actions toward Marcy were justified over the woman's direct threats against Dylan, so she's my first stop. After breakfast, I bundle Dylan in his cutest baby bunting, tuck him in his carriage, then *Birgit* and I set off to "visit" with Lady *Nuada.* At the last moment, I grab the leather belt I bought for Declan. I tell myself I'll use it as a prop of sorts while I tell my side of the story, though, truthfully, it's really there for me to hold so my in-laws don't see my hands shaking. Fear is frowned upon at *Dun Siorai* and the weak get eaten.

Halfway to the solar parlor, Lady *Nuada's* usual spot for post-breakfast tea, I have second thoughts and head for the kitchen instead. I explain to the nanny that this change of plans is so that I can check if his Lordship's orders regarding *Buaf's* care have been followed, but I'm pretty sure she can see right through my delay tactic.

Cook is surprised to find me in her kitchen at this time of the day and her inability to look me straight in the eye makes it pretty likely she's already heard the rumors about what went on at the *Ostara* faire. She fusses around finding me a clean chair and sets up tea and cinnamon scones to fill the awkward silence. *Buaf* is nowhere to be seen, so I feel it's a good time to discuss the boy's situation, my way of avoiding the real elephant in the room.

"We were on our way to see Lady *Nuada* and so I thought I would stop by and check if Lord *Mac Nuada's* directives regarding the boy were being attended to," I say.

"Aye, my Lady," Cook answers. I can't tell if the woman is relieved not to have to talk about my public embarrassment or disappointed not to have the scoop straight from the horse's mouth. "The boy has had a proper bath, a set of clean clothes, and a new pair of boots, though the later weren't no small feat, my Lady, him havin' that vera' odd sixth toe." She makes the Fae sign for the evil eye to which I make a face.

"There's nothing 'odd' about an extra finger or toe, Madame Cook. It's actually quite common among Mundane babies," I explain. "It often runs in families but can also sometimes just happen spontaneously during fetal development. Which leads me to my next question. "How did the boy come to be living here at *Dun Siorai*? What became of his parents?"

Cook hesitates a moment too long, as if she's not comfortable discussing the topic. Wiping her hands in her apron smock, she pulls up a stool next to me, settling in for her tale. "The story, like the boy himself, is a strange one, ma' Lady. He was brought here in the wee hours of the mornin' by Himself of all people. I had just started preparin' the day's *bricfesta* (breakfast) when the man stomped in, a wailin' *bairn* in his arms."

"Wait," I interrupt. "By 'Himself' do you mean Lord *Nuada?*"

"Aye. His Lordship said he found the babe abandoned in the woods surroundin' *Dun Siorai* when he was out huntin' wolves that had ben' menancin' the farmers. He was no too happy about the situation but grumbled that as Lord he could not in good conscience leave the par' thing to get eaten...even if the boy was undoubtedly a foundlin' of...unnatural parentage."

The story is horrific yet fascinating and I can't help but feel sorry for a child who's had such a rough beginning through no fault of his own. "Poor kid. I agree it's not the best of circumstances, but I don't understand why you'd call his birth 'unnatural.' Surely, it's not just because of that extra toe?" I ask. "That would just be ridiculous."

"It weren't just the toe, ma' Lady. The boy was still wearin' his caul, torn open only wide enough to allow him to take his first breaths, with his birth cord yet attached, it bein' all rough cut and bloody as if the *bairn* was just hacked from its *mathair*. Only a monster would leave a babe in such poor condition, newly fresh from the womb. No decent Fae would do such a thing...not even the *Formoire*."

Her statement is no lie. The spiritual philosophy of almost every race in the Otherworld, Fae or otherwise, held to the sacred tenement that new life was divinely created. Offspring were considered the highest gift of the Universe, the end all to a species' very survival. Even the most primitive and violent cultures, like the warrior *Formoire*, cherished their children. Someone leaving a newborn infant out in the elements as was done to poor *Buaf* was in a special category of evil all by itself no matter what corner of the Otherworld you hailed from. "And no one ever discovered who'd left the baby in such a horrible condition? I would think that the Black Knight wouldn't rest until he found the culprit responsible for such reprehensible behavior."

"T'weren't no Black Knight in *I Idir* durin' that time, Lady *Mac.* The old one had violated Her Highness's law about citizens forcin' themselves on innocent males and females. It was revealed that the man had been usin' his authority ta' impose seduction without consent upon a number of the kingdom's less powerful Fae. That sorta thin' ken' no be tolerated. The Morrigan herself executed the man in front of *Crann Bethadh* far' all ta' witness. T'was quite the bloody spectacle with the Knight's head rollin' across the stone walkway far' no less than *dha chos* (two feet). I don't even like remembern' it," she says, pulling a cloth from her apron pocket and wiping her eyes before continuing with her narrative. "Soon after that, our current Black Knight pledged his service to *I Idir.* What a blessin' that was! Have ya' as of yet met the man, ma' Lady? He is a bonnie fine specimen of Otherworldly justice, ain't he? Him bein' the Merlin's own seed as well as the *Banphrionsa's* mate, and all. Trust me, if that babe was found today, our new Black Knight would be like a hound ta' fox ta' find those evil-doers."

I have enough people gossiping about me already. I don't need to add fuel to the fire so I forgo mentioning that I've met our impressive Black Knight...more than once and on an "up close and personal" basis. *I Idir's* intelligence network, led by the man himself, is not common knowledge in the kingdom and those of us in his employ know to keep that information to ourselves. Still, I agree with Cook. If that baby had been found today, those behind his heinous abandonment would surely be brought to justice. I've learned firsthand that the Black Knight is not a man to trifle with. "Yes. I've heard that *I Idir's* Hand of Justice is one hundred percent committed to his task." I respond, then attempt to bring the subject back to the boy. "So, the child's been here ever since?"

"Aye. Leza the washwoman had just given birth to a *bairn* herself, so she acted as wet nurse ta' the babe. The rest of us took turns fosterin' him until he was able ta' care far' himself at *Dun Siorai* and thus earn his keep. He is full of mischief that one, but he is good of heart. Never speaks a sassy word ta' any of the staff and is always takin' in injured wee creatures and nursin' 'em back ta' health. Though I can't say I am as fond of that little *madra diabhal* (demon dog) that he's claimed as his own. That creature is no more than a four-footed *gadai* (thief)! The pointy-eared hell-hound has stolen more biscuits from ma' table than I care ta' talk about."

Her description *of Buaf's* canine pal makes me smile. "The pup is high-strung, no doubt about that, but the two of them do seem devoted to one another. We'd never have found the boy in that hole the other night if the dog hadn't led us to him. I can't imagine who would leave such a dangerous open pit like that. Anyone could have fallen in," I say in the little dog's defense.

The woman shrugged her shoulders. "I suppose the gardener was lookin' to trap some vermin. Somethin' has been scavengin' the spring offerins' for a few weeks now. I'm sure old Geoff would never knowingly put any of the family or staff in danger."

According to Declan's description of the pit, it didn't sound like it was any type of small animal trap, but I don't make my suspicions known. "I'm just glad we didn't end up with a tragedy here," I comment, though honestly, I'm not really sure if anyone at *Dun Siorai* would have shed any tears over the loss of the poor kid. "I'm glad then to see that his Lordship's directives were met. Has the dog been given shelter in the barn as well?"

"Yes, ma' Lady. Lord *Mac Nuada's* personal groom has seen to it that the little demon has a warm bed near his Lordship's stalls. Unfortunately, the boy has now decided to sleep with the dog in the barn rather than his usual spot here in the kitchen. He claims his dog is lonely without him," Cook said, shaking her head in disgust. "I hope Lord *Mac* will not blame me for the boy's silly attachment."

"No, I'm sure he won't, Cook. My husband has a soft spot for animals as well, especially his horses. I can fully see him sleeping in their stalls as a boy."

" 'Tis the truth ya' speak, dear Lady. His Lordship has a vera' gentle heart. No wonder he's taken such an interest in *Buaf*. The boy is not unlike him in that manner."

Her comment pokes at my subconscious and makes me realize how little I know about my Tax Man's life as a boy beyond what he's told me about The Ritual. However, those are stories better left for another visit. Even without a watch or a cell phone to remind me of the time, I know I've been here in the kitchen for far too long. Because of our forced proximity in the last month of my pregnancy, I'm familiar with my mother-in-law's daily habits. She'll soon be finishing up her late morning tea break and then will be off taking care of the day's business. I can't put off facing the music any longer, so I rise to leave. "Thank you for all the information, Madame Cook. I'll be sure to let his Lordship know that you have done as he asked. I know he'll be appreciative of your loyalty and attention to detail."

Cook flushes a warm pink color, and drops a curtsy. "Thank you, Lady *Mac*. I'm sure you know how fond I am of yar' *Mo Shiorghra* and how much bein' a part of *Dun Siorai* for all these years means ta' me."

"Your affection surely shows, good lady. House *Nuada* is lucky to have you here in the kitchen where your talent knows no bounds," I say.

She blushes again, then quickly turns to wrap some newly baked scones and a small crock of freshly churned cream in a piece of laundered muslin. Handing the parcel to me she adds, "For when his Lordship returns this afternoon. To go with his tea. They are known ta' be his favorite...buttermilk with candied orange peel. I make 'em special for *Mac Nuada* every spring when the preserved winter orange peels have finally reached thar' peak sweetness."

Her kindness toward my Tax Man tugs at my heart. "What a treasure, Madame Cook. Without a doubt I can assure you that his Lordship will especially enjoy these. I thank you from the bottom of my heart for thinking of him." Tucking the scones and cream in the foot pouch of Dylan's carriage, the *scathach* takes over and maneuvers the pram out of the tight confines of the kitchen and into the estate's main hallway with me right behind her.

WISDOM 22

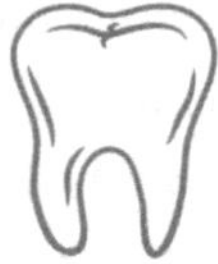

Dog Gone It

"I suppose there's no putting this off any longer, *Birgit*," I say when we are out of Cook's ear shot. "It's such a beautiful day, let's take the garden path to the solar parlor. I'd like to avoid the prying eyes and questioning looks of the staff if I'm able," I suggest. "I'm surprised Cook didn't ask me about yesterday's events."

"It wasn't as if she didn't desire such a conversation, my Lady," the *scathach* laughed. "But I think she speaks the truth when she says she is fond of your Lord, and thus yourself as well, being that you are his true *Mo Shiorghra*. I am sorry to tell you but it is my belief that all of *Dun Siorai* is already abuzz with the news of your encounter with that black-hearted *breagadoir* (liar)."

"Of course, they are," I mutter. "Because that's the way it usually goes for me." I sigh and add, "I suppose I better meet with Lord and Lady *Nuada* pronto and see if I can't do some type of damage control."

The three of us casually stroll the cobblestone pathway. The day is unseasonably mild with a warm sun and a cloudless blue sky, and if I didn't have In-Law Armageddon hanging over my head, I would have thoroughly enjoyed a long walk around *Dun Siorai's* sizable gardens. With its just greening flower beds and attractively shaped topiaries, it's one of my favorite spots in the Tax Man's large ancestral home. The conversation with Cook still lingering foremost in my mind, I try to imagine a boy-sized Declan wandering these same paths, while at the same time anticipating our son doing the same someday in the future.

Lost in my daydreams, I don't see the small terrier following us until we almost reach the east entrance to the house that leads to the Solar Parlor. I stop and call him. "Good Morrow, wee *Seamus.* Where is your young Master this fine day?"

The pup wags his tail and comes close enough to allow some personal attention. I put my handbag on the ground next to me, the ill-fated belt for Declan sticking out the top of it, and bend down to pet the dog's head and scratch behind his ears. "I don't care what anyone says, *Seamus.* You're a sweet little thing, aren't you," I coo at him in the same voice I use with Dylan.

The puppy sits up on his hind legs and yaps, his tail waving back and forth like a metronome. "I think he's asking for a treat," *Birgit* comments.

"I think you're right," I say. "But I don't think I have anything to give him." Declan's scones come to mind, but before I can decide to break a hunk off to toss to him, the cunning little thing leaps forward and grabs the leather belt from the top of my purse. Without hesitation, the dog is off and running like hell away from us in the direction of the house, the buckle of the belt clanking behind him. "Sonofabitch! You come back here, you damn little thief! I didn't go through all that trouble to buy that frickin' belt so you can run off with it!" I yell at the dog.

"I can chase him, Lady *Mac*," *Birgit* offers. "I am vera' fast."

With Marcy's threats against Dylan still foremost in my mind, I decide I'd prefer her with my son instead. "No. You stay here with Dylan. I'll track him down. He knows me so maybe he'll let me get close enough to take the belt back."

"As you wish, good Lady. Dylan and I shall remain here and wait for your return," the *scathach* replies.

I take off in the direction of the blasted dog, but when I get to the east entrance walkway, he's nowhere to be seen. From outside the open gate, I hear a few barks, so I step inside the covered passage and try to place from which direction the sound came from. This is a section of the house I'm least familiar with as it contains mostly storerooms, larders and pantries that I've yet to have reason to explore. It is the furthest byway from the main entrance and butts up against a wooded expanse, and though I've been to the Solar Parlor that sits several floors up, I've never been down in the rooms below. Once my eyes adjust to the darkness of the windowless hall, I see the four-legged fiend several meters ahead, my belt still in its mouth, tail wagging, as if to goad me into chasing him.

I move slowly, trying not to scare him off in the hopes I can get close enough to grab the end with the buckle.

"Nice doggy. Good *Seamus*. Good boy. Give Rosie the belt and I'll give you a treat." I wonder as I say this if Fae canines are capable of distinguishing a lie, as I didn't think to bring any of those orange peel scones with me to bribe him. The pup sits himself down and lets me get almost to him before immediately racing further down the winding pathway. I chase after him around corners, stairways, and closed doors until we both come to a dead end, a brick wall signaling the end of the line. "You got nowhere to go, doggo! Give me that damn belt!" My voice bounces off the walls and echoes down the passage.

Seamus stays still, as if seriously considering all his options, then sprints past me towards a heavy wooden door to my right that is open just a crack. I grab at the end of the belt as the canine scampers by, but, slimy with dog drool, it slips from my hand, leaving me with no choice but to follow him inside the room. The space is dark, musty and covered in multi-generational grime, the only light coming from a very small square window with bars in front of it. "Damn it, you bad dog! Let's end this stupid game. I'm tired of chasing you and this room gives me the creeps."

The fact that there are chains fastened to heavy hooks, green with the patina of age, and thus indicating their makeup to be a blend of zinc and copper, better known as brass, doesn't help with my high "ick factor" reaction. As a tooth fairy, my very limited magical abilities don't show themselves during the daylight hours, but even though it's not even noon, I can feel the oppressive push of the metal alloys against my Fae spirit. I try hard not to think of Declan being surrounded by this feeling day and night during the entire time he was held by the North Koreans, but the knowledge, nevertheless, leaves me queasy.

Pushing further into the space, I note two cell like niches, each closed in by more brass bars and the sudden realization of the nature of this place hits me like a brick to the head. This is House *Nuada's* dungeon, a throwback to the dark times when House fought against House in a landscape of mistrust and violence. Thankfully, the layers of undisturbed dust and the green patina of the brass are proof that the space hasn't been used as such for a very long time, but the vibrations of misery and hopelessness still circle inside these walls. That's when I notice the crude cot inside one of the small cells, covered in a pile of furs and blankets that look new and have the distinct odor of jasmine and vanilla. There is also a small table with an empty bottle of wine and two used pieces of expensive stemware, that, unlike everything else down here, is not covered in dust, with one glass showing a tell-tale lipstick stain. It becomes obvious to me that someone has recently been using this space as a rendezvous location, a lovers' nest for trysting in complete privacy despite the shit load of mood-busting, negative energy the space exudes.

I catch the dog with the corner of my eye, running toward the very back of the dungeon where he is stopped by a lowered portcullis covering a dark tunnel that leads to no place I'm anxious to explore. Finally, the mangy mutt is at a disadvantage with absolutely nowhere to go, the brass grate keeping him from disappearing into the dark passage. "You didn't have to make this so difficult, Master *Seamus*. You've gone and lost one of the few friends you actually had around this place. Now, hand over that feckin' belt!"

Before the dog can obey, there is the echo of footsteps in the hallway just outside the dungeon and the soft murmuring of voices. The dog's ear's stand straight up at the sound. He instantly drops the belt, turns and squeezes his furry body through an opening at the bottom of the portcullis, then trots into the darkness, leaving me frozen to my spot.

I grab the ill-fated leather *crios* (belt) where the pup finally relinquished it, while frantically looking for somewhere to hide, hoping against hope that whomever is coming down the passage isn't heading for the old dungeon. I'd be hard pressed to explain why I'm down here snooping around. The wine cellar is also at this end of the house, so I cross my fingers that the footsteps belong to a member of the staff in search of a specific lunch-time bottle, but as the sounds come closer, I distinguish that the voices belong to both a male and a female, and without a doubt I realize the pair is on their way to their secret love nest.

With nowhere to go and the only other exit bringing me face to face with a pair who definitely won't be happy to find me waiting for them, I spy an old wooden trunk pushed against the wall in the second cell. Something inside my head, Herself perhaps, strongly warns me not to reveal myself. With thanks to all the goddesses I claim, I find the crate to be empty except for a collection of dirt and spider webs. I quickly climb in, tucking my gown around my legs, while I pull the heavy top down over me.

WISDOM 23

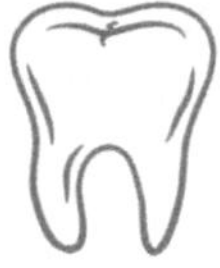

Hide And Peek

THE INSIDE of the trunk smells like rotting wood and moldy rags and I don't even want to think about all the rat poop I'm undoubtedly sitting on. The thin spaces between the planks that make up the sides and top of the chest allow for a miniscule amount of light and air to filter in, but are much too narrow to allow me any kind of decent view of what's going on outside. All sound is muffled, so it's almost impossible to hear specific conversation or to identify the speakers by their voice other than to distinguish that they are male and female. However, when my visitors move from the front of the dungeon to the cot in the cell across from me, there's no mistaking what's going on outside my hiding place.

I would stick my fingers in my ears to further block it out if there was some feasible way for me to move my arms enough to be able to get my hands anywhere near my face. Unfortunately, it's a tight fit and my elbows are firmly wedged next to my body. Shifting around is bound to cause too much noise so I am ungratefully treated to the whole audio track of the…uhmmm… "romantic interlude" going on in the cell across from me.

I'd be the first to admit that I'm not what one would call "worldly" regarding sex. Most of what I know has been garnished from movies, television, a handful of smutty romance novels, and very limited personal experience. It's true that my destiny with the Tax Man has happily broadened my world in that regard, but voyeurism is apparently not in my wheelhouse, especially not the audio kind. I do not perceive the moaning, grunting, and flesh-slapping noises to be in the least bit…titillating. As a matter of fact, instead of conjuring up erotic images, I find myself taking bets on how long it will be until the ratty, old cot completely falls apart from all that monstrous bouncing.

Inside my hidey-hole, I make general assumptions that offer little in the way of helping me identify the people involved, which is probably for the best. Logic dictates my lovers are members of the *Dun Siorai* household who I am bound to run into at some point. I think I would find it hard to look them in the eye if I knew for a fact that I was privy to their most intimate moments. Plus, it's none of my business who's boinking who, though I figure that having them choose such a dismal place to have their rendezvous means their love affair is probably illicit.

Still, stuck in this stinky trunk with my anxiety running high over being caught, it's hard for my mind not to characterize the lovers using their sounds. The woman is without a doubt a moaner, which could explain why the two of them have selected such an isolated spot with thick walls. She's loud, with a scale-like crescendo that gets higher pitched with every one of her partner's thrusts. In a strange way, her mewing reminds me of the song "Memories" from the Broadway musical "Cats," high pitched and warbling, which in turn makes me wonder if she might be faking all this supposed "passion." Or maybe I'm just a bitch, disgruntled because I don't usually provide such a rousing vocal audio track during sex and thinking maybe the Tax Man would prefer if I did.

Her partner has excellent staying power, I'll give him that, though I wonder what will end up giving out first… his equipment or the ancient cot. I hypothesize that the male is older and substantially heavier than his paramour by his ragged breathing and the dangerous creaking of that poor make-shift bed. At some point, his breathing turns to panting and I start to have some serious concern that the guy is on his way to a full-fledged heart attack, which would be a nightmare for everyone involved, myself included.

When they finally finish in an orchestrated duet of passionate yowling and growling, I have to bury my face in my boobs to keep from giggling out loud. Perhaps it's a symptom of mental hysteria brought on by the thought of being caught, but I find my current situation hilariously comical. Who else but good old Rosie Parker could ever end up being the hidden audience of someone else's private porno fantasy. I can't wait to tell Declan the whole uproariously funny story, though I'll probably wait until we're released from our postpartum celibacy. Just in case he finds it…well…hot.

I hope with every fiber of my being that these two are not the type to lay around in post-coitus afterglow. I am stiff from sitting in this one tight position and I really have to pee. In addition, I'm guessing I've been gone a really long time and no doubt *Birgit* has begun to worry over my failure to return. I breathe a sigh of relief (but not too deep of a breath…it really stinks in here) when I hear both parties sit up and begin to shuffle around, putting themselves back into some presentable order. I peer through the slats, but all I can see are booted feet with silver tips on the toes and the bottom of a green wool cloak with an embroidered hem, which I surmise is rather fancy apparel for working staff.

The couple is silent as they go about their dressing and eventually the man leaves without so much as a goodbye. The woman lingers a few minutes longer, lounging by herself on the cot for reasons I can't figure. Then, she stands up and reaches for something up on the bed. I hear the jingle of coins and wonder if I have misread this entire encounter. The man leaving payment means an entirely different scenario and somehow makes what I just witnessed seedier than an illicit romantic rendezvous.

I wait several minutes after the woman leaves to be sure all parties are completely gone from the passageway before escaping from the trunk. I am sore and stiff from being in that awkward position for too long, and my face, neck and back are sweaty from the lack of fresh air. I shake out any errant rodent poop from my gown and tuck a few stray hairs back into place before turning to leave. Relief fills me at being free of that nasty dungeon and I am halfway to the east exit when I realize that I've gone and left behind that damn, cursed belt. Turning around, I head back to the awful place. As predicted, the belt is right where I left it…at the bottom of the trunk. "Declan better love this feckin' thing for all the trouble it's caused me," I mutter to myself.

That's when I see something glittering on the floor of the cell that catches my eye. I walk over and pick it up. It's a single stud earring; a substantial sized, square-cut emerald set in yellow gold. Without thinking the whole thing through, I tuck the piece of jewelry into my pocket, figuring I will leave it someplace near the east entrance in case the woman comes back looking for it, which I believe she will most definitely do. It's a valuable piece and worth a hefty sum.

This time I make it out the east exit before I am spotted by a young member of the House's security team. "There you are, Lady *Mac Nuada*! We've been looking all over for you."

I'm a tad annoyed that I'm being hunted down like a lost pet. "I didn't know it was necessary for me to let Security know my whereabouts each and every minute of the day," I say, sounding overly bitchy even to my own ear.

The young man bows, then adds, "I apologize, my Lady. It seems your *scathach* was very concerned over your…disappearance. I am to tell you that she and Master Dylan have gone back to your quarters and that his Lordship has returned from *Asgard* earlier than expected and is awaiting you there as well."

The news that Declan is home safe and sound makes up for all the shitty things that have happened to me in the last two days. "Thank you for the information, young

Master. I'll head there immediately. And I'm sorry if I sounded a bit…harsh. It's been a trying day."

The teenager blushes and gives another bow. "No apologies needed, Lady *Mac.* House *Nuada* security is always at your service."

Smiling, I give him a wave and then take off toward the main entrance, thrilled to have my husband home and thus completely forgetting all about the emerald earring in my pocket.

WISDOM 24

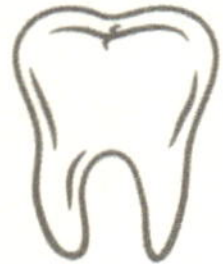

Hammered

NOW IN A HURRY TO see my darling Tax Man, I take the most direct route back to our family quarters, not giving much thought to the sideward glances thrown my way by the estate's staff. As I see it, no matter the actual truth, the Fae inside *Dun Siorai* are going to believe whatever it is they want to believe, and my fretting about it is simply a waste of energy. In hindsight, I suppose that some of those curious looks I received were not only in response to my *Ostara* faire shenanigans, but possibly had something to do with what awaited me in my home space.

I see my husband's cousin first, sporting a purplish-black, doozy of a shiner around his left eye, as well as several cuts and bruises marking his handsome face. He freezes when I walk into our parlor, then gives me an

embarrassed bow, careful not to draw additional attention to his battered self. I have no time to question him
over the hows and whys of his appearance before Declan
sweeps in from our bedroom, shirtless, his midsection
wrapped in white linen bandages that are leaking a tell-
tale spot of spreading red. "What the hell happened?" I
blurt, not bothering to hide my alarm.

His Lordship doesn't grace me with an answer, instead
stepping up and embracing me in a bear hug while lifting
me up off the ground. "There she be, ma' sexy mate. I have
missed ya' somethin' fierce, Lass, and I am vera', vera'
happy ta' be home." Declan plants a sloppy kiss on my
mouth, his tongue forcing its way inside while he takes
my left hand and places it directly on the crotch of his
leather riding breeches. He's not lying. Every inch of him
is "vera, vera' happy."

My husband is no slouch in the romance department,
but the Declan Fitzpatrick I know and love has always
been a complete stickler about observing the proper
protocol required of his title unless he is in the relaxed
company of his very close friends. This is outwardly lewd
behavior in front of not only Duncan, but also Birgit, who
I can see standing in the nursery doorway, another *Sidhe*
woman in the process of delivering our afternoon tea, and
his *athair's* page, Corvot, who is tapping his foot impa-
tiently, waiting, I assume, to deliver a message that's
undoubtedly from Lord *Nuada*. This lustful public
demeanor is totally not part of the Tax Man's normal
behavior, and my anxiety ramps up by several notches. I
wiggle myself out of his embrace while wrestling my hand

off his "vera happy to see me" package, but not before I smell an odd odor that adds to my confusion.

I move in closer to have another good sniff which results in Himself trying to feel me up. The last thing I want to do is further embarrass him in front of all these people, so I pretend to hug him while whispering in his ear. "Hell's Bells, Declan…have you been drinking?" I ask, more shocked than angry.

He pulls away, slightly swaying on his feet, before putting up his right thumb and index finger to measure out a small portion. "Just a wee bit, Lass. A man needs a pint of fortification far' a long ride home, don' he?"

"I suppose in some cases, Sweetie…but you're not much of a drinker, remember? You've told me you don't care for the taste and it usually makes you sick." He doesn't answer, just looks at me with a stupid, snockered grin on his face.

I turn to Duncan, who sees the look I give him and suddenly becomes overly interested in the laces of his riding gloves. Not relishing this audience, I try to nonchalantly prop my wobbly husband against the wall while I deal with the needs of the other people in the room. I send *Birgit* into the nursery to get Dylan's bath ready for me, instruct the kitchen maid to leave our tea covered on the dining table before dismissing her, and accept the rolled parchment from Corvot's hands, who leaves our quarters shaking his head in disgust as he undoubtedly races back to inform his Lordship of my husband's inebriation.

Duncan gives me a bow before attempting to flee what

I'm sure he realizes will be a full-blown interrogation from yours truly. "I will be on my way as well, my dear Lady. I am hoping to return to the Mundane world this afternoon," he stammers.

"Not so fast Duncan. I need some answers before you go slinking off," I mutter.

My husband's partner in crime looks toward his Lord, who has eyes closed and is leaning precariously too far to the right, destined to fall over sooner than later. "We war' just blowin' off some steam, Lady Cousin. Your Lord is much frustrated over no bein' able to go after those Korean bastards. We only meant to have a single pint with ar' breakfast, but then those *Asgard* pigs thought it necessary to call us out. These days, My Lord has little patience far' that kind of disrespect flung his way. One thin' led to another…some punches were thrown…and we could no let those bastards best us, could we? I have never seen his Lordship pub brawl so grandly. He seemed ta' enjoy kickin' thar' asses vera' much."

"Seriously, Duncan? You think coming to blows in some seedy tavern is normal behavior for my husband? We both know very well that Declan doesn't drink…his 'yar' body is a temple' is the philosophy behind his athletic life. Don't stand there with that innocent expression and try to tell me that you haven't noticed Lord *Mac's* been acting strangely since he's returned from North Korea!"

The *gancanagh* shifts his weight from one foot to another and looks away, uncomfortable with talking smack about his Liege Lord. He shrugs, trying his best to act casual. "With all that happened ta' the man, I would think some *fearg iarmharach* (lingering anger) is ta' be expected and...pardoned...by all who care far' him."

I'm sure Duncan doesn't intend to make me feel guilty about not having more understanding over my husband's ordeal, but his comment pokes at the dread I'm already harboring and I lash out with more venom that I'd normally use with someone I call a dear friend. "Where do you get off lecturing me on how I should feel about all of this, Duncan Fitzpatrick! He is MY husband! MY fated mate! You can't even begin to understand the bond between us and you never will! You're not here when he wakes up in the middle of the night in a cold sweat, lashing out at imaginary enemies. Yelling out words in North Korean that I don't even understand! And those are only on the nights that he CAN sleep. More often than not, he spends the entire night wandering from room to room or just staring out the window into the darkness. This is more than just normal PTSD, Duncan! Something is seriously wrong with my Tax Man!"

"'Tis enough, Lass," my husband mumbles from across the room. Taking a few unsteady steps, he flops down onto a nearby divan. "My cousin is not responsible far' ma' own actions, Rosie Love. T'was ma' idea to stop at that pub and it was I takin' the first swing. Yar' dumpin' yar' feminine anger on the wrong man."

I don't like feeling "ganged up" on, especially in a place that's supposed to be my home, nor do I care much for my husband's sexist description of my rightful anger. "I think you should go now, Duncan. It's best that this discussion remains between my husband and me."

Duncan looks toward Declan, as if looking for

Declan's permission to leave, an action which only infuriates me more. "I said go, Duncan. Shoo! This is none of your damn business."

With his head hanging off the end of the couch and his eyes closed, the Tax Man gives a wave. "Aye. Best ya' go while ya' ken', cousin. I may be a mite indisposed but I ken' still handle the sharp claws of ma' own Lady Tiger."

"As you wish, ma' Lord," Duncan says. Then, giving a polite bow before leaving, he adds, "I am deeply sorry if I have hart' yar feelings, Lady Cousin. T'was surely not my intention. I know that his Lordship's welfare weighs heavily on yar' mind."

I don't respond to him, waiting until I hear the door close, signaling that Duncan has left our quarters, before sitting down on the edge of the divan next to him. I try to keep my voice down, knowing the *scathach* can probably hear us from the nursery. I take his left hand in mine, the knuckles swollen and bruised from his earlier activities. "Declan...Sweetie...you have to listen to me. This is getting serious and I'm starting to really worry about you. The constant nightmares...the insomnia...this strange behavior...it's not like you. I'm pretty sure you're suffering from extreme Post-Traumatic Stress Disorder and I don't think we can handle this on our own. Something is very, very wrong and I think we need to consult with Dr. Brannigan."

Declan opens one bloodshot eye and looks at me before closing it again. "There's no need ta' be botherin' Robyn over any of this, Lass," he mutters, struggling to form the words. "I'm already aware of what the problem is. It ken' no be fixed."

His comment catches me off guard. "Wait...what does that mean? Of course, it can be fixed. You're *Tuatha De Danann*," I argue. "Nothing takes your people out." He doesn't, however, respond to my comments. That's because the Tax Man is now passed out cold, head back, mouth wide open, and snoring like a frickin' lumberjack.

WISDOM 25

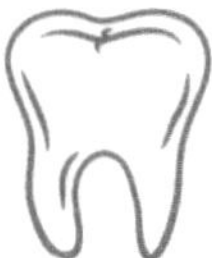

All Pain, No Gain

I TRY MOVING Declan from the divan in the parlor to our bedroom, partially for his comfort and partially so he's not as visible should anyone come to our door. But even with *Birgit* helping me, we can't get Lord "Drunk as a Skunk" to stand on his own, and despite the *scathach's* unusual strength, we refrain from her throwing him over her shoulders or the two of us carrying him by his arms and legs simply out of concern for my husband's lordly dignity. I know once he's sober, my Tax Man would be mortified at the notion of being hauled around like a sack of horse feed.

Instead, the two of us put him into a lying position on his right side, the physician in me worried about the possibility of him choking on his own vomit, which according to the tales he's previously shared with me about the few times he's been drunk, is a distinct possibility. I pull off his boots and damp socks, stick a bed pillow under his head, and wait for the effect of the Fae ale to wear off.

By this time, Dylan has woken from his nap, so I change and feed him first before *Birgit* and I settle down to eat our own lunch. It's the first opportunity I have to speak to the *scathach* about what kept me so long in my attempt to retrieve the leather belt from *Seamus* the dog. At first, I contemplate telling her the whole truth, but then something inside my brain, a clawing memory just out of reach, keeps me from being honest about what I'd inadvertently seen and heard in the old dungeon, at least until I'd spoken to Declan about it. As an alternative, I give her a long, convoluted tale of how I got lost in the maze that makes up the east wing underground rooms and then spent time wandering around the wine cellar marveling at all the exotic and expensive choices House *Nuada* curates. The story sounds dumb even to my own ears, but the nanny smiles politely and doesn't pry, only commenting that she's very glad I was able to get the belt back in one piece.

We are nearly finished with our meal and lingering over tea and cookies when my husband suddenly sits up and runs for the bathroom, his hand over his mouth. Both of us hear his enthusiastic retching, and even though I know he'll be self-conscious about having an audience, there's not much I can do about the lack of audio privacy. Our family quarters are spacious, but the shape of the estate's roof line and our flat, ten-foot ceilings work to amplify the acoustics, so the sounds from one end of the space echo throughout all of the rooms, something I will need to keep in mind when the Tax Man and I are finally able to resume our…uhmm…marital activities. Up until now, we've had the luxury of it being just the two of us, so noise wasn't ever an issue. With the nanny joining our family, it's something the two of us need to keep in mind.

His Lordship wanders out of the bathroom looking wretched. *Birgit* politely gathers up the remains of the meal tray, guessing that her employer is certainly not up for solid food. She offers to set the dishes in the hall for the staff to pick up and then makes plans to take Dylan out for a late afternoon stroll around the estate for some fresh air, which I understand is an opportunity for her Lord and his Lady to have some needed privacy. Without a word of greeting, Declan heads for our bedroom where I assume he plans on wallowing in his hangover misery.

Truthfully, I've been in the same situation as my dear husband, albeit it's been probably ten years or better since a night of partying led to a day of suffering. But I still remember how miserable I was and how I just wanted my college roommates to leave me the hell alone. However, the message scroll left by Declan's *athair* simply cannot be ignored any longer. As sure as the sun rises, it contains some mention of my embarrassing actions of the day before. I need to present my side of the story before my husband hears the details from his father. Even more importantly, we need to discuss, once and for all, the effects my *Mo Shiorghra's* PTSD symptoms are having on his general well-being and our lives as a family.

It's no surprise when I find the Tax Man lying on his stomach, stretched horizontally across the entire bed, his left arm hanging over the side and his face buried in the mattress. No doubt he just walked up to the bed and fell in. It's not a good position for someone "fishy around the gills." Sitting on the edge of the bed, I give his shoulder a light shake. "Declan? Sweetie? Are you awake? That's not the best way to lie down when you're hung over."

He mumbles into the mattress. "If ya' love me, Lass, ya' will go away and leave me ta' ma' misery."

"It's not good to lie on your stomach. You might aspirate your own vomit. You need to lie on your right side. It's been proven to help with post-drinking nausea."

My suggestion does not get a look of grateful appreciation, nor any attempt on his part to change positions. "I will take that inta' consideration, Dr. Parker," the Tax Man says, stressing, out of sarcasm, the word "doctor." But right now," he continues, never raising his head, "I'm beggin' ma' lovin' wife...ma' *Mo Shiorghra...* ta' leave me be. Past experience has shown that I will no doubt feel better by dinner time and then we ken' talk 'til our mouths bleed."

I've come face to face with cranky Declan on a handful of occasions in the past nine and a half months of our whirlwind romance, so I understand that when my true love asks to be left alone, it's probably best to do so. Unfortunately, I don't have the luxury of playing the game his way today. This being the Otherworld, I'm certain that Lord and Lady *Nuada* have been made aware of Declan's public brawl in *Asgard*. My husband's un-lordly behavior, combined with my own social *faux pas* at the *Ostara* faire, in the company of the *Banphri-onsa,* no less, makes us certified targets for the wrath of House *Nuada*. Buying myself some time before coming clean, I decide to tackle the PTSD issue first. "I'm sorry you're feeling awful, Sweetie, but that makes it more important than ever that we talk about your very normal reaction to what happened to you in North Korea."

I can see his body stiffen at my words. Talking about his kidnapping is extremely difficult for my husband, which I'm sure is the main reason he's unable to move forward from the horrible experience. He rolls over, throwing an arm over his eyes to shield them from the late afternoon light pouring in through the west windows of our bedrooms. "I have asked ya' with all the kindness I can muster in this condition ta' simply leave me alone for a while, Rosalinda. Yet ya' insist on havin' yar' own stubborn way. If ya' want so bad ta' talk, then talk we shall, but I'd prefer to begin by hearin' how ya' came ta' be causin' such a public spectacle with that damn Kilcrabtree woman after I specifically asked ya' ta' stay away from her while I was gone."

Declan's use of my full name, and the terse, arrogant Lord *Mac Nuada* tone of his comment cuts right through me. Jumping to conclusions and blaming me for something that wasn't my fault is not what I've seen from him before, and it takes every bit of my self-control not to tell him to kiss my ass before stomping out of the room. Common sense dictates that his snarly behavior has more to do with the North Korea and the aftermath of his binge drinking than with me, so I calmly reply, "As you wish, my Lord." My use of his title earns me a disgusted grunt, but I ignore it. "May I respectfully suggest that perhaps you might want to attend to this missive from your Lord *Athair* before we proceed with my unfortunate narrative?"

I hold out the parchment that I carried into the bedroom with me.

The dramatic sigh of annoyance I get in return is worthy of an Academy Award nomination, as is his long-suffering, poor-me expression. He pushes himself to a sitting position next to me, swinging his legs over the side of the bed before taking the scroll from my hand. His countenance doesn't improve as he scans the words before rolling it back up without showing it to me. "We are expected in my *athair's* study at *ocht sa trathnona* (eight in the evening), no doubt for a first-rate tongue-lashing and the opportunity for his Lordship to dish out an abundance of personal humiliation," Declan explains with more bitterness than I have ever heard him use in regards to his father.

"Oh boy," I reply. "I can hardly wait." I sit silent after my comment, waiting for an invitation to begin my defense of yesterday's actions, but it doesn't come. Instead, he reaches for me and pulls me into his lap. "I am sorry, Lass. Ya' deserve better than this from yar' *Mo Shiorghra*. As you say, I have been a mite out of sorts and not ma' self." I try and hold my breath without it being obvious because, frankly, the Tax Man doesn't smell all that great. The combination of sweat, vomit and alcohol is a bad mix, and in this intimate position, this is in no way the stuff of romance novels.

"You don't need to apologize, Tax Man. I know it's going to take time to get past this but we will fight through it together...you and me... and put what happened in North Korea behind us," I say with heartfelt conviction in one long breath.

I expect him to agree with me while reinforcing in his own words, this belief that what we're experiencing now is just a rough patch for the two of us, a bump in the road that we'll eventually conquer and emerge from stronger and more committed. But he doesn't. Rather, he loosens his embrace on me and the look I see in his eyes scares the shit out of me. Through our mental bond, I acutely feel his sense of hopelessness, a dark void of apprehension and grief. Then, he abruptly slams a mental shield in place, cutting me off from his innermost thoughts while rising from the bed's edge. "I'm in desperate need of a long hot shower, Love, along with some soul searchin' and quiet reflection. I know 'tis a lot ta' ask, but I'm pleadin' for a few hours of solitude. Can ya' give me that? I promise that when we return from my *athair's* verbal floggin', we will talk about everythin' ya wish ta'discuss. Can ya' do this far' me, ma' Sweet Rosie Lass?"

WISDOM 26

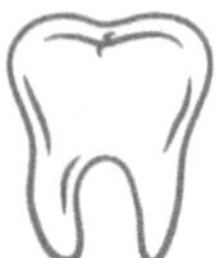

Shared Thoughts

I DO as the Tax Man asks. I leave him be. This is no small thing as I am beside myself with worry over what is going on with my husband's frame of mind. I have limited knowledge of PTSD, though had I been back home in Salem, I would have simply googled the information I needed. Here in the Otherworld, I'm without any resources, or at least any that I would feel comfortable enough to discuss my mate's intimate personal problems with. I contemplate trying to arrange a meeting with Duncan somewhere private to try and get some additional insight regarding Declan's behavior, but quickly quash any such idea. Going behind my Beloved's back seems terribly disloyal and would put my husband's cousin and best friend in an incredibly awkward position. There's also the thought that perhaps I could speak privately with Dr. Brannigan one on one when he comes for my postpartum exam, but being the consummate medical professional Robyn is, I doubt he would discuss Declan's mental health without my husband being part of that conversation.

With few alternatives, I have to hope that whatever the Tax Man is dealing with is something he will eventually share with me. In the meantime, I vow that I will be the most loving, most patient, most supportive spouse that ever walked this Earth...both sides of it. Looking for something else to dwell on, I await *Birgit's* return with my son, with plans to spend a long time cuddling and cooing him until he's ready to be fed and settled in for the first of his longer evening naps. Then, I spend a great deal of time writing a lengthy letter to my older sister, Claire, which Rory Dell, Declan's new associate, will deliver to her on one of his many trips back and forth.

I miss Claire something fierce, especially during this time when I could really use her calm and logical demeanor in the midst of all these mega-changes in my life. I also have a deep level of guilt over leaving my sister with the full responsibility of my father's care. Though he is in a top-rate nursing home environment, we have always shared a schedule for bi-weekly visits mixed in with regular day outings. With me hidden away in the Otherworld, this duty falls exclusively to Claire and her husband, Scott, who have two children of their own in addition to serious job demands.

If it weren't for Mel's weekend visits to *I Idir*, I would be totally cut-off from the world I called "home" for most of my life. She and Duncan have been forced to keep apart in the Mundane world by order of the Black Knight's security protocol, thus making their weekends together in

I Idir a time-pressing, whirlwind of romance. Despite the limited span these Otherworld visits provide, my BFF always tries to spend a few hours with me over the course of her two busy days, filling me in on what's going on at my practice and generally reminding me that I'm not alone in this forced exile.

I remind myself to be grateful for all the true blessings I've received...my husband's return to me safe and mostly sound...our healthy baby boy, peacefully asleep in his nursery...the family and friends back in the Mundane World who love and support me...and this unique opportunity to deeply discover my Fae heritage and practice the life-spirit philosophy I claim to so faithfully believe. Thus, by the time my Tax Man leaves his self-imposed solitude in our bedroom suite, I'm mentally fortified and soulfully-prepared to put on a calm and reasonable demeanor as I attempt to explain to him what happened with that Kilcrabtree woman at the *Ostara* faire.

Truthfully, I half expected to have a slight foot up on Declan, mentally and physically, since I hadn't spent several hours drinking myself silly. During the few times I remember being hungover, it seems to me that it took longer than a handful of hours to feel like myself again. I have no doubt that after a night of partying, I always looked a little gray and sweaty in spite of any sleep I might have grabbed. Much to my surprise, Lord *Mac Nuada* emerges from the bedroom looking like the cover model of GQ magazine if they had decided to publish a Renaissance Faire issue. Being his *Mo Shiorghra,* I suppose I might be a tad prejudiced, but hot damn, my man looks good. No. Not good. Like vera', vera' good. Awesome, in fact.

There's no trace of a sweaty, gray pallor, no blood shot eyes, or any sense that he's still suffering from nausea. The re-opened cut on his lip is healed, along with the few purplish-black bruises along the jawline he was sporting a few hours ago. Because hair grows faster here in the Otherworld than it does in the Mundane (don't ask me to explain why... it's complicated), the nearly shaved head that Declan returned from North Korea with is now sporting shoulder length ginger hair, which, still too short to braid, looks mega-hot pulled into a neat little man bun at the back of his head.

There is little doubt Lord *Mac* is dressed to impress ahead of our meeting with his *athair.* Attired in House colors, this is an ensemble I haven't seen before; soft doeskin breeches, tight where they ought to be, in a deep maroon shade, topped by a crisp cream-colored linen shirt and an overly long tunic vest in a rich golden-rod hue, perfectly finished with his favorite, knee length, leather dress boots.

From day one, I've always been a sucker for "Brooks Brothers Declan" in his custom-made suits, tortoise frame glasses and expensive loafers, but when I see him here in the Otherworld, clothed in the trappings of his heritage, I fully realize that this is my *Mo Shiorghra's* true identity, the real Lord *Deaglan Mac Nuada*, the one who can trace his lineage to the ancient ones of the *Tuatha De Danann.* It's an impressive sight, and I can't help but give a very unlady-like wolf whistle. The Tax Man smiles and leans down to kiss me. Because the sun has already set, and my limited tooth fairy magic is alive and well, I feel a slight tingle when our lips touch, his overpowering energy meeting mine. I look up at him with a tilt of my head. "Are you using *glamour* magic?"

Putting his thumb and forefinger together in the same gesture he used earlier this afternoon, "Perhaps a wee bit," he admits with a wider grin. "I will not go willingly inta' the lion's den with my beloved Lady on ma' arm without a few weapons in ma' arsenal."

"So, you believe it's going to be a...difficult discussion?" I ask, already knowing the answer.

Declan gives me a very loud snort. "What da' you think, Lass?"

I give a pointed look toward *Birgit*, who is rocking our son in a chair only a few feet away, obviously in hearing distance. *"Are you sure it's safe to discuss his Lordship in front of Birgit?"* I mentally ask.

"I would trust Magda's own granddaughter with ma' life, Love, and with yars' and Dylan's as well. Har' loyalty lies entirely with me...with our family. She will no betray us. Ever. This I know as the truth. Ya don't have ta' worry about speakin' honestly 'round the scathach." He returned to a vocal conversation. "I expect ta' be soundly brow-beaten, insulted, belittled and threatened. I am entirely used to his Lordship's scoldins'. I have been on the receivin' end of plenty of them and am still here to speak of it. I do, however, hold some worry over what he will attempt to throw at ya'. Rest assured, father or no father, Lord or not, I will no allow him ta' disrespect ya' in any such way."

I'm a tad shocked at his bluntness. Up until now, although Lord *Nuada* has been less than gracious to either of us, Declan has always gone the route of dutiful son and heir. Even when his father has been at his worst, my husband has followed the protocol of respect and obedience that is expected of him. Part of me is inwardly cheering at my Tax Man's refusal to swallow his *athair's* vile words. The other logical part reminds me that this is yet another example of Lord *Mac's* changing personality since the trauma of North Korea.

My husband takes our son from his nanny and settles himself in his favorite chair. Offering a finger for Dylan to grab onto, he says, "Perhaps ya should relate ta' me...in yar' own words... the events of yesterday's encounter with that *ni maith* (no good) liar."

"What have you heard so far?" I ask, wondering if the truth has already been embellished.

"Some bits," he replies, "but I'd much prefer ta' hear the whole story from ma' beloved *Mo Shiorghra*." His expression is blank, giving no of his emotions away.

It's then that I note that he isn't wearing his favored dress belt, the one I've seen him wear every other time we've traveled to *Dun Siorai*. Or any belt for that matter, which I find to be highly suspicious and an outright clue that my husband has obviously heard more of "the tale" than he's letting on. I weigh the idea of not giving him the belt at this particular moment, simply because I wanted my special gift to be a surprise, but at this point, the damn thing has caused me so much trouble, I'm ready for my thoroughly punished good deed to be over. "Hold that thought," I say, as I head toward my wardrobe in our bedroom. "I'll be right back."

I take the etched leather belt from its hiding place and

make my way back to the parlor. Despite all the irritation the gift has caused me, I still think it's a lovely piece and the musical notes worked into the Celtic design is custom made for Declan the music lover. With the belt hidden behind my back, I say, "Before we discuss my...unfortunate encounter yesterday, I have a gift for you. An early *Ostara* present."

"Is that so?" he asks with a far-from-innocent grin along with that crazy single arched eyebrow.

He signals for *Birgit* to take Dylan from him so he can accept my gift. I stick it out in front of him. "For you, my Lord...a small token of my heart's affection...even when you are away."

He reaches out, but instead of taking the belt from my hands, he grabs hold of my wrist and pulls me into his lap. "You are gift enough, Sweet Rosie Lass, though I am deeply moved by your wantin' ta' surprise me with yar' lovely *bronntanas* (gift)." He kisses me again, the brush of his magic tickling all my physical senses. At this moment, I wish so hard that the three of us could be away from *I Idir...* back home in Salem, nestled cozily on the overstuffed sofa we picked out together before our handfast. The sense of want I feel...the burning need to be gone from here...is so pressing that I find it almost too difficult to breathe. I also must not be shielding very well, because the Tax Man squeezes me tighter and I hear him whisper in my head, *"I know, Lass. I wish things were different as well."*

There's another voice humming in my brain. One that comes to me with the sound of cawing birds. *"You need to be strong, little tooth fairy mama. More now than ever. Trust the path set before you."* My heart goes from aching to practically stopping in my chest. I've been hearing sounds in my head since the birth of my son and Declan's safe return. Sometimes it is the tinkling of small bells, often accompanied by the light lilt of female laughter. Other times I hear full sentences, words of encouragement, advice and even warning. I know very well who the voice belongs to; remember clearly what I exchanged for my *Mo Shiorghra's* return, and though it's more than a little disconcerting to have her always floating around in there, I'd do it all over again. Without hesitation. However, these words, about staying strong, frighten me.

I brush away my fear and instead focus on my conversation with my husband. Pointing out to him the musical notes hidden in the complicated Celtic design of twists and knots, I say, "I saw this and knew it was made for you, Declan…for your love of music."

The Tax Man runs his hand over the tooled design imbedded in the leather, following the lines of a Treble Clef with the index finger of the hand that is not wrapped around my waist. "'Tis a work of art, Lass, a Masterpiece for sure. I will treasure it always." A smile graces his handsome face, but the joy doesn't reach his eyes, highly out of character for a man who has always been thoughtful to a fault. I try not to have hurt feelings while double-checking my mental shields, lest my disappointment at his reaction somehow leak out. "Thank you, my Love. Yar' token of the heart will be ma' true source of strength this evenin'. Now," he adds, as he settles me more comfortably in his lap, "why don' ya' tell me how ya' came to be brawlin' at the faire grounds with the Wicked Witch of *I Idir.*"

WISDOM 27

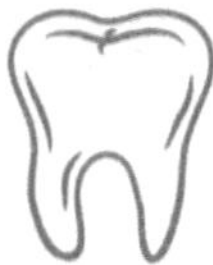

Knockin' *Nuada* Off His Pedestal

OUR MEETING with Lord *Nuada* goes as badly as expected. We are not offered seats and thus are required to stand for the entire length of the man's winded diatribe, which by my guess, goes on for at least thirty plus minutes. During that excruciatingly uncomfortable tirade, I am called "ungenteel, uncultured and lacking even the most miniscule sense of proper protocol." Except for the moment I have to take an involuntary step backward in an attempt to dodge his Lordship's projected spittle in the midst of his most furious rant, I mentally congratulate myself on remaining staid and letting his words roll off of me as if I were made of Teflon, even when he insinuates that Dylan is in need of a nanny because I am a "vera' lazy *mathair* and all-together too focused on moving up my social station by acting as a pet to The Royal Family." I even have to fight the inclination to smile and gloat over the notion that everything the pompous ass is spewing is most likely going straight to the ear of The Morrigan listening in my head.

However, all of my calm, aloof posturing goes straight out the window when Lord Heartless Bastard goes after my Tax Man, and when he calls Declan a "poor excuse for a Lord's heir" and blames him for "allowing his sorry, incompetent self to be captured by inferior Mundane beasts." I completely lose it. I step forward, finger pointed and let the man have a piece of my mind. Things deteriorate from there, and before long, my husband has to literally pick me up and carry me out of his *athair's* study while I continue to rain down more threats and curses on the man than I can ever hope to fulfill in a normal lifetime.

The Tax Man doesn't put me down until we are nearly back to our family quarters, plopping me butt first on a padded bench tucked in an alcove and then settling himself next to me. I know I've crossed every Fae protocol line and could technically, according to ancient Otherworld law, be imprisoned by his Lordship for disrespect. I think back to that icky dungeon and let myself feel a tiny seed of fear. "Look, Declan...I'm sorry...I know you warned me ahead of time about reacting to your father's vitriol but...what he was saying to you..."

I look over to see Declan with his face in his hands, his body shaking, and now I'm truly worried that my absolutely inappropriate behavior towards my husband's *athair* has brought him to tears. "Oh goddesses...I'm so sorry...please, Sweetie, don't cry."

He pulls his hands away from his face, and though his eyes are wet, they don't match the huge grin on his face.

Yes, he's shedding tears…but they're tears of mirth as he tries to hold in his laughter. He puts both hands on the sides of my face and pulls my lips to his. He kisses me, long and deep, then says, "Ah, Rosie ma' Love, you are the light in ma' par' soul. I have not laughed this hard in a long time. 'Tis good to feel something other than worry and regret." He drops his hands from my face. "Did ya see how angry his Lordship got when ya' called him a *"sean gabhar righin* (stubborn old goat)?" The Tax Man scrunches up his face, narrows his eyes and puffs out his cheeks while pretending to chew some cud. "He surely did resemble that ole' billy goat that sits out in the pasture beyond the stables, the ornery one that bleats when ya' try ta' get near him. Ya' know that old goat bit me one time when I was a wee lad, but it no did stop me from trying ta' keep annoyin' him…just like I do with ma' *athair*," he says, as he starts laughing all over again.

I am, of course, one hundred percent relieved to see jovial Declan instead of the cranky one, but part of me is more than a little confused over this change in his behavior. Since we've first met, Lord *Mac Nuada* has pounded into my head the idea that his father was more than just his father: His *athair* was also his Liege Lord and therefore was entitled to the utmost respect and obedience no matter the situation at hand. Now here he was…making silly goat faces in reference to his old man. I'm not sure what to think.

It doesn't help my confusion when my husband dries his eyes and stands, sticking out his hand in an offer to help me up. "Thank ya, sweet Rosie, for lightnin' my dark mood. I will never be able to tell ya' how much yar' courageous defense of me in the face of his Lordship's wrath means ta' me. I will ever be mindful of yar' little tiger claws as long as I shall live, Mrs. Fitzpatrick."

I stand up and take his hand in mine. "You are most welcome, Mr. Fitzpatrick. Now, I don't know how you feel about imbuing 'the hair of the dog that bit you,' but I could really use a shot of that fine Irish whiskey that you keep in your study."

The smile momentarily slips from his face, but he recovers it quickly. "Aye, Lass, I do believe this will be a night for findin' solace in the *Uisce Beatha* (Water of Life)."

Declan is quiet as we walk the rest of the way to our quarters. I assume his comment regarding the need for alcohol this evening was in reference to the long trial that was both yesterday and today. How very wrong I was. If only it had been that simple.

I attempt to carry Declan's upbeat attitude from a few moments ago into our quarters, shouting out ahead of me as we walk in, "Okay...it's time to bring out the good stuff! We have successfully made it out of his Lordship's study in one piece!" I expect only to find only *Birgit* and our son waiting for us, so when I see the visitor through the arched foyer leading to the parlor, I stop short. "Robyn?" I ask, not understanding what the doctor would be doing in *I Idir*... at *Dun Siorai*...so late in the evening. "What are you doing here?" I blurt out. I look across the room to where the *scathach* has our baby in her arms and make an immediate conjecture. "Wait...is something wrong with Dylan? Why didn't anyone come get me?" I demand, as I sweep my son from the nanny's arm and begin to give him a close inspection.

WISDOM 28

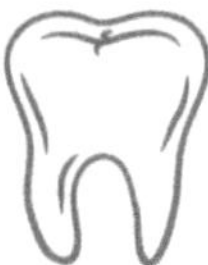

Walking the Path

"Your son is fine, Dr. Parker," Brannigan said. "In fact, I just gave him a thorough check-up. He's doing great; up nearly a pound in weight and over an inch in length. All perfectly normal."

I turn to his nanny with a questioning look, but she shakes her head in the negative. "Okay. I give up then. Why are you here so late in the evening?" I quiz the doctor.

Declan, who hasn't said a word since we've walked in, takes Dylan from my arms and hands him to the nanny, who with a nod to everyone gathered, takes my son off to his nursery. I'm about to demand answers when the Tax Man takes my hand in his and says, "Robyn is here, Lass, because yar' husband is a coward. He's here ta' explain things ta' ya' that I can't begin ta' make ma' mouth speak."

I stare at him, confused, his words to me sounding as if they are coming from across the room and not from where he's standing directly in front of me. "I don't understand," I stammer. "How are you some kind of coward? That's a ridiculous sentence. None of you are making any sense." I rant. "Please…can someone just tell me what this is all about!"

The doctor points to the sofa. "Perhaps we could all sit down."

"Stop treating me like a blathering idiot! I'm a grown woman…a medical professional. Just tell me what the problem is."

"Please, Rosie Lass. Don' make this any harder than it already is. Please come sit down and let Robyn speak," Lord *Mac* suggests.

I narrow my eyes at both males, trying to keep them from seeing just how petrified I am, and take a seat on the Chesterfield-style settee. Declan sits next to me and takes my hand in his again. His palm is sweaty and his right knee is jiggling which he only does when he's extremely tense. Everything around me feels like a tragic movie scene where the main character is about to get bad news. All we're missing is the ominous music. "Okay. I'm sitting," I say, raising my hands in mock surrender. "Someone better explain to me what's going on."

The Doc looks at my husband who gives him a slight nod of his head. Robyn clasps his hands between his knees, leans forward and looks at me. "How much do you know about the science behind magic, Dr. Parker?"

WTF? This is about magic? "Only the most basic of facts," I state. "As you're aware, my education was entirely in the Mundane world, from elementary level on. Being a tooth fairy, I never had the… 'opportunity' to attend any of the magical study programs here in the Otherworld." What I really wanted to say was that I wasn't allowed to attend them because the *Sidhe* elite hold prejudice against Fae without long, ancient pedigrees and inner circle connections.

The way they both look away tells me they know exactly what I'm inferring, but neither man brings it up. Instead, Robyn tries to over compensate. "Still, I have no doubt an intelligent woman like yourself understands that magic is the result of extremely powerful neurons in the Fae brain that allow for manipulation of the energy in the material world. Magical ability and skill is a biological anomaly of all the inhabitants of the Otherworld that isn't shared by our human counterparts in the Mundane world."

"I'm aware," I say, folding my arms across my chest. "I did undertake a pre-med track before dental school, Dr. Brannigan. I know well enough how the human brain works, and it was my understanding, except for areas in the prefrontal cortex, human and Fae brains were basically very similar. And as much as I usually enjoy 'talking shop' with you, Doc, I hope you're not offended if I tell you to stop the hell stalling and get to the damn point!"

"I am not at all offended, Dr. Parker...Rosie," he says, switching to my given name which I have invited him to use on multiple occasions, an offer he doesn't normally take me up on. That's how I know that whatever he's going to tell me is so awful, he's trying to soften the blow. "If you'll allow me a little leeway, I feel that it will help you better understand the issue at hand. You are correct. The human and Fae brain are a near match until we study the prefrontal cortex. It's only in the past two hundred years or so that researchers in the Otherworld have been able to learn more deeply where the seat of magical ability lies in the Fae brain. It should come as no surprise to you that it mainly originates in the prefrontal cortex, the central point for all cognitive functions in both humans and Fae. In the case of the Fae population, there are twenty times as many neurons firing in that area of the brain, allowing for deeper focus and concentration than what is humanly possible. That is where we believe the ability to manipulate energy exists."

The Tax Man's leg, smashed up next to mine, is now doing a complete fox trot, making the whole sofa cushion bounce. Between my husband's agitation and Robyn's serious brain talk, I begin to make my own "cognitive connections." "Hold on…" I say, as I look first at Declan and then at the doctor, "are you saying that my husband has suffered some type of brain trauma in North Korea and that it's damaged his magical ability?"

Again, there's this look between the two men that makes me feel as if they're tip-toeing around my "delicate" nature. Granted, I was a tad more emotional during the nine months of my pregnancy, but I have never been, nor will I ever be, a shrinking violet of feminine sensibilities. "Look, I'm tired of all this posturing," I say. "Just spit it out, Robyn. Obviously, there is something going on with my husband. Something beyond normal Post Traumatic Stress Disorder. I need for you to give us your professional diagnosis without sugar-coating it. I want your honesty…as both our physician and our friend."

"Truthfully, I'm not trying to 'soothe' you, Lady *Mac*,"

the Doc says. "I just want to be sure that you understand completely what I'm going to tell you…because, as you've said, you are both my patient and my friend. Again, brain study in regards to magical ability is a fairly new area of study for Otherworld researchers. For eons, magical skill has been clothed in the mystique of divine intervention and getting permission from the Powers That Be to study it from a scientific vantage point has been exceedingly difficult. You yourself know how hard the Fae hold to ancient tradition. The idea of pinpointing the 'seat of magic' is abhorrent to many, many Otherworldly cultures, so all of the information we've been able to gather regarding magic and the brain is relatively recent. We had no idea that the Mundane population was seeking the same knowledge. Hell…we didn't even know that they'd made the connection to the brain's prefrontal cortex and its role in magical ability."

My stomach begins to churn with the acid of anxiety as I put more and more of what the doctor is saying together. "The only way the Mundanes could have realized this is if they'd been able to…to study a Fae brain," I say, not wanting to fully accept the indications of my statement.

Robyn looks as solemn and angry as I have ever seen him. In his professional role, he is the calmest, most non-ruffled man I'd ever met. But the information he is sharing with us tonight has him extremely agitated, which makes me dread the rest of this conversation even more. "That is exactly right, Rosie. Apparently, various Mundane governments have been abducting Fae living in the human world and using them as lab rats to try and determine if augmentation with surgery and extra Fae stem cells to the prefrontal cortex could increase magical ability. We assume they had hopes of being able to reproduce this ability in human subjects and thus 'even the score between the two races,' as the humans crudely put it. I'm sure you can imagine what a disaster that would be for the future of the Otherworld."

An ugly thought crosses my mind. "Does this have anything to do with what happened to me last summer? With Eric Ashton and the Chechens? I thought the Mundane terrorists were only after the DNA in baby teeth?"

My husband finally pulls out of his silent observation. "Aye, Lass. The theft of the gathered baby teeth was only a side distraction to keep us from discovering the real reason for the abductions. Though they were collecting the Fae DNA in the dental pulp of the teeth, they were also specifically targeting tooth fairies because they believed them ta' be the best test subjects; they had some minor magical ability, and thus some extra Fae neurons. The terrorists hoped with thar' research they could turn the tooth fairies inta' 'super magical beings,' and eventually do the same far' human fetuses who had been plied with extra doses of Fae DNA stolen from mixed-blood baby teeth."

"That's disgusting!" I add, not wanting to think of how close I came to being some terrorist-held lab rat. I recall with overwhelming uneasiness how frantic the Tax Man had been about my safety during those earlier weeks... and how shitty and unreasonable I acted toward his over-protectiveness. I squeeze his hand, letting him know I remember and he squeezes mine back, and when he does, he drops his mental shield and opens the line of thought between us. It's then that I realize what all this is all about. Why Robyn is actually here tonight.

A physical ache burns in my chest like nothing I've ever experienced before, and I feel like my throat is completely closing up. Every breath seems like it's being choked off. Had I not had the medical background I do, I would have been absolutely sure that I was in the midst of a heart attack. But I understand that this is no cardiac arrest. This is a full-blown panic attack over the realization that my beloved, my *Mo Shiorghra*, my darling One and Only, has been a victim of the North Korean brain altering research program. My face crumples and I can barely push the words out as I grab for his other hand. "Oh Declan," I squeak.

The look on his face makes me woozy. Every ounce of anguish, suffering and uncertainty is written on the planes and angles of his beautiful face. I desire only to fall into his arms and weep until next Tuesday…until I haven't a tear or a sob left in my entire body. Before I can make that happen, I feel a zap to my own head, almost like an electrical shock. It immediately clears the weight of emotion from my thoughts, and my physical symptoms disappear as well. I hear Her voice as clearly as if she were sitting next to me. *"This is no time to fall apart, little tooth fairy. Your Mo Shiorghra's future depends on your strength at this very moment. As I have foretold, your paths are not easy ones, but the Universe has wisely chosen that you should walk them together. Trust in this truth."*

"But I don't know what to do! What to say!" I whimper inside my head.

"Of course, you do, tooth fairy. Trust in the pure love and devotion you have for your fated mate.

Just as suddenly, the voice disappears, but I feel as if I can speak without falling apart. Still holding my Tax Man's hands, I turn to the doctor. "How bad? What's the overall prognosis?" I ask, sounding more like Dr. Parker, D.D.S., and less like Minnie Mouse.

Dr. Brannigan rubs a hand over his face. "It's too early to say. We don't have a complete understanding of the complex medical cocktail they injected into Lord *Mac Nuada*'s prefrontal cortex. We collected as much data as we could before Herself completely destroyed the facility. We're still trying to process it all. From what we can tell so far, they were able to increase the number of neural pathways, which also increased some cognitive abilities, but also destroyed or damaged others. Declan still has a lot of brain swelling and until some of that heals, we won't be able to get a clear reading on what's what. In addition, there's no telling what will happen long term. Fae physiology is very complex with the ability to self-heal, but as the Otherworld has never used living souls in their research, we don't have a lot of past data to lean on."

"Have you done an MRI?" I ask, shocked at how calm I sound despite every part of me wanting to scream.

"We attempted a brief one while you and your baby were still at the hospital, but MRI imaging to that level of neural views is in the early stages. Only a few hospitals in the Mundane World have that technology, and unfortunately, most of them are located in countries that are not overly friendly toward the Fae. Once the swelling decreases, we have some Fae magical techniques available to us that we can employ that will allow for a better 'look see' of what's going on with the neurons in Lord *Mac's* frontal cortex."

My stomach is doing flip flops, but nevertheless, I throw my arms around my *Mo Shiorghra's* neck. "Oh Sweetie, I'm so, so very sorry this happened to you. But we're going to get through this. You and I together. We can face whatever fallout comes from this terrible situation."

The grief in his face is almost too much to bear, and I am sure that without the extra boost of The Morrigan's ancient juju, I would have already completely fallen apart. "I love ya' to the depths of ma' soul, Rosie Lass," my husband says, "and I thank the Universe every day for allowing me to have these months with ya' by ma' side... for given' us a son through the love we have for one another. But ya' heard what Robyn said, Rosie Love. There's no way of knowin' what I'll become...what deviant traits I will develop because of their evil experimentation. I love ya' too much ta' burden ya' with a life that will undoubtedly bring ya' nothin' but disappointment and..."

I put a hand over his mouth, not caring if the doctor finds my actions toward a lord of my husband's standing inappropriate. "Don't say it, Declan! Don't you dare say what I think you're going to say! You promised me when we left Salem to come here that you would never, ever say such a feckin' stupid thing like that again! Are you seriously trying to challenge the Universe's decisions?"

He gently takes my hand off his mouth and kisses it. "I love that ya' are willin' to defend me at all costs, *ardaigh mo stor* (my darling rose), whether it be at the hands of ma' mean-spirited *athair* or simply the will of Fate that we sadly ken' not change. You have too kind of a soul ta' realize that bad things happen through no fault of our own. 'Tis my duty and right ta' protect ya' from makin' long reachin' decisions out of yar' strong feelins' far' me."

I pull my hands away from him. "No, Declan Phineas Fitzpatrick! It is not your damn 'duty' or your feckin' 'right' to tell me how I'm supposed to feel. I'm a grown woman. An adult in both the Otherworld and the Mundane. When I said I loved you, I meant it forever. I vowed that we would walk our paths together, hand in hand, wherever they lead us. I don't give a rat's ass about any archaic Otherworld nonsense surrounding your damn handfasting traditions." And that's when I "know." Just like Herself promised. I know exactly what I need to do to keep my husband moving forward on the path he's destined to walk. The path Fate meant us to walk together.

I stand up, my body stiff from being tense and sitting in one place for so long. Pointing fingers at both my Tax Man and Dr. Brannigan, I order, "I don't want either of you to move a single, solitary muscle until I get back. Do you understand me?"

WISDOM 29

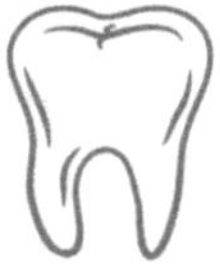

Decisions, Decisions

ON THE WAY to our bedroom suite, I stop by the nursery with an urgent request for *Birgit*. "I'm in desperate need of an ink mage," I say. "Do you know someone who'd make a house call on such short notice…at this time of the night?" The *scathach* glances over toward the cradle where my son is sleeping. "There's three of us here, including Dylan's Black-Knight-trained father and his equally trained obstetrician. I think we can hold down the fort while you arrange this for me," I explain. "I wouldn't know where to begin to look and there's no way I could slip out of *Dun Siorai* unnoticed."

"I do happen ta' know one. He's the best in the business if you're interested in unbreakable ink magic. Quite an artist as well," the nanny states.

"Do you think he'd come at this ridiculous hour?" I ask, hoping I don't sound as desperate as I feel. "And be discreet as well?"

"For House *Nuada*? I believe he most certainly will, though he will require a big…incentive," *Birgit* warns. "Master Finn is vera' fond of good livin'."

"The cost is not a problem. Make whatever deal you feel is fair on my behalf. I'll need him here in our quarters as soon as possible and with a plausible cover story should anyone stop you on the way back."

The *scathach* nodded her understanding. "I can do this for you ma' Lady. I will leave immediately."

"Thank you, *Birgit*. You've surely been goddess sent! I mean that! I'm so glad you're part of our little family."

The young woman smiled, dropped a curtsy and then just disappeared. I double check that the baby is still asleep and head toward the Master suite. I knew exactly what I'm looking for and where to find it. Grabbing the carved wooden chest, I lift the lid, finding my handfast contract lying there in a bed of maroon satin along with the thick cords that are a symbol of our union. It crosses my mind how ironic it was that in those last few days before Dylan was born, after that ridiculous proposal offered up by the kid from House *Badh*, I had, for some strange reason, decided I needed to read up on *I Idir* law regarding my handfast commitments. Well, at least the first two dozen pages or so. Then I smile and shake my head with understanding. No. Not irony. Not for a follower of the Old Ways for whom "coincidence" is no more than an imaginary concept. This was purposeful action, the Universe nudging me in the right direction during those anxiety fraught days, so that I would be ready with answers when faced with tonight's challenge.

I walk back to the parlor, the chest in my arms, to

bewildered expressions on the faces of both men. My husband looks more than just confused. He's gone a shade paler, his shoulders slumping, obviously reading the situation entirely wrong. "I had hoped with ma' whole heart, Lass, that once ya' heard the news about ma' wretched injuries ya' would be willin' ta at least give me the remainin' days of our handfast contract before' makin' yar' decision. But I wholly understand. I am not the same man ya' pledged yar' life to on that summer day. I will not fight to keep ya' to a commitment ya' don' desire."

I put the chest down on the table in the center of the room, and walk over to my husband. Taking him by the shoulders, I give him a good shake. "For Pete's sake, Declan Fitzpatrick, sometimes you can be a real yutz." Then I kiss him on the mouth, befuddling him even more. "I have no intention of breaking our handfast contract," I announce. "In fact, I'm initiating my right to call for *An Banna Siorai*"

It takes his Lordship a few short seconds to work out what I'm trying to say. "The Eternal Bond?" he asks with a voice that's barely a whisper. "Surely ya' don't understand the entirety of what yar' demandin', Rosie Lass, else ya' would no make such a huge commitment ta' a man in ma' damning position."

"That's where you're wrong, Tax Man. I know perfectly well what *An Banna Siorai* entails. I've read all the documents." I mentally cross my fingers knowing full well I didn't read every word of them. But I perused the important stuff, got the gist, and that's enough for me. "As your *Mo Shiorghra,* Your One and Only, it's my right to ask for it...and your right to refuse me. So, I'm asking you, Lord *Mac Nuada*...will you take the bond with me?"

Relationship commitments and the legality of them are completely different in the Otherworld than they are in the Mundane. Most Fae couples start with a "handfast," a year plus a day time period in which they live as mates, afforded all of the similar legal standards of husband and wives under the laws of the United States. At the end of the 366 days, the female partner (if there is a female partner; the Otherworld laws are slightly different for same-sex couples where no children or heirs can be biologically created between the joined couple and where no titles are involved) has the right to end the commitment according to the terms of their handfast contract. If the couple wishes to remain together after the 366 days have passed, their handfast contract is destroyed by flame and a new long term marital agreement is drawn. There is no such thing as "divorce" in Otherworldly culture or law. Once a new marital contract is signed, the couple pledges to stay together no matter what, promises being sacred to the Fae. Still, over the years, and in a nod to the Mundane world, loopholes and clauses in the law were added to allow for dissolution of some marital contracts due to a wide range of reasons, most of them centering on a political or treasonous nature.

There is also a very ancient magical covenant called, in the Old Language, *An Banna Siorai* (The Eternal Bond), though I'm sure it has similar names in different Otherworldly cultures. This magical covenant supersedes all other laws and traditions regarding the joining of two souls and is meant to follow the lovers into the afterlife.

Legend states that some of the Universe's most well-known couples, such as Marc Anthony and Cleopatra, Percy and Mary Shelley, and even Napoleon and Josephine, were all joined in an eternal bond, though since they have never returned from the afterlife to verify this, the concept is often regarded as a myth. Still, among the Fae, it is considered the highest form of love and devotion, a no-escape pledge that supposedly even the Grim Reaper can't undo.

There's no doubt that this request of mine is something my *Mo Shiorghra* never expected. He stares at me with parted lips as if he wants to speak but has no idea what it is he wants to say. Running a hand through his hair over and over again, a typical "Declan is stalling" trait, he finally draws me to him in a tight embrace and presses his lips to the top of my head. "My Love," he says, choking up on every syllable, "I am humbled by yar' generous offer and love ya' more than I could ever come up with the words to say. Never was a man so richly gifted through no effort of his own. Yet, it would not be right far me ta' let ya' make such a huge decision that will follow ya' even after yar' death in light of the news ya' just received. Would ya' consider waitin' a few months until we reach the end of the handfast term? If I am still functionin' in an acceptable way, I will joyfully undertake *An Banna Siorai* with ya'."

I push away. "You're missing the whole point, Declan! I want to do this immediately! This very night...so that you...and everyone else...fully understands that I will stand by you, be your *Mo Shiorghra*, no matter what may come in the future. We'll face the fallout of your North

Korean tragedy together…in whatever manner we must. Otherworld law only stipulates that we must be handfasted for a minimum of six months before taking this next step. We've been together for eight. There's nothing holding us back."

His Lordship is a man torn; his deep feelings for me and our family pulling him in one way, the nobleness seeded in his character pulling him another. "Why does it have to be tonight, Rosie? 'Tis a big, big decision. Can we not even sleep on it?" he stammers.

"You have doubts about your feelings for me, Tax Man?" I ask, knowing fully well I'm not playing fair. Truly, I don't have a single solitary doubt that my *Mo Shiorghra* loves me with every fiber of his being, but I need for him to realize that our love is stronger, more meaningful, than anything that happened in North Korea.

Doctor Brannigan, who up until now has been uncomfortably privy to this intimate conversation between mates, finally speaks up. "Perhaps I should let the two of you discuss this in private."

"No, Robyn. You need to stay put," I command.

"My Lady Love, the par' man has had a long day. He came to *Dun Siorai* at ma' request ta' help me tell ya' the truth. It's vera' late. I'm sure Robyn would like ta' return home," Declan argues.

I wriggle out of my husband's arms. "You're an official Prince of Avalon, are you not, Doc?" I ask him. "And a descendant of The Lady of The Lake?"

The doctor turns a slight pink, uncomfortable with any title other than his professional medical one. "Yes. I am both of those things. Why do you ask?"

"According to the laws regarding a bonding ceremony, we need someone of royal blood to stand witness. I was hoping you might do this for us?" I ask.

I'm pretty sure that the poor man doesn't want to be drawn into what he sees as a personal discussion between my husband and I, but Robyn is first and foremost a damn good guy. "If the two of you decide this is really what you want to do, then I would be honored to stand as your witness. Although, in truth, Dr. Parker...Rosie...I agree with your husband that maybe you should take twenty-four hours to clarify your decision."

"Ya' see, Rosie. Even Robyn thinks we should take this a bit slower," the Tax Man adds

"Well, I'm not asking Robyn to take the bond with me. I'm asking you," I counter.

My husband doesn't like to be put on the spot and he gives me his cranky look, but then drops it immediately for another delay tactic. "I believe that ya' are unaware that we each need a personal witness ta' lay hands on us durin' the ceremony, and more importantly, an ink mage with enough skill and know-how to properly cast *An Banna Siorai*. 'Tis not an easy or common spell, Lass. It is a highly specialized casting. I personally don' know anyone who has undergone The Eternal Bondin', and off hand, I cannot think of any mage that would be available to cast it in a twenty-mile radius. This idea that ya' could gather everyone ya' need here in the wee hours of the night is probably far too unrealistic for ya' ta' make happen, no matter how much I adore ya' for thinkin' ya' could."

The Tax Man's naysaying has nothing to do with his recent brain trauma. This is Declan just being Declan. The man hates to be wrong. Ever. And he will use any argument, no matter how silly, to get you to agree with him. In the past, I've just given in on most things just to keep the peace. But not this time. "Sorry Lord *Mac*. I regret to inform you that on that point you are incorrect. I have arranged for everything we need to make this bond happen...here and now." I barely get the final word out of my mouth when Duncan Fitzpatrick pops into the room, dirk in hand and holding a defensive pose, followed in mere seconds by an anxious Mel. "Voila, Tax Man! Witnesses," I say, pointing to our friends. "Royal Official-check. Your witness-check. My witness-check. Now all we're waiting on is our ink mage."

"I am sorry, ma' Lord," Duncan says, more than mildly confused as he slides his dirk back into his belt. "I have no idea what's going on, though I am vera' glad to see that none are in peril. Lady Rosie sent a mental message that she needed me to return to *Dun Siorai* immediately."

"Same here," Mel said, crossing her arms across her chest. "I would have been here sooner, but because of the time change, I'd just gotten home from work when I got Rosie's message. I needed to change clothes first. Traveling through the veil in heels is a major pain in the ass. So, what's going on?" Seeing Robyn Brannigan in the room, she added, "Doughnuts to Diapers! I hope Dylan isn't ill?" I can't help but smile at Mel's version of an obscenity. She holds fast to the Otherworld belief that all words have power, so she has her own version of curse words that she believes avoids the notice of the Universe.

I'm not wholly sure who knows the truth about what happened to Declan in North Korea, and it's not my place to tell anyone, so I skate around the truth a bit. "I'm sorry if I alarmed either of you. Believe me, that wasn't my intention. I just wanted my dearest friends to be part of something wonderful." I look directly at Declan, knowing that Mel and Duncan are waiting for more information. I hear my husband laugh in my head. *"Ya' play games better than Lugh Himself, Lass. Touche, Little Tiger."*

"I thank ya' both far' answerin' ma' Lady's call so quickly. 'Tis no emergency, other than a woman with her heart set on love. Ma' Rosie has asked that we be joined in *An Banna Siorai* this vera' evening," Declan explains. "She says her heart ken' no wait for the end of the handfast contract and that she is followin' the will of the Universe. I believe she has asked ya' here to be our witnesses."

Mel's response is to throw her arms around me in happiness, while Duncan slaps Declan's back in obvious excitement, then forgetting protocol, throws his arms around his cousin in an exuberant bear hug. "Girl, that is so mega-romantic" Mel squeals, "like something from a long-ago fairytale. Imagine loving someone so much you want to be together even in the afterlife! I'm so happy for you, Rosie Posie!"

The way Duncan is looking at my husband is a sure sign he understands the reasons behind my urgency in calling for The Eternal Bond. Putting two and two together and recalling the way my husband's cousin was so anxious not to answer my questions earlier this evening, I assume that Duncan is fully aware of what happened to Declan in North Korea. It makes sense, as he was a member of the tightly secretive security team that rescued Lord *Mac Nuada*. As he embraces my husband,

and I can hear him say, "I am beyond happy for you, my Lord. How you must feel knowing that yar' Lady will be by yar' side no matter what happens. You are truly the richest man I know."

The Tax Man looks up at me with eyes so full of emotion I can barely breathe. "Aye, Cousin," he says, "the richest and the luckiest. Blessed be!"

WISDOM 30

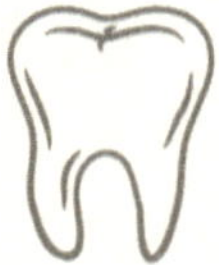

Eternal Mates

WE GO from the pure adrenaline of that special moment with Mel and Duncan to a subdued hurry-up-and-wait mode. Although our friends came as soon as they were called, it doesn't work that way with mages, especially those who work in ink and consider themselves artists as well as spell casters. Because dark magic (spells and such that rely on secondary sources like rituals, runes, and totems), is a far rarer gift among the Fae than the common personal white magic, mages are typically prima-donna types and pick and choose who they deem to cast for. As of yet, I have heard nothing from *Birgit* regarding her ability to convince the talented Master Finn to come to *Dun Siorai*. As one hour of tense patience ends and another begins, I feel as if I'm losing the adrenaline that was keeping my buoyancy alive over this decision. Declan and his cousin kill the time by playing draughts, a game that resembles American checkers, while Mel has her nose buried in one of my husband's favored Mundane crime thrillers.

Me? I just pace, until Doc Brannigan, bored himself, suggests we take care of my postpartum appointment earlier than the date we had planned next week. I note my husband's interest in this conversation and he gives me a blush-inducing wink from across the room. I don't blame him. He's as anxious for the "green light' regarding our "marital" activities as I am. It's been a really long dry spell for us both, and in light of everything going on, an intimate encounter might be just what the doctor ordered. Literally.

It's always a bit weird when Robyn goes from friend to physician, but his professional demeanor and matter-of-fact conversation, which never includes anything personal during a formal visit, always puts me at ease. The "appointment" is over quickly and as I leave the bedroom that we've used as an impromptu exam room, courtesy of a little of the Doc's personal magic, I can give my Tax Man the thumbs up in answer to his questioning looks.

Unfortunately, there's still no sign of the *scathach* or the ink mage, and I start to truly worry whether this bonding will actually take place tonight as I'd hoped. Apparently, Dylan has also woken while I was with Robyn, fussing and whimpering for his middle-of-the-night feeding. I take him from Mel's arms and head for the nursery, where for the next forty minutes or so, I care for our son; feeding him, changing him and rocking him back to sleep, all the while setting myself up for what I expect will be disappointment. I'm just about to join my comrades in the parlor and send everyone home when I hear additional voices, one of which definitely belongs to our nanny.

The ink mage is not what I had expected. To obtain the title of "Master," a mage must successfully complete several difficult trials designated by the leaders of their particular magical guild, and even then, only after years of training and apprenticeship. Master Finn looks far too young to have already earned his title, though there's always the chance that he is the recipient of his own anti-aging spell. If I had to guess, I'd say he was in the same age range as Declan and Robyn, somewhere in his mid to late thirties. Unlike many of his counterparts, whose overdone apparel heralds their abilities, Master Finn is plainly and simply dressed in an unadorned linen robe the color of cocoa, the only symbol of his status being an expensive looking, wide, silver belt etched with intricate Celtic patterns. He is carrying a leather case which I assume holds the tools of his trade.

Birgit does the introductions following traditional protocol. "Lord *Spideog,* Lord and Lady *Mac Nuada,* may I present Master Ian Finn, one of *I Idir's* top ink mages."

The sorcerer gives a perfunctory bow. "I am most intrigued, ma' Lords and Lady, as to why ya' would have need of an ink mage at such an unusual hour of the day, though ma' dearest *cara* (friend) insisted that this meeting was of the most important nature."

"I am grateful for your attendance to House *Nuada,* Master Finn. My Lady and I wish to partake in *An Banna Siorai,* which as you are aware, requires a skilled mage to complete the ink work for such a binding, especially when both parties are already marked as each other's *Mo*

Shiorghra. The spell must be added seamlessly to the original, keeping the magic intact in the original artwork, while adding this new bonding to the overall design. 'Tis known to be a difficult casting."

The mage nodded, his face an expressionless mask. "I am aware, ma' Lord. Difficult…and expensive."

"The cost is irrelevant to me, Master Mage. I consider it money well spent for such an all-encompassing magical bond," my husband responds.

"I assume, then, that Lord *Spideog* of *Avalon* is in attendance as your royal witness according to Otherworld Magical Law? And that you have furnished two witnesses of *Sidhe* birth?"

It sticks in my craw that as a tooth fairy and not considered *Sidhe,* I would be unable to act as a witness for the very casting I will be a central part of as Declan's *Mo Shiorghra.* The discriminating rules surrounding the Fae cultural magical hierarchy are completely out of touch with reality and excludes a whole portion of the Otherworld population. Tonight, however, is not the time for railing against the social injustice of magic, especially in the presence of a staunch believer of such prejudice. I keep my mouth shut and try to smile without grimacing.

"We have all the necessary witnesses," says my husband, "and we are anxious to begin if you are willing to work the casting. Obviously, your presence here at such an unusual hour will be generously rewarded."

"That's good to hear, my Lord. Let us begin by examining the original bond. As your House's heir, I assume that you received the first image and spell during your Ritual?" the mage asks.

Declan rolls up the right sleeve of his chemise exposing the familiar band of Celtic knotwork. The mage pulls out what appears to be a normal magnifying glass, but when he places it over my husband's tattoo, I can see vibrant reflections of color in the glass which I imagine is the expression of energy within the Ritual spell. Seeing the intensity of Declan's armband, I am anxious to know if the wolf head sigil inked on my right shoulder blade will reflect with the same potency as his.

"This spell was very well done, ma' Lord. May I ask who cast and inked it?" Master Finn questions.

"T'was Master Brendan. He also inked my *athair's* Ritual, though I believe he has long since retired."

"Aye. I have never met the man personally, though I have certainly heard of his skill. 'Tis a shame he decided to take on the path of a *dithreabhach* (hermit). Many could have benefitted from the sharing of his knowledge." The mage turns to me, "I will need to see your ink as well, Lady *Mac Nuada*. If it is located in a…delicate location… we can do all the casting discreetly in privacy with only your witness in attendance, though Lord *Spideog* will need to be present for the actual bonding."

"My image is on my right shoulder blade, Master Finn, so there's no need for privacy. As for Lord *Spideog*…he's our family physician and delivered our son, so I'm pretty sure I have nothing left to hide from him." The doctor turns a light pink color and my husband runs a hand through his hair and looks away while Mel gives a whispered snicker over my comment. Despite eight months in the role of Lady *Mac Nuada*, I have yet to concede to all the verbal protocol commandments.

Master Finn, on the other hand, must find my candidness refreshing. He nods his approval. "Excellent, dear Lady. That makes this so much easier without having to drape body parts. May I examine your mark?"

I had assumed in advance that the mage would need access to my *Mo Shiorghra* ink, so after my appointment with Robyn, I'd changed into a low backed kirtle that I wear without the intended chemise and the usual corset, leaving my entire dorsum bare and then covering all that exposed skin with a short bolero sweater. I wouldn't win any fashion awards, but at least I was ready for the mage to work. I pulled off the knitted jacket and turned around so that I was now facing Declan while allowing Master Finn a good view of the inked wolf sigil.

The Tax Man's moss green eyes go instantly to mine and he reaches out to take my hand. The moment he touches me, I can feel every one of his warring emotions. They ran the gamut from pure unadulterated joy...to grateful pride...and finally a simmering, underlying wash of doubt and anxiety. I squeeze his hand without breaking eye contact, and say silently to him., *"This is meant to be, Declan. I am as sure of that as any soul can be. We need to trust the path the Universe has laid out for the two of us. Haven't you said the very same thing to me on many, many occasions since we've met? Now you need to put away your doubts and put truth behind your words."*

"I do not have all the answers, sweet Lass. I am not even sure that I ken' formulate the right questions. But I do know one thing. I will love ya, Rosie Parker Fitzpatrick...here in this world, and in whatever the next life brings. This is ma' truth."

I have no doubt I would have wept like a baby at that

moment had I not felt strange, rather cold fingers tracing the mark on my back. My husband has run his hand over the inked sigil on my shoulder blade, following its dark strokes over and over again, dozens of times in our intimate moments. His magic brushing up against mine always leaves a low current of energy, not much different from the tingle and tickle of static electricity. What I feel now is completely different. It was as if the mage was untangling the lines of the design, separating them into individual strands and closely examining them.

I give an involuntary shudder and no doubt Master Finn can sense my wariness. "I apologize, Lady *Mac*. I am aware that this examination can feel a tad invasive. But to add new threads to an existing spell, I need to see where all the ends travel and where they meet." After a few minutes of this odd experience, the ink mage pulls his hands away. "I predict that adding this new bond to your band of knotwork should be an easy cast, your Lordship. The spell on the Lady's sigil, however, is far more complex. I expect it to be a mite more challenging to incorporate this new ink and have it connected seamlessly to the original in both a magical and artistic way. Have you had any other magical ink castings, my Lady?" he asks me.

"No," I shrug. "This is the only one,"

"Any Mundane tattoos? Butterflies, hearts or the like?" he questions.

I shake my head in the negative. I don't mention that although I had always admired body art, I'd been too cowardly to consider having it done to myself.

Master Finn makes a face. "I feel the need to mention,

Lady *Mac Nuada*, that inking is not an entirely pleasant experience. I will be placing the pigment beneath your skin, which will require my pricking through the top layer of your epidermis over and over again. It will not be anything like when your *Mo Shiorghra* sigil was transferred. I can try a light pain-blocking conjure, but as the process is part of the bonding, I cannot completely block your body's reaction to it."

My husband interjects. "Master Finn speaks honestly, Lass. Ink castin' can be vera' painful at times. Are ya' sure this is what ya' want to do?"

Truthfully, I'm not crazy about what I'm hearing. But this whole thing was my idea, and I refuse to be deterred by the idea of a little pain. "Oh, for Pete's sake," I comment, "I just delivered a nine-pound baby last month. You want to talk about pain? Childbirth is not for cowards."

"I can attest to that," Robyn says. "And you handled that like a warrior, Dr. Parker. I'm sure you can get through this as well."

Like I said before; Robyn Brannigan is one of the good ones. "I can handle pain with the best of 'em, Master Finn. Let's get this show on the road," I say.

* * *

Declan, as the male, goes first, simply because that's the way the ritual is worked. There's a minimum of preliminary magic; a large circle is drawn around my husband and I with some type of natural chalk on the hardwood floors, red beeswax candles stand lit at the points of the four elements in the circle, while incense made from rosemary, cedar and vanilla fills the air space of the parlor. Before beginning, Master Finn pricks the index fingers of both of our left hands with an *athame* (ceremonial knife) and squeezes several drops of our joined blood into the dark burgundy colored ink he has selected for the new spell. The trained medical professional in me tries not to think about the chances for infection when mixing body fluids with ink and inserting it under the skin. Doctor Brannigan doesn't seem concerned, so I take comfort in that.

Then, the artist goes to work, adding lines and curves to the already intricate pattern on my husband's bicep while whispering a repeated combination of words that makes no sense to me. For the most part, whatever pain the mage's activities might be causing my *Mo Shiorghra*, it doesn't seem to affect him. He chats amicably with all of us while Master Finn goes about his work, and I see him slightly grimace only once or twice.

The Tax Man's part of the spell is over quicker than I expect, and suddenly I find myself face down on my stomach, spread across the divan, with the ink mage hovering over me. Declan takes hold of my left hand so that I can squeeze it when the pain gets intense. That doesn't last long. I soon end up squeezing so hard, my poor husband's hand goes white from lack of blood flow. Letting go of Declan's hand, I instead grip the sides of the narrow couch and burrow my face into the throw pillows to hide the agony I feel.

At first, everyone around me tries to act as a cheer team, but eventually I ask them, none too politely, to shut the hell up. Someone adds background music to the mix and I gratefully try to breath my way through the waves of pain according to the rhythm of the song, much in the same way I panted through my labor pains with Dylan. Just when I think I can't bear to go on, Master Finn announces he is finished.

Declan helps me up from the couch, and notes my red, watery eyes. "Ah, Love, I am sorry beyond words that ya' were in so much pain. Ya' are ma' brave wee tiger and I will not ever forget yar' courage tonight."

I know he's trying to be romantic and sweet, but all I can think about is the Tylenol Three that Doc Brannigan promised me when this was over. I wave his words off, wanting the whole thing to be done. Master Finn covers our new artwork with an Otherworld style of "Saniderm," a cling wrap style of clear bandage that keeps ink leakage and plasma inside while allowing oxygen to reach the skin. I'm relieved to see some nod to sanitation, but then the sorcerer pours out some powdery substance into his palm and blows it over the tattoos. So much for infection prevention.

There are a few additional magical words spoken by Master Finn while Declan and I clasp hands, wearing our handfasting cords, and still within the casting circle. Then, the ink mage blows out the candles and scuffs the lines of the chalk circle. I'm surprised that Declan and I aren't required to make any personal declarations, but thrilled that no one expects me to profess my undying love when my entire back feels like it's on fire. Even with that reprieve, I'm not free to collapse into a miserable heap. There is an abundance of paperwork that everyone attending needs to sign, which to my mind seems utterly ridiculous. Who in the Universe will require paperwork in the afterlife?

No one is more relieved than I when Declan hands the mage a small parcel of what I assume is *I Idirian* gold tokens as payment and escorts him to the door. The lunar clock on the mantle states that it is nearly 4:00 AM and I have little doubt everyone in the room is beyond exhausted. Dr. Brannigan states his intention to return to the Mundane world, while Mel and Duncan take up the offer of hospitality in our guest room. Having a few private hours together in the middle of the week is an unexpected treat for them, and Mel gives me a thumbs up sign as she and her lover retire for whatever is left of the night.

My husband and I check on our son before heading to bed, finding him sleeping peacefully in his cradle, his nanny near him on her own bed. Seeing us, she whispers, "Congratulations, Lord and Lady *Mac Nuada*. Blessed be."

"Thank you, *Birgit*. We are most grateful ta' ya' far' bringing us Master Finn," his Lordship says in a hushed tone, careful not to wake the baby. He places a small pouch on the dresser near her. "Please accept this gift from ma' Lady and myself."

"'Tis not necessary, ma' Lord. I am happy to serve yar' family in any way I ken'," the *scathach* replies.

"Then think of it as a way of sharin' our joy. I have seen ya' admirin' my boot knife. Perhaps ya' might want to purchase one far' yourself…in remembrance of this special occasion," my husband suggests. A deadly weapon seems like an odd token of a love celebration to me, but the Fae do seem to hold a strange affection for sharp, pointy things.

The nanny bows her head. "Thank ya,' Lord *Mac*. 'Tis a fine suggestion. I will treasure your gift always along with the memory of this night."

I stifle a yawn, the effects of the Tylenol Three kicking in. Declan puts an arm around my waist, careful to avoid touching any part of my upper back as we walk to our own room. I need his assistance in pulling my clothes over my head and slipping on a nightgown. Every movement causes a stabbing pain to the sore skin around my shoulder blade reminding me that sleeping on my back is probably a no-go tonight.

We get as comfortable as we can in bed, Declan avoiding any pressure on his right bicep, me staying on my side and avoiding having anything touching my right shoulder blade. I lean over and kiss him. "Doc gave us 'the green-light' for 'matrimonial activities,' as he so delicately put it. Robyn tries so hard to stay professional," I say, with a grin.

Declan laughs and kisses me back. "He is a fine man... and a good friend. I owe him much. He has worked vera' hard ta' keep me from complete despair over this situation."

The mention of what we face covers the two of us like a nighttime blanket. "Why didn't you tell me, Declan?" I ask, trying not to sound accusatorial. "I could have shared your worry."

"That is exactly why I dinna tell ya', Love. Ya' spent those last weeks before Dylan's birth in a constant state of anxiety. Then, ya' were ripped from yar' vera' home. How could I add yet another layer of unhappiness ta' yar' already full plate," he explained. "I thought I'd wait until the Doc had a better idea of what ta' expect goin' forward, but ya' were gettin' more and more concerned 'bout ma' odd behavior. I felt I had no choice but ta' tell ya' the truth. I am vera', vera' sorry that I dinna' trust that ya' could handle news this overwhelmin'. I was surely wrong. Ya' are ma' wee tiger and stronger than most men I know. I should have realized it sooner."

I feel that familiar ache in my throat over his words, but I'm too tired and too sore for a boo-hoo. Instead, I make silly tiger growling noises and run my hand down his chest. "This tigress has dirty thoughts on her mind," I say, as I twist my body to be able to travel my hand further south. The movement causes a red-hot, iron poker stab of pain to explode across my back. I can't help but gasp.

"As ya' can tell from yar' explorations, Love, no one wants ya' more than me at this vera' moment, but I'd vera' much would like any moans coming from ya' to be from pleasure, not pain. We've waited this long. What's a handful more hours," my Tax Man says.

"I'm sorry. I didn't realize it was going to hurt this much. I'm sure I'll feel better tomorrow," I reply with more hope than I feel.

"Yar' more than worth the wait, sweet Rosie Lass." He opens his arms wider. "Come cuddle closer so I can hold ma' Eternal Love in ma' arms as we rest." I inch over a bit and he carefully tucks a bed pillow behind my back while wrapping his arm under my butt. This works only because I am inches shorter than he is. "Comfy?" he asks.

"Perfect," I say. "I love you, Declan."

"I love ya' too Rosie. Always and forever. Now try and get some rest before the sun rises on this new day. We can talk more tomorrow." He sighs and closes his eyes.

I try to do the same, but the events of this past day play in my mind like a video on a loop, and I find it hard to shut down my brain. Pacing my own breathing to my husband's steady counterpart, I fall into that fuzzy, twilight stage that happens before you slide into deeper REM sleep. Out of nowhere, a single memory pops into my head, a snapshot image from the carousel of the day's incidents. My eyes instantly pop open and I'm wide awake, murmuring under my breath, "Sonofabitch! Those boots…those damn stinkin' boots!"

WISDOM 31

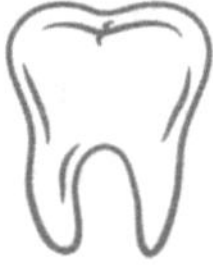

Slainte

I'M wrong about feeling better the next morning. The burning feeling has now turned to a rhythmic throbbing and even the softest chemise I own feels like I'm wearing a sheet of industrial grade sandpaper. Even though Master Finn used a breathable clear bandage, the idea of the lightest spray of water touching that sensitive area is out of the question, so I settle for a sponge bath instead.

Declan, on the other hand, feels perfectly fine, normal enough to complete his normal morning run and work-out, followed by his regular shower, though he admits to using lukewarm to cool water for more than one reason. It's times like these I truly envy his *Sidhe* heritage with its ability to heal from just about any injury or physical setback so quickly. Even here in the Otherworld, my tooth fairy bloodline doesn't give me much of a boost in that category, especially during the daylight hours.

Between the pain from the new ink, the lack of sleep,

and the revelation that came to me in the early morning hours, I am surely not up to taking on the role of Miss Mary Sunshine, not even when Mel and Duncan join us at the breakfast table, all lovey-dovey and dewy-eyed. Okay. I'll be the first to admit that perhaps I'm a tad bit jealous over what I'm sure went on within their bedroom suite that did not go on in mine.

On top of that, I haven't had a chance yet to speak with my Tax Man about the repulsive connection I made in those moments before falling asleep, and it's imperative I do so as soon as possible. But how does one go about telling one's husband that his *athair*, his own flesh and blood, the Lord to whom Declan has sworn his complete allegiance to, is a lecherous, philandering, no-good cheat.

Originally, my mind didn't put two and two together when I first saw those silver-tipped boots on the man's feet as he ranted at us in his study last night. I was too busy doing my best to appear repentant, at least until he started ripping into my beloved *Mo Shiorghra*. I got a real good look at those boots as Declan carried me out of his *athair's* study over his shoulder, but it wasn't until I was attempting to shut down my head and fall asleep that I recalled that I had seen the exact same trim on the feet of the male lover from my trunk hiding experience in the dungeon.

This is, of course, not an appropriate topic to discuss with Mel and Duncan over breakfast no matter how good of friends they are. I have no doubt this information will crush my Tax Man, and knowing my husband as I do, having other people there when I tell him is a bad idea. As it turns out, the other news of the day overshadows everything.

In hindsight, it did seem that our two closest companions appeared unusually giddy this particular morning. They'd always been an "affectionate" couple, open to sharing their attraction to each other to the general public without any kind of reservation, but this morning, their amorous behavior went beyond the norm. Still, I wasn't prepared when a bottle of champagne and four crystal flutes appeared on the table out of nowhere. My first thought was that the Tax Man had conjured it up in response to our taking the Eternal Bond the night before, but a glance at his face, just as confused as mine and slightly green at the thought of more booze, put that thought to rest.

Duncan Fitzpatrick looks at my best friend, and then turns to us. "We have wonderful news we wanted to share with you both first...our dearest friends and family."

I know what he's going to say before the words leave his mouth and I can feel Mel's eyes on me, waiting for my reaction. Though I love my husband's cousin like he was my own family, Duncan is an Otherworld *gancanagh*, a type of Fae incubus and known in the old language as a "love talker." He is courageous, compassionate and sexy as hell, one of the prettiest men I've ever seen, but he can't change what he is. Women are like a moth to the flame around him, an edge I happen to know the Black Knight uses as an asset within his intelligence network. Mel and I have already been through a major blow-out over her relationship with Duncan, and it's only by the blessing of the Universe that we were able to mend our broken friendship.

The man at the heart of this disagreement opens the bottle of champagne. "Lord and Lady *Mac Nuada*…in witnessing the true depths of what love means through your actions last night, you have inspired my own Lady and I to dwell on our own relationship. We understand fully that a love as strong as the kind the two of you possess requires brave and selfless hearts, and the Lady Sparks and I firmly believe that we are up to that challenge."

Underneath the table, the Tax Man is squeezing my knee and I can hear him clearly in my head. *Do not make the same mistake twice, Love. This is yar' chance ta' show the Universe that you have learned the lesson It set out ta' teach ya. Use whatever strength ya' need ta' be happy far' them and keep yar' negative thoughts ta' yourself.*

I know my husband means well. I was miserable when Mel and I weren't speaking to each other several months back. But I feel like he's scolding me, something I never like in normal circumstances and especially find annoying when I feel so lousy. Plus, we just became an eternally bonded couple. Shouldn't he take my side over this debate?

I get an immediate response. *"What I feel far' ya, Rosie, has nothin' ta' do with Duncan or Mel. They must walk their path in the same way we are walkin' our own. Do not say some-thin' ya'll regret when ya' come ta' realize that the heart wants what the heart wants and no well-meanin' advice will change that."* I pull up the tightest shield I can which is akin to my slamming a door in his face. Despite my negative reaction, the Tax Man finds my hand in my lap and entwines his fingers through mine.

While all this is going on between Declan and myself, Duncan has poured champagne into all four glasses. He takes his own flute and raises it toward his Liege Lord. "Lady Sparks has lovingly accepted my proposal to hand-fast. I ask far' yar' blessings on this match, ma' Lord."

Declan lets go of my hand and raises his own glass and says, "Not only ma' blessing, Cousin, but ma' deep felt wish that you and yar' lovely Lady are blessed with all the happiness the Universe can offer."

Everyone pauses and looks at me. I lock eyes with Mel and I can see the hope and love in her eyes. She is trusting me not to ruin this moment for her, and though I still feel strongly that this is a mistake that will eventually crush her soul, I can't be the one to take away her happiness and excitement. I raise my own glass and give the traditional Otherworldy toast in my role as Lady *Mac Nuada*. "May your mornings bring joy and your evenings bring peace. May your troubles grow few as your blessings increase. May the saddest day of your future be no worse than your past. And may your hands join together in a love that will last."

"Blessed be," my husband adds. We all drink from our flutes, even Declan, who takes only the tiniest of sips, yesterday's hangover still fresh in his mind, and me, who just wets my lips to be polite because I'm a nursing mother. There are hugs and handshakes all around and Mel proudly shows off her ring, a platinum band set with an oval ruby the size of a US quarter.

Mel pulls me to the side. "Are you really happy for us,

Rosie? I know you think Duncan is incapable of being a good mate because of his heritage, but you don't know him like I do. He truly loves me. I can feel it here," she says pointing to her chest. "Just like you know that Declan is the only one for you."

"You know I love you, Melly Jelly," I say, using her childhood nickname. "And if Duncan makes you this happy, then how can I not be just as happy for you." It's not totally a lie. I DO want my very best friend to have the wonderful life she deserves. I'm just not sure that as much as Duncan wants to be able to give that to her, he'll be truly able to squelch several generations of basic Fae biology that runs through his veins. But today is not the day to even think this thought, lest something leak out from behind my shield.

"I'm so blessed to hear that, Rosie Posie, because I want you to be my Matron," my dearest friend says as she hugs me again. "I know Duncan plans on asking Declan as well, so you'll be able to stand for us together."

I force a convincing smile to my lips, which I'm sure would earn me an Academy Award nomination. "I'd be honored, Mel. We both will. Thank you for asking me," I gush.

We finish our breakfast amid talk of the upcoming handfast, though nothing about it has been set in motion. Duncan still needs to meet with both fathers, though I don't foresee Mel's dad objecting. Despite both of my BFF's parents being firm in their *Sidhe* culture, they have always struck me as very modern thinking. Unlike a lot of the hoity-toity Fae types of *I Idir*, they will embrace Duncan's diverse family history with the same grace as they always accepted mine. The happy couple will also need to meet with the mages of both their respective Houses, *Nuada* and *Manannan,* to determine the most advantageous dates for their joining before a final date can be set.

Amidst all the conversation, Mel checks the clock on the mantle and determines that she needs to return to the Mundane world. Duncan offers to see her safely back. After last minute bites of breakfast and a few extra sips of champagne, the couple says their goodbyes and disappears through the Veil, leaving Declan and I alone, though not long enough for us to talk things over. *Birgit* joins us in the dining room, Dylan in her arms as is our usual morning routine. Declan takes the baby from her to cuddle before our son demands his morning feeding from me.

Watching Declan interact with Dylan almost every morning is my favorite time of the day. His love for our infant son is so intense that I have no doubt that even the *scathach* is privy to his deepest emotions despite any personal shields my husband uses to hide them. The two of them engage in very direct eye contact, which is something unique to Fae newborns that doesn't happen with Mundane babies of the same age. Whereas I usually speak out loud to our son, his *athair* speaks to him mentally, though neither of us is one hundred percent certain if our baby boy can actually comprehend what is being said by either of us. Most authorities on Fae infant development believe the child only picks up on the emotion of the speaker and not the individual words, though some gifted infants seem to actually respond to specific words, a telling sign that they have exceptional cognitive ability at a very early age. I like to believe that our beautiful boy is one of the gifted ones.

When I was pregnant, Declan would often sing to my belly, insisting that our "Pay-not," the name we gave him before he was born, could hear his tunes. Truthfully, Dylan would actively kick when his father sang to him, so maybe my Tax Man wasn't wrong. The thought comes to me at that moment how strange it is that now that our son is out here in the world, my husband doesn't sing to him. No lullaby, nor any of the sweet folk tunes he was apt to hum on a regular basis. In fact, except for routine dusting by the housekeeping staff, the custom baby grand piano in our parlor, along with the hand-made, ornate Celtic harp, both of which are Lord *Mac's* prize possessions, haven't been touched since we arrived four weeks ago. I think to ask the Tax Man about it, but I don't want to interrupt his "special time" with the baby, and, like a great deal of topics we desperately need to talk about, my questions regarding his sudden lack of interest in music, gets pushed to the side.

WISDOM 32

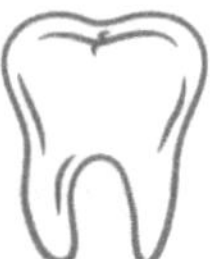

A Change to the Schedule

PART of the overall discontent regarding my forced exile into the Otherworld lies in the simple fact that I am bored; mind-numbingly, unenthusiastically, bored out of my mind. I worked throughout a large portion of my pregnancy until a single bad decision at 35 weeks put me under doctor-ordered, general bedrest. That last month or so was filled with anxiety over my missing husband and maneuvering around daily life with my mother-in-law so that I had no room on my plate to miss going to work every day.

When we first arrived at *Dun Siorai,* I was a brand-new mommy, spending every minute, waking or not, taking care of our infant son. Then we hired *Birgit,* a decision I don't regret for one single minute, especially with that evil bitch, Marcy Kilcrabtree, dogging our lives like a bad case of food poisoning. But the situation does leave me with plenty of extra time, empty hours that I end up using to fret about the multiple issues facing our little family. In addition, I miss my work. I love being a dentist to my young patients. It gives me personal satisfaction and makes me feel as if I actually make a difference in helping kids get over their fears of regular dental health. There's nothing in my role as Lady *Mac Nuada,* here at *Dun Siorai,* or anywhere within *I Idir* itself, to replace the energy I used in my profession. My one and only "walk about" as a guest of the Royal entourage was a complete disaster, and I doubt the *Banphrionsa* will be extending me another invitation anytime soon.

Today is a perfect example of my bland existence. Mel and Duncan have already returned to Salem, Dylan's been cuddled, fed and tucked in for his morning nap, and Declan has just announced his plans to spend the day with Rory Dell finishing up work for a handful of Mundane clients, an intention he's just dropped on me. "You're working ALL day?" I ask, trying to keep from forming a disgruntled pout.

" 'Tis the end weeks of tax season, Love. Probably ma' busiest time of the year. SOME people do like ta' pay their taxes on time, ya' know," he teases. The Tax Man puts his hands on my shoulder tops and kisses my cheek, careful not to brush up against the new ink.

"Ha ha," I answer, not holding back my sarcasm. "You're a real hoot, D.P. A regular comedian."

"I thank the Universe everyday far' yar' decision not ta' give Uncle Sam his fair due, Rosie Lass. T'was the spark that brought us together. Eternally," he adds with a wink. "Besides, I guessed that after all the excitement of last night, yar' lack of sleep, plus the ache of yar' new ink, ya' would want ta' take the day easy and rest."

"That's all I do is sit around and rest," I complain. The statement is not entirely true. Both yesterday and the day before were not what anyone would call restful, certainly not with my unexpected and undesired role as Lady Voyeur. However, I suppose I secretly thought that after taking such a big relationship step only a few hours ago, my One and Only would have planned to spend the day with me in some type of romantic pursuit.

I'm not holding a decent shield so my thoughts are right there for my husband to hear telepathically. "I am vera' sorry, Love," he answers out loud. "I had no idea ya' had such a monumental gift in store far' me last night, otherwise I would have made arrangements with Rory far' another day. But I expect him any moment now, and it would be rude ta' abruptly cancel without notice. Plus, we do need ta' finish up this work sooner than later. I will send him home at a decent hour and the two of us ken' have a nice, romantic dinner. Anythin' ya' like. Ask Cook far' something special so we can celebrate appropriately...just the two of us."

He's right. He had no idea I was going to propose *An Banna Siorai*. Hell! I didn't know I was going to sign on for something that monumental without any discussion or debate. I'd just gone along with my instincts. It wasn't fair to make Declan feel guilty over a decision I made completely on my own and out of the blue. "It's fine, Sweetie. Dinner sounds lovely. I'll let Cook know," I reply, sounding far more enthusiastic than I feel. It will be a romantic dinner that won't lead to much of anything unless my back miraculously heals in the next several hours.

I curl up in my favorite chair in the parlor, the one next to the window that offers the best natural light, a needlework project in my lap, but I just can't get myself interested in it. My attention wanders outside the window where down below, the kitchen boy, *Buaf,* is trying to teach that misbehaving, demon dog to play dead. Maybe it's because I miss my young patients, or maybe it's because I'm a mom to a son of my own, but seeing the kid always hits me hard in "the feels." The tone in his voice and his overall body language when the dog refuses to *"lui sios"* (lie down) as ordered, reminds me so much of the Tax Man when we first met that it makes me smile as I recall that air of lordly annoyance whenever I disagreed with him. It's funny to see the same personality traits in the orphan boy, as if he were not just a kitchen lad but a Lord himself, ruling his own make-believe House.

Whenever I see *Buaf,* I always wonder how Declan was as a boy. There aren't, of course, any Mundane style photographs of a young Lord *Mac Nuada* as a child of the kitchen lad's age, or even as an infant or toddler, for that matter. There is one family portrait over the mantle in Dragon Mama's suite in which my husband appears to be in his mid-teens, if the peach-fuzz dusting of golden-red facial hair is any indication. His youngest sister, Meghan, is a babe in Lady *Nuada's* arms in that portrait, and as I recall, she was near seventeen when she tried to murder me before our handfasting, thus making Declan approximately sixteen years old when that portrait was painted. Even at that young age, I can see his *Tuatha de Danann* bloodline in the way he holds himself, the air of regal confidence that comes with a thousand years of royal Fae heritage.

As if the Universe is privy to my thoughts about my husband's dysfunctional family, there is a knock at the door to our quarters. As per our preference, we don't employ full-time, in-suite staff, so I answer the door myself and find Master Hobart, my mother in law's page, on the other side, message in hand. It's an official summons thinly disguised as an invitation requesting me to share lunch with Lady *Nuada,* alone, in the southwest atrium at just past noon. It's not as if this turn of events is totally unexpected. Being side-lined by yesterday's thieving dog and amorous lovers, I never did accomplish facing her as I'd planned. Making Dragon Mama wait to take her turn at scolding me won't help matters any so I send the sour-faced page back with an answer that I graciously accept her "kind invitation."

Before heading toward our suite to agonize over what I should wear, I stop by Declan's study to let him know my plans for the afternoon have changed. Because Rory Dell, his associate, is working with him, I don't go into a lot of detail about the invitation. Nonetheless, my husband understands what I am in store for and gives me a sympathetic look. "Are ya' sure ya' are up for such a… demandin' social engagement, ma' Lady? Today of all days?" he asks. "I know that yar' feelin' a bit under the weather this morning."

"I'll be fine," I reply, both of us knowing that my words are a lie. "She wants to dine with me alone, so I'll be leaving Dylan here with *Birgit.*"

The Tax Man nods his approval, but in to my mind he adds, *"If ya need rescuin' from my sweet mathair, just ask. I'll come save ya' from the mighty dragon's lair."*

I consider how he rescued me from my loud discussion with his father; picking up all 154 pounds of me off my feet and throwing me over his left shoulder as he stomped out the door without another word. I'm guessing it did little to improve the whole father-son relationship, but from my vantage point, the experience was rather romantically swoony. *"Only if you promise to go the caveman route and throw me over your shoulder again,"* I tease.

Lord *Mac* grins and peers over the tortoise frame glasses he doesn't need but likes to wear when he's in "Tax Man" mode. *"I would carry ya' all the way to Asgard and back if ya' asked me to, Love, but I wouldn't promise to keep ma' hands ta' myself."* He gives me a salacious wink, and adds, *"Seriously, if things get heated and ya' need me to extract ya' I want ya' to promise that ya will call for me. As ya' are aware, my mathair can be difficult."*

I smile, shields up while thinking to myself that a postpartum mommy with a severe lack of sleep and her back on fire can surely give as good as she gets.

WISDOM 33

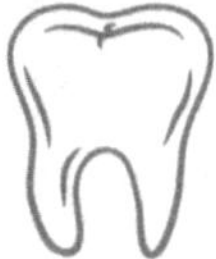

Saving Seamus

IN THE SHORT time Declan and I have been together, I have come to learn that when dealing with his family I should always be ready to wear a thick skin and expect the socially unacceptable. Today's lunch with my husband's mother, however, goes beyond the normal Fitzpatrick dysfunction I've previously witnessed and straight into the downright weird. The first half hour we are together is spent, as anticipated, with Lady *Nuada* listing all the ways in which I have embarrassed the House over these past few weeks and her reminding me several times over that although I had produced an "above average" grandson and heir for House *Nuada*, my low-born, tooth fairy status required me to work twice as hard to gain respect among my mate's peers.

It's on the tip of my tongue to remark that I've met several of my mate's peers and they all like me just fine, but during the time I spent with Lady *Siobhan* before

Dylan was born, I gained an understanding that it is best to let her spill all her venom as quickly as possible so as to allow the rest of the conversation to proceed to a more reasonably peaceful subject. Unfortunately, we never get to that point.

Somewhere between the beef consommé and the spring salad of pea shoots, watercress and early radishes, we are interrupted by the estate's head gardener and a junior member of House *Nuada's* security team, who has a filthy, barefoot *Buaf* by his shirt collar while his mischievous dog, *Seamus*, is being pulled along behind him in a small animal cage on wheels. Both men give a crisp bow, and when the kitchen lad doesn't follow their lead, the guard pushes on the boy's back with such force that *Buaf* falls forward to his knees, making the dog in the cage go wild with barking. "I am most sorry to bother your dinin', ma' Ladies," the armed man says over the dog's yapping.

Dragon Mama gives the young man a scathing look, which in turns causes him to turn a deep shade of pink. "Whatever could be so important that you find it necessary to disturb our lunch, lieutenant? And why is that wretched mongrel inside my house?"

It is the gardener who speaks up. "My deepest apologies, Lady *Nuada*. We would have easily handled the problem ourselves, but you see, the boy...well...he claims that he and this four- legged fiend are under the personal protection of Lord Tond Lady *Mac Nuada*."

It's a good thing I'd finished chewing that last leaf of watercress when I did, otherwise I would have undoubtedly choked on it over the kid's bold-faced lie. Both the boy and the dog look at me with panicked eyes, their whites fully showing, silently pleading for my help. Lady *Siobhan* looks at me with that trademark eyebrow just like someone else I know. "Is this true, Lady *Mac Nuada?*" she asks, not bothering to hide the annoyance in her tone.

As I've said, I have a soft spot for kids. There is no way I'm leaving *Buaf* to the mercy of those two angry men who are obviously manhandling him, though I can't say I have an equal amount of sympathy for that obnoxious dog after what he put me through yesterday. "I'm afraid it's true, Lady *Mathair,*" I fib. "I have taken a genuine interest in the lad." The boy shifts his eyes to me and then to the ginger-colored terrier. "And the dog as well. By the request of my Lord Husband, of course, who is well known for his fondness for animals." I add, quickly throwing Declan's name into the mix.

"Lord *Mac Nuada* has offered this foul-smelling urchin his protection?" Lady *Siobhan* asks, looking me directly in the eye and daring me to lie to her again.

I was never much good at folding, even when I know every card in my hand is a loser. I smile sweetly. "Yes, dear Lady. As you are aware, my husband has a soft heart. He sees potential in the boy."

Dragon Mama smirks at me and I can't tell whether she's looking forward to calling me out, or impressed that I had enough guts to repeatedly lie to her. That old myth about the Fae being unable to tell a lie is a lie itself. No one tells a whopper easier than a *Sidhe.* Lady *Siobhan* turns her attention back to the two men. "What trouble was the boy causing when you found him?" she asks them.

"T'was not the lad so much as it was that horrid dog. He has dug up the spring petunias for the thard' time this week, good Lady. And when we rounded up the dog ta' finally do what needs ta' be done, the boy fought us like a rabid weasel…bitin' and kickin' like he had lost his vera' mind," the gardener complained.

Buaf raises up his head to look at his accusers, twisting and fighting the guard's hold on him. "They was gonna' drown *Seamus* in the garden's well, nice Lady," the boy shouts at me, his voice cracking with emotion. "I coulda' not let them do such a horrid thing ta' ma' good boy. I told them that the two of us belonged under Lord and Lady *Mac Nuada's* watch and they 'aught not be thinkin' ta' harm *Seamus*. His Lordship even gave this dog a spot in the barn near his own harse'. Lord *Mac* would surely be vera' angry if someone hurt this wee doggo."

I jump into the conversation. "I can vouch that all of what *Buaf* says is true, Lady *Mathair*. My Lord Husband did have his groom set a special place for the dog in the barn near his stallion. So, I suppose it does prove some type of real affection for this animal."

Lady *Nuada* sighed. "*Deaglean* was always hauling home injured animals when he was a lad. Nasty, half-dead, rejects. It would seem he hasn't lost that part of himself." She rose from the table and walked over to the boy, picking up his chin and turning it every which way to examine his face. Frowning, she asked, "Are you *Sidhe,* boy? It is hard to tell under all that dirt."

The kitchen lad shrugged. "I donna' know who or what begat me, Lady *Nuada*. Cook has called me a changelin' and has forbidden me ta' use ma' magic. She says it will only put ridiculous notions in ma' par', addled head."

She looked the boy up and down, and when she noticed his odd foot with the sixth toe, she abruptly dropped her hand from his chin. Stepping back, she narrowed her eyes. "Filthy, stupid and cursed besides. How old are you, boy?"

"I only know that I 'ken remember six different Solstices, ma' Lady. Other than that, I donna' know the day or year the Universe first sent me," he answered.

Dragon Mama glared, baring her perfect white teeth in a snarl. "If what you say is true, Lady Rosalinda, and this boy is under *Mac Nuada's* watch, then let the two of you deal with his curse. Get him out of my sight this very minute, lest I not only have the four-legged mongrel drowned, but this changeling fiend as well."

WISDOM 34

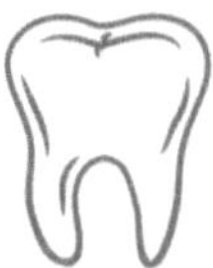

Explanations and Ramifications

DRAGON MAMA'S threat leaves me with no choice but to drag the kid and his misbehaved dog back to our quarters. I tell myself that this will be a short-term solution until Lady *Nuada* "cools off," though, personally, I'm not really sure what has got her so riled up in the first place. I realize eight-year-old boys and growing puppies can mire themselves in bad choices, and the dog's constant mischief can truly be annoying. However, my mother-in-law's reaction to the dug-up petunias seems a tad extreme even for *Siobhan* Fitzpatrick.

The two partners in crime follow solemnly behind me, the boy using his tattered rope belt as a leash for the dog. "Perhaps you should have put *Seamus* on a leash sooner," I suggest. "Then we might all not be in Lady *Nuada's* bad graces."

"I am vera sorry, Lady *Mac,* far' throwin' ma' *fadhbanna* (problems) on ya. *Seamus* is vera' sorry too. He just likes to dig an awful lot." The kitchen lad wagged a finger at the terrier. "See what trouble ya've gotten us into, boy? Ya' nearly got us both drowned."

"I'm sure no one really meant they would actually drown the two of you. I just think they meant to scare you is all," I say. "Their threats were meant to shock you so in the future, you'd be frightened and both try to behave better from now on. All life is sacred here at *Dun Siorai*," I lie, my mind going back to the several attempts on my life during my previous visits.

Buaf shakes his head in disagreement with me. "I donna' mean ta' sound like a gagglin' goose, Lady *Mac*, but I knows far' a fact that ole' man Tyber, the gardener, threw a whole litter of *cait leanbh* ("baby cats") straight into that well. He said they was nothin' mar' than a nuisance and Lord *Nuada* dinna' need useless mouths ta' feed."

I suck in my breath over the kid's statement. They drown poor, defenseless animals at *Dun Siorai*? The Tax Man and I are going to have a serious discussion about that. But first, I have to figure out how to explain to him why I've returned with two extra house guests in tow, both of whom stink to high heavens.

The doors open for me as soon as I arrive, the wards set to allow our little family automatic entry. Before I can get my whole story straight, his Lordship comes out of his study, obviously surprised that I've returned so soon. His eyes meet mine first, with me wearing what must be a guilty expression across my face, then turns his scrutiny to the kid and the dog. He leans in the doorway, his arms crossed over his chest and an amused lift to his lips.

"Ken' I assume there's a helluva' good story ta' follow?" he asks.

Buaf bows so low, he almost tips over while yanking his dog to a sitting position. "'Tis all ma' fault, yar' Lordship. I dinna' keep a good hand on ma' boy *Seamus* an' he went and dug up ole' Tyber's petunias. The ole' *gruaim* (grump) wantad' ta' drown ma' dog, and and I woodna' let him. I gave as gad' as I got," the lad admits.

Lord *Mac Nuada* leaves his post in the doorway and comes closer to the three of us, making a face when he gets near enough to get a good whiff of the pair's odor. Still, he speaks to the boy with calm authority. "And do ya' think it is right far' *Seamus* ta' be ruinin' Master Tyber's hard work?"

Buaf hung his head in shame. "No, ma' Lord. *Seamus* needs ta' learn ta' behave better and not ta' dig up the gardens." With a bit of fire in his belly, the kid looks up and adds, "But he is just a wee pup, yar' Lordship. He donna' know no better. If anyone deserves ta' be drowned, it shad' be me 'cause I shad' have been watchin' him closer and trainin' him better."

A flit of emotion crosses my husband's face. "Rest assured, lad, there'll be do drowin' of anyone or anything here at *Dun Siorai*."

I hold my breath, waiting for the boy to tell Declan about the kittens, but thankfully, he doesn't. I think that is a conversation best left for when the two of us are alone. Instead, the kid bows low again and says, "I am forever in yar' debt, Lord *Mac.* Someday, when I am bigger and stronger, I shall swear ma' loyal allegiance as yar' man."

The corner of his Lordship's lip turns up again at the

boy's bravado. "I look forward ta' that day, young *Buaf*. But first, ya' must tell me how ma' lovely Lady came to be part of yar' trouble?"

I open my mouth to explain, but Declan puts a hand up to stop me. "I would vera' much like ta' hear the lad explain."

Apparently, the Tax Man is on a roll, so I play along. Dropping a curtsy, I reply much too sweetly. "As you wish, my Lord." I feel a pang of sympathy for the kid. I, myself, have been in Lord *Mac's* crosshairs on a few occasions, feeling like a thief with his hand in the till while the shop owner looks on with deadly calmness.

The boy turns a bright shade of pink as I watch him mentally contemplate whether he will tell my husband the real truth of why he's here with me now, or will he attempt to spin the story to his own benefit. His little toothpick leg is jiggling in nervous tension, a physical reaction I've often seen in my husband as well. I try not to crack a smile. It's a fact that since the night Declan rescued *Buaf* from that deep pit, the child's held my husband in a state of exalted hero worship. Admitting his dishonesty and facing my husband's disappointment will be difficult for the poor kid to bear.

The kitchen lad looks up at my husband who towers over his child's small form like a fairy-tale giant. *Buaf* is wearing the saddest, most pitiful looking expression I've ever seen on his young face. If that isn't bad enough, next to him, the dog has dropped to his belly and is staring up at Declan with perfectly miserable, puppy dog eyes, his shaggy head between his paws. The kid sniffs his sadness away in Academy Award fashion. "Yar' Lady is part of ma' troubles only because she is the kindest, the most beauti-ful-est, the wisest and surely the most bravest Lady in all of *I Idir*, ma' Lord."

Declan puts a discreet hand over his mouth as if he is contemplating the boy's words, but I can tell from the merriment in his eyes that he's trying very hard not to laugh. Sounding every bit the Lord of the Manor, he puts his hands behind his back and says, "I vera' much agree with ya' lad. Lady *Mac Nuada* is surely a prize, and I consider ma'self a lucky man, but that does no explain how or why I find ya' and yar' dog in ma' private quarters."

With a deep sigh of weariness, the boy confesses, though he wears his discomfort over the truth like a heavy millstone around his neck. "I am here, ma' Lord, because I am a no gad', low-life, *breagadoir* (liar) who does not deserve yar' mercy."

When the boy doesn't explain, the Tax Man prods him on. "And what is this supposed lie you told, Master *Buaf*? I would like clarification."

With another dramatic sigh, the kid continues. "They said they was gonna' drown ma' *Seamus* and make me watch, ma' Lord. They told me they was gonna' hold me over the side of the well by ma' ankles and make me view it all as ma' par' dog took his last breath and slipped under the water. I could no let them do that, yar Lordship. I would rather have had them drop us both in the well. I tried fightin' them, but they was too much far' me. So, ta' make them stop I told them that me and *Seamus* were under the protection of you and yar' nice Lady. At first, they no believed me, but then Master Tyber said that he had seen Lady *Mac* talkin' ta' me on more than one occasion and that maybe they'd better check before they commenced with the drowin'. Just in case."

This was a part of the story I hadn't heard. The thought that they'd not only drown the child's pet but make him watch as it happened makes me physically ill and I have to swallow back the bile that rises in my throat. I see my husband's aura darken, as well as the tight set to his jaw. Rage isn't Declan's norm, but there's no doubt *Buaf's* story has deeply angered him. Still, he retains his outwardly calm demeanor, choosing his words carefully, and not for the first time do I think about what an excellent member of the Ruling Council he'll make some day.

"We do not practice such unjust cruelty here at *Dun Siorai*, lad. I am sorry that you were made to believe we did. It is a discussion I will have with the men themselves. But you must understand, Master *Buaf*, that a man's word should be as solid as the sword in his hand. Lies beget treachery, and treachery leads to chaos. A man's honor is above all things."

"Aye, ma' Lord. I understand," the boy replies. "T'was wrong of me ta' lie, especially in yar' name. If ya' want ta' have me whipped, I will understand, but I will take double the strokes if ya' just pardon ma' *Seamus*. He donna' know any better, yar' Lordship, and I ken' no stand far' him to suffer far' ma' spoilin' him."

Okay. Now I just want to collapse in a puddle of mushy, mama tears, which is why I would not make a very good politician. I can't help but wear everything I'm feeling in my body language and facial expression. *"Please*

Sweetie, be gentle with this kid. He just loves that dog to the point of distraction," I mentally suggest.

Declan doesn't answer me. Instead, he squats down to the boy's level. "I am not a believer in physical punishment, lad. Especially not far' boys who know the difference between right and wrong and are willin' ta' own up ta' their mistakes. However, we must make this right, lest everyone at *Dun Siorai* believe ya' ta' be 'a no gad', low life *breagadoir.'* Ya' donna want that kind of cloud hangin' about yar' name, do ya'?"

"No, ma' Lord. I do not want folks ta' think I am dishonest. But I donna' know how ta' fix what I said now that I went ahead and said it," the boy admits.

"We shall have ta' make yar' statement the truth then, Master *Buaf.* As of this vera' moment, you, and wee *Seamus*, are under the protection and guardianship of ma' Lady and ma'self. I will make sure everyone at *Dun Siorai* is aware of this fact. That is, of course, if this be somethin' ya' believe ya' ken' live with lad?"

The child blinks several times, unsure as to whether he was being played as a fool. Eventually, coming to the belief that my husband meant what he'd just said, *Buaf* whispers as if he thought that if he said the answer too loudly the offer might evaporate. "Aye, ma' Lord. 'Tis more than I could have hoped far.'"

"Good. I am glad we could resolve this problem. Going forward, you will live here while ya' train to be a page until ya' are old enough ta' choose yar' own path. In yar' spare time, ya' will work with Tybalt the Hound Master on trainin' *Seamus* to behave properly as a house dog."

"A page, ma' Lord? I am *naire* (embarrassed) far' ya ta' know that I ken' no read nor write," the kid stammered.

"Then you will learn. As ya' said yourself, ma' Lady is the kindest, loveliest and smartest Lady in all of *I Idir.* I am sure she will be willing to help you in yar' quest," my husband tells him, giving me a conspiratorial wink.

I smile, loving my Tax Man even more in these past few moments, if that's even possible. "Of course, I'll teach you, *Buaf.* We'll have you reading and writing in no time."

The boy beams and the dog wags his tail as if he can sense his Master's joy, which maybe he can. "When shall we begin, Lady *Mac?* I am ready this vera' minute."

His Lordship shakes his head. "I think befar' we can start any lessons you and wee *Seamus* must begin by lookin' the part. No good page looks...or smells... like he lives with the pigs."

"I just need a bucket and an ole' rag, ma' Lord. I'll have us both cleaned up befar' ya' ken whistle a merry tune," the lad says, nearly dancing a jig in his exuberance.

"I was thinkin' of something a little mar'...complete," Lord *Mac* says. "A hot bath for you, and an entire groomin' far' yar' pup. His coat is matted and his nails need ta' be trimmed. A visit with Master Tybalt is in order." The boy hesitates, his fear at being separated from the dog obvious, so Declan quickly adds, "Ya' have ma' word that no one will harm yar' pup, lad. *Seamus* will be returned ta' ya' in a few hours. In the meantime, ma' good Lady will help ya' with yar' own bath."

This time, the eight-year old's fear turns to general horror. He bends over to whisper in Declan's ear, though the kid is loud enough for me to hear. "With all due respect far' yar' generosity, ma' Lord, I no ken' get nekked' in front of Lady *Mac.* I am a man, yar' Lordship. She is a high-born Lady." he explains "She should not be veiwin' ma' manly parts."

How the Tax Man is holding in his laughter, I'll never know, but I can hear him chuckling in my head. "I see. That is a problem." He points to *Birgit,* who has stepped out of the nursery with Dylan in her arms to see what all the commotion is about. "How about if *Birgit* helps you with yar' bath. She is ma' son's nanny, and he is a boy as well."

Our new page shakes his head in the negative. "Though he be a Lord himself, yar' own son is a wee *bairn,* ma' Lord. 'Tis not the same. Our parts are different, I think. Plus, the nanny still be a lady."

"But *Birgit* is also a *scathach,* lad. A trained warrior. She ken' fight alongside any man and hold har' own if not best him outright," his Lordship explains.

"Truly?" the kid asks, not hiding the awe in his voice.

"'Tis the truth, lad. And if ya' come take yar' bath like a gad' page, I will tell ya' about the time I trained with the Lord Warrior himself," the nanny promises.

"Do ya' mean ta' say that ya' have sparred with *Cu Chulainn* himself?"

"Aye," *Birgit* answers. "He is all they say he is…and then some."

"Then I will come with ya' and take a bath. But ya' must promise not ta' tell people ya' have seen me nekked."

Birgit raises her hand in solemn vow. "Ma' lips shall remain sealed over yar' nekkedness. I swear."

Buaf bends down to address the dog. "We are to

become pages, *Seamus*. 'Tis a more better path far' the two of us. No more talk of drowin'. You be a gad' boy and take yar' bath with Master Tybalt and I will see ya' in a little while."

Birgit hands me my son and sticks out her hand for the ex-kitchen lad to grasp. The boy puts his small, grimy hand in the nanny's as they walk down the hall toward the largest of our guest bathrooms, allowing me to finally let out the biggest of sighs.

WISDOM 35

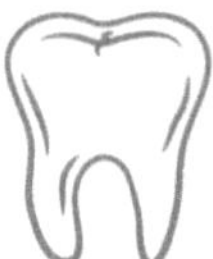

A Bigger Family Tree Don't Come Free

I DON'T EVEN WAIT until the two of them reach the bathroom before throwing my arms around my husband's neck. "You, Declan Fitzpatrick, are, without a doubt, the most wonderful man in the entire world. Both of them," I add, pressing my lips against his for a kiss he generously returns.

"Then ya' are no upset, Lass?" he asks. "Taking guardianship of the boy and adding him ta' the household is a big step, not ta' mention ma' offer ta' have ya' teach him ta' read."

"How could I ever be upset over such an honorable and compassionate gesture, Sweetie? You saw a child in need and you reached out to him. In my eyes, that makes you more of a Lord than any ancient bloodline. No doubt this is part of our path. Blessed be," I say, spiritually over-whelmed by my husband's generosity. "The boy's story about what they planned to do to him and the dog made me sick to my stomach. I would like to see those two jerks dangled over that well."

"Aye. It was all I could do ta' hold ma' temper and not attempt some justice of ma' own," Declan admits. "Since North Korea I seem ta' have a much shorter fuse. Robyn is not sure if it is just normal stress related ta' ma' experience or a result of ..." His words trail off, and my heart breaks for him. "But I ken' no go runnin' off ta' discipline ma' *athair's* men, especially since this decision ta' take the lad in with us will undoubtedly ruffle some feathers in the household."

"I'm not sure why what we do within our own family is anyone else's business?" I ask, knowing full well that everything in the Otherworld is everyone's business. The Fae breathe gossip like humans take in oxygen.

"Ya' know the culture here is complicated, Love. Our generation is not apt ta' change a belief system that's been around far' multiple generations," the Tax Man explains. "By the way," he adds, "Why in *Dubnos* (Celtic version of Hell) is the boy still walkin' around barefoot? I thought ya' told me Cook found him some boots."

"He DID have boots the last time I checked. I asked him the same thing on the way here. He explained that although one boot was just fine, the other pinched his *ladhar an diabhal* ("devil's toe"). It doesn't matter how many times I've tried to explain that the extra toe is a quirk of genetics and not a reflection of who he is as a person. The poor kid can't seem to take my word for it."

"Old beliefs die hard here, Love."

"I get that, Declan, and I can understand a young, uneducated child believing that shit, but your mother as well? Didn't you tell me that she studied at the Sorbonne before she met and handfasted your father? She undoubtedly has enough Mundane science background to know a random toe is not an evil 'curse,' yet she carried on like an insane woman when she noted *Buaf's* extra appendage. Threatened to drown him if I didn't get him out of her quarters."

The Tax Man looks away and bites his lower lip, a unique Declan "tell" when he's keeping bad news from me. I've been on the receiving end of "that look" several times, and not once did the information he was forced to reveal make me happy. "What?" I ask. "What are you not saying." He doesn't answer and so I repeat myself, a little terser sounding this second time. "I know that look Declan. That damn lip biting. Didn't we just have this conversation about not keeping things from each other? We took the frickin' Eternal Bond. I expect you to always be open and transparent with me, no matter what."

Before he can answer, there is a knock at our door. The Tax Man obviously knows who's on the other side. He picks up the dog, who, remarkably, has stayed exactly where the boy has left him, and gives Master Tybalt, the kennel boss, entry. The two chatter away in the old language with Declan giving the Hound Master instructions on *Seamus'* grooming and subsequent training. Although my Gaelic is better than it was when we first met, when the "natives' speak it here in *I Idir*, they communicate so quickly I have trouble translating all the words. I can, however, pick out small pieces of the conversation in which my husband calls that four-legged-doggie-terror our new "family pet." Goddesses help us.

Once Tybalt leaves, Lord *Mac* turns his attention back to me. "Give me a minute ta' send Rory Dell home to the Mundane world, then come join me in my study, Love. We'll talk in there where I can add extra wards for privacy," he instructs as he walks away.

I don't like the sound of that. Not one little bit. I count to a thousand and then head for the study. His associate is gone and Declan is moving around to all four corners of the room casting an extra layer of security on a space that is already as guarded as a prison. "You're making me nervous, Tax Man. What's with all this cloak and dagger nonsense?"

He shuts the door and gestures to a spot on the leather settee, placing himself next to me. I start wrapping my finger around the end of my braid, my own outward anxiety "tell." "I don't wish ta' see ghosts where none may exist, Lass, but I have some...concerns about the wee lad. I understand vera' well the science behind a genetic anomaly. As ta' the wee lad, I am disquieted by the unique coincidences in his case," the Tax Man admits.

"Coincidences? How so?" I question, my heart rapidly beating though I'm not fully registering why that is.

"His Lordship, my *athair,* has an extra toe. On the same foot. My twin had one as well. It is apparently a quirk in the *Nuada* line, one I myself do not have, though I was half-expectin' our own Dylan to have one as well." My husband pauses, waiting for me to make my own connection.

I blink several times as I put his information together in my head. "Are you saying that *Buaf* might be a *Nuada?* That the two of you might be related?"

The Tax Man bites his lip again and that's when I figure out what he's inferring. "Feckin' hell, Declan! Are you saying he might be your...?" I can't make myself finish the sentence; can't possibly force the damning words to flow from my mouth. Dylan is Declan's son. His only son. Our son. Logic kicks in and I propose a reasonable argument. "That's impossible. You took The Ritual. You insisted to me that conceiving a child with anyone but your *Mo Shiorghra* was impossible within the perimeters of the magic involved. He can't be yours. There must be another *Nuada* male floating around out there that no one knows about."

"I do not know of any, but everyone is related to someone at *Dun Siorai.* 'Tis not impossible, I suppose," he consoles. My anxiety must be rolling off of me in waves because my husband takes both of my hands in his and squeezes. "I am sorry ta' cause ya' more worry, Rosie, ma' Love. It seems I do little more than upset yar' vera' soul. If it give's ya' any peace, there are more reasons that negate ma' being the boy's sire." I don't respond so he continues. "The child physically appears ta' be in his eighth year. As ya' of all people probably noticed, he still has most of his baby teeth. I've done some discreet poking aroun' and ma' sources say the child first appeared at *Dun Siorai* the same fall that the Hunter's Moon appeared later than anyone ever remembered, not risin' until after *Samhain.* It was unusually dark in color and bein' superstitious folks considered it an ill omen. That would have been eight years ago last autumn."

Declan lets go of my hands and begins pacing the room. "That was the same year I was in Tibet. At the Sakya Monastery. I had reached a point in ma' life where I had lost hope that I would ever find ma' true path in life or whether I'd ever find ma' One and Only. It was suggested by our current Merlin that I spend a year studying with the monks at Sakya, who are fully aware of the Otherworld's existence and can help some of us come ta' terms with our life path. I was in residence at the monastery from the start of the traditional Mundane New Year of January 1st until the following Solstice. Celibacy is mandatory for all postulants. I lay with no females during those twelve months. So, if *Buaf* was born in the fall of that year, I ken' no' be his *athair*".

I'm about to breathe a sigh of relief when my brutally honest husband adds, "But if the boy is younger or older than we think…" This time it is his turn to let the words fall off, uncomfortable with saying them as well.

"It still doesn't make sense. Why bother with The Ritual if the damn thing doesn't work?" I growl.

"I have no answers to that, Lass. I hope to hunt down the elusive Master Brendan, the ink mage who cast my Ritual, as well as my *athair's*. Perhaps he can offer some explanation."

And just like that, Lord Callum Fitzpatrick *Nuada* becomes the elephant in the room, and when it comes to metaphorical elephants, Rosie Parker always needs to feed them some peanuts. "I don't want to be disrespectful or offend you in any way, Declan, but have you considered that just maybe...your father is the boy's sire?"

He stops pacing and turns to me. "Aye, Love. I have considered that possibility, and as much as it pains me to say so, I have learned things about ma' *athair* that leave me with unease."

The Tax Man doesn't expound on that comment, leaving the door open for me to tell him what I should have told him earlier when I made the connection the night of our Eternal Bond. "There's something I have to tell you, Sweetie. It's about something...odd...that happened before you arrived home from *Asgard*." Then, before I can chicken out, I rapid-fire spill out the story of how I chased the dog into the dungeon; of how I hid in the trunk and overheard what I heard and saw what I saw through the open spaces in the planks; and finally, how I recognized those same unique boots with the silver toe trim on his own father's feet.

At first, my husband doesn't say anything in response to my tale, seemingly deep in thought, so we sit in silence as several minutes tick by on the hands of his wall clock. It crosses my mind that in my haste to get the story about the dungeon out, I may have forgotten to mention the emerald earring that I found and am still in possession of.

Before I can add that tidbit of information, we are once again interrupted by knocking, this time at the door to the study. It's *Birgit,* accompanied by our newest page, freshly scrubbed and smelling of citrus and pine, his once ratty, tangled auburn hair now neatly combed and braided down his back, and somehow wearing perfectly sized doeskin leather breeches and a linen tunic. His little feet are stuffed into flat moccasin-style slippers trimmed in soft rabbit fur. Dressed this way, he looks every bit the small child he is. More startling is the fact that with the dirt and grime washed from his small, handsome face, there's no denying his *Sidhe* ancestry. His high Fae bloodline is clearly written across the planes of his face. A face that resembles the one standing next to me.

WISDOM 36

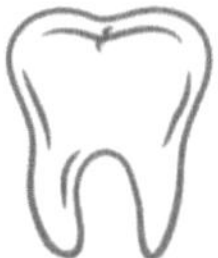

The Whispers of Mothers

THERE'S A SAYING HERE in *I Idir; "glaonna na fola."* It's in reference to family ties and in the old language means "the blood calls," a central part of the Fae spiritual philosophy that the individual self is, foremost, an extension of one's family legacy. As someone who was raised entirely in the Mundane world, where self-awareness and personal achievement are paramount to a successful and happy existence, a belief that mandates your path in life is exclusively determined by all those who came before you is more than a little hard to swallow.

It's my husband's opinion that I process the concept of *glaonna na fola* too simply without truly understanding the real connections between souls that share a bloodline. Though he's spent an impressive number of years studying in the human world, Declan's soul, who he is and what he believes in, is entirely rooted in the Fae Otherworld. Lord *Mac Nuada* is absolutely convinced that his "self" is made up of pieces of every family member that ever came before him, and that a piece of his soul now rests in our son, Dylan. He claims it is the sole reason that when he first encountered *Buaf* a few nights back, my husband felt a solid connection between the orphan child and himself, though he had no logical understanding of why he felt this way.

Maybe it's the Otherworld magic that creates this bond, or maybe there is some other biological reason the Fae seem to instinctively know their own. It might explain why my own mother was so miserable in her self-isolation in the Mundane world, cut off from the "blood" that undoubtedly still called to her even after she'd turned her back on her Fae heritage. Still, even now, though she's physically gone from me, a day doesn't go by where I don't feel her presence in my life, so maybe there's more to this "calling of the blood" than I'd like to admit.

I'm telling you all of this to hopefully explain how easily the child, as well as that ornery dog, have made a home with us, both physically and within our hearts. Logic would dictate that the addition of an outside child and a puppy to a household might naturally come with a sense of "stranger awkwardness," but in the case of *Buaf* and *Seamus*, the two seemed to blend naturally into the fabric of our daily lives.

That's not to say there weren't some needed adjustments and compromises. We had originally planned on the boy taking one of the larger guest suites as his room, with the stipulation that the dog was to stay in his own pet bed near the parlor fireplace. Despite *Buaf* agreeing to those terms, the following morning, we found both he and *Seamus* squeezed into the tiny dog basket in the parlor. After a long talk with his "Liege Lord," a compromise was made; the boy would take the much smaller, unused servant's quarter connected to the nursery. Because that room was absent of any of the beautiful, hand-knotted rugs that were more like artwork throughout our home, an allowance was made for the dog to sleep in the room with him, though Lord *Mac* drew the line at *Seamus* sleeping in the bed with the boy and the dog basket was thus set next to it.

The child was blessed with a sunny disposition, eager to please and especially astute for someone with such rough beginnings. For the time being, Declan and I have decided not to go public with our suspicions regarding the boy's heritage. At my husband's insistence regarding his family's security, it's also been determined that, for the present, both the boy and the dog should keep a very low profile, staying exclusively near to our family quarters and not roaming the estate. Gossip being what it was in *I Idir*, there was little doubt that news of our taking guardianship of the orphan and the dog was common knowledge among the staff at *Dun Siorai*. Still, the longer we could avoid any direct confrontation with Lord and Lady *Nuada* about the boy's status, the better it would be for everyone involved, at least until we could ascertain more of the truth regarding *Buaf's* birth and his strange arrival at *Dun Siorai*. The Tax Man, being a highly trained intelligence officer, is excellent in gaining insight into the truth folks want to hide. If anyone can get to the bottom of this eight-year mystery, it would be my hubby.

I knew he'd attended a hush-hush meeting at *Crann*

Bethadh, and hosted another closed-door session with Duncan here at home. When I asked what might be going on, my fated mate simply kissed me and asked me to trust him to tell me everything when "the time was right." Grrrr. I'll admit, I am not a happy camper over being left out of the discussion, but even in the short time we've been together, I've learned that when D. P. Fitzpatrick, aka Lord *Mac Nuada,* makes a decision, he does not usually change his mind no matter how hard you might work at getting him to do so.

At the very least, my new teacher role helps fill some of the empty boredom of life in the Otherworld. The kid is surprisingly bright, quick to conquer the letters of the English alphabet in less than two days and then moving on to the consonants and vowels of the Old Language spoken here in *I Idir.* I'd initially planned on having him first master reading and writing basic English before moving on to the more difficult Gaelic, but the child was determined to learn them both together and nothing I said could dissuade him. It was only a day or two later that I realized that it was for his "Liege Lord" that the new page had become determined to conquer printing out the letters by his own hand.

Between our new family members not staying in their own beds at night, and the lingering burning of the new ink added to my shoulder blade, Decan and I have yet to find time and privacy to properly exercise Doc Brannigan's "thumbs up" regarding resuming our spousal intimacy. Despite some hot and heavy foreplay, we'd not actually consummated our newest relationship bond. Truthfully, I was starting to get a bit cranky about his holding back, but in hindsight, I am glad I kept my snarky mouth shut on the topic, lest I might have ruined the Tax Man's big surprise, which came unexpectedly this very morning.

I should have suspected something was up by the way the kid and my husband kept exchanging secret glances over the breakfast table while the boy kept slipping the dog his bacon under the table. "I'm feeling a bit left out this morning. Is there something going on that I'm not aware of?" I ask, addressing my question to *Buaf*.

The boy giggled before answering. "Oh no, Lady Rosie. I am just feelin' happy this fine morn. There be no secret in place. None at all," he says as he looks over to my husband and grins.

I eye Declan, who just shrugs, his face not giving anything away. "I know nothing more than you, Love," he fibs, then gives me a cheeky wink.

"Okay. I guess I'm not in on the joke," I tease. "Iced out by two of the men in my life. I hope Dylan won't start laughing at me when I go to feed him."

The child looks at me in all seriousness. "Oh no, ma' Lady. Dylan be just a wee, sweet *bairn*. He is no privy ta' manly secrets. Not yet anyway."

I hide my smiles under my napkins. "You're right, Master Page. Dylan is content to simply eat, sleep and poop. I'm guessing he doesn't hold on to any secrets."

Apparently, my saying "poop" at the breakfast table tickles the lad's fancy, and he chuckles loudly, which considering his sorry state a few days ago, warms my own heart. He stands and politely asks, "May I be excused, Lady *Mac*? I must attend ta'…things."

"Of course, Master Page. I will see you in the parlor at 9:00 sharp for your lessons."

The kid gives a formal bow before heading off in the direction of my husband's study. "I believe that's my cue to exit as well," my husband says as he stands, then leans over to kiss me. "I have 'things' to attend to as well."

"Should I be worried about all these so-called "things"?" I ask.

"Define 'worry,'" he laughs, as he follows after the kid.

* * *

At ten minutes before nine, Lord *Mac Nuada's* young page enters the parlor dressed in regal Otherworldly formality. He's attired in the House's favored maroon and gold, his usually slipper clad feet now clad in a pair of short leather boots that look suspiciously custom made to accommodate his extra toe. *Buaf* carries a satin pillow in his hand which holds a rolled parchment and a sweet-smelling, gardenia look-alike, the Fae floral symbol for fated mates.

The child walks with deliberate steps, concentrating on keeping his back straight and the pillow steady. When he reaches my chair, he attempts a wobbly bow, catching the scroll and the flower with one hand before it slides off the slippery fabric. "A message far' ya', Lady *Mac,* from his Lordship."

I have to bite the inside of my cheeks to keep from grinning. The lad looks so adorable I just want to pick him up and hug him, though something tells me he wouldn't find it a compliment in his new position. Instead, I politely take the flower and the parchment off the pillow. That's when I notice the lettering on the outside. In what is plainly a child's careful scrawl it says, "To the lovely Lady Rosalinda Fitzpatrick *Mac Nuada* from her ever-loving Lord *Mac Nuada*." I know how much tongue-biting effort went into printing out all these letters. It's such a sweet gesture on both their parts that I can't help the ache in my throat. "This is excellent penmanship, Master Page. Quite impressive for such a new student."

His face is beaming and I never wished more since coming to *Dun Siorai* that I had a working cell phone with a camera so I could capture this moment. "You must open the message, ma' Lady, far' I am ta' bring a response to ma' Lord."

"Of course," I say as I slide off the ribbon and unroll the parchment. The note is written in Declan's neat hand and it says,

> *My dearest Lady Love,*
> *Your devoted Mo Shiorghra and Eternal*
> *Mate wishes the pleasure of your loving company*
> *tomorrow. Would you be willing to share your*
> *day with me? We would be gone from 10 in the*
> *morning until approximately 4 in the afternoon.*
> *I await your response with a heart set afire.*
> *D*

My toes involuntarily curl in my shoes. The Tax Man is the king of sexy, mind-numbing, seduction planning. If the kid notices my face is pinker than it was a moment ago, he doesn't comment. I roll the parchment back up and place it on the table next to the flower. "You can tell his Lordship that I would be most honored to accept his lovely invitation. I shall be ready at 10:00 AM tomorrow."

"I will tell him, ma' Lady," he says, racing back to his "Liege Lord." Then, remembering he hadn't bowed before he left, he faces me, bends at the waist then literally skips out the door like the eight-year-old he is, whistling a cheerful tune while mashing the satin pillow under his arm.

Declan Fitzpatrick can keep secrets better than anyone I know. Understanding this in advance, I still spend the rest of today trying to wrangle even the tiniest bit of information out of him regarding the details of our day together. I believe my attempts at subterfuge are rather clever, but the Spy Master sees through each and every one of them and manages to outmaneuver every query I put forth. "How should I dress tomorrow?" I ask with an air of false innocence.

"Wear yar' favorite gown," he replies without adding a single detail.

"Will I need a light cloak? Or maybe some riding gear?"

"If those things become necessary then I shall be happy ta' provide them far' ya, Lass" his Jr. Lordship answers.

"Perhaps I should have Cook provide us with a basket of goodies? A bottle of wine, maybe?" I question, batting my eyes and winding the end of my braid around my finger in obvious flirtation.

"Tomorrow's fare has already been handled," he says with a smirk, "but I'm impressed by yar' feminine perseverance."

"Well, can you at least tell me if I'll need indoor shoes or outdoor shoes? I'd rather not ruin my best slippers," I whine, frustrated at getting nowhere.

He leans over and kisses my cheek. "If necessary, ma' Love, I would carry ya' ta' *Dubnos* and back ta' prevent ya' from ruinin' yar' lovely *slipeirs* (slippers)." Then he has the damn audacity to snicker.

"You know, D. P. Fitzpatrick, sometimes you can be insufferable," I mumble, earning me a full-blown chuckle and a clownish bow. After that, I just give up with my interrogation and instead let my mind mull over all kinds of deliciously possible, steamy scenarios.

That evening, despite my anticipation of finally having some premium sexy time alone with my husband, I fall asleep easily and stay that way until I hear Dylan fussing for his night feeding. Call me crazy, but I love this special time shared with my baby in the sacred quiet of the night. It's just Dylan and I, bonded together in the *glaonna na fola* (the call of the blood). In these early hours, sitting in the peaceful, inky blue darkness of pre-dawn, my mind wanders to another child sleeping safely in his bed just a few feet away and to the mother he never knew. My maternal heart breaks for her loss, and his, even while I question how she could ever leave her baby boy in the woods to die.

This mournful mood stays with me long after Dylan

falls asleep and I return him to his cradle in the nursery. As is her routine, *Birgit* is now awake, cross-legged on the floor of the nursery and deep in meditation. At her request, I don't disturb her daily spiritual journey. I tuck Dylan into his *chliabhan* (cradle) and swaddle him in the manner he prefers, then quietly tip-toe out of the nursery. I poke my head into *Buaf's* room to check in on him. The boy is curled up in the fetus position, one small foot sticking out from under his blanket, his left thumb tucked inside his mouth. The dentist in me worries about the damage to his teeth while my mama heart wants to cuddle the baby still in him. *Seamus,* in his basket next to the bed, picks his head up in greeting, then yawns and resettles himself in his puppy nest.

I return to my own bed feeling unsettled. Declan stirs as I slide into my spot and throws out an arm to pull me in closer to him. Even within my mate's embrace, I don't relax. My mind keeps returning to that other mother, the one whose blood must surely call to that sleeping little boy.

WISDOM 37

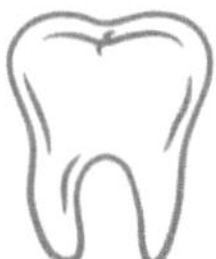

Declan Scores

GETTING DRESSED FOR MY "DATE" with his Jr. Lordship turns out to be a major project, ending with half of my day gowns spread all over our bed and the rest hung over armoire doors and chairs. It's lucky for me that my husband exited our quarters directly after breakfast on some errand he's refused to discuss. The Tax Man is a neat freak and viewing the mess I've created in our bedroom would have had him grinding his teeth. On the other hand, if he'd been here at home instead of out and about, he no doubt could have righted the disorder with a magical wave of his hand, a job that will take little ole' tooth-fairy-me a considerable amount of time during these daylight hours.

After an hour of fussing, I finally decide on the same dress I wore to the Ostara Faire. Despite the awful memories of that day, I still love the gown, and frankly, of all the ones I've tried on, this is the one that makes me feel less the doughy, postpartum mama, and more the tempting, spring-kissed maiden. To change up my look from that awful day, I venture to wear my hair in a complex cornet braid around my head, with tiny fresh wildflowers tucked in between the woven strands. Happily, I know just where to find the blooms I need.

In exchange for a heart-pumping, uphill hike and some muddy boots, I return to *Dun Siorai* with a handful of lightly scented, five petaled flowers, similar in appearance to the southern-grown jasmine of the Mundane world, but with a deeper, sweeter scent. The braiding itself is complicated and takes me nearly an hour to finish, but I'm more than pleased with the final results. Not only do the tiny white blooms offer a gorgeous contrast to my copper-colored hair, they whisper a delightful fragrance every time I move my head. It's all these things together that makes me feel lovely and just a little bit giddy when Lord *Mac* arrives back home at precisely 10:00 AM.

He pauses in the archway separating the foyer from the parlor and stares at me standing there, before putting a dramatic hand over his heart. "The sight of ya' nearly makes ma' par' *croi* (heart) stop, Lass. I ken' not imagine that I've done anythin' in ma' life ta' deserve such a treasure as ma' mate."

"You make me blush, my Lord," I reply, putting a hand to my own proudly displayed chest.

He's across the room in three long steps, pulling me to him and nuzzling my neck. "Only a blush, ma' Love? Then I surely need ta' 'up' ma' game."

Despite it being late morning, a low point for tooth fairy metaphysics, I physically feel the pull of energy between us, the electric static of his powerful, personal magic brushing up against the shadow of my lesser reserve. Our auras are now wrapped in a deep blanket of soul-centered love while they bob in a layer of pure lust. If this is how it is between Eternal Mates, then the two of us are in for a very special day. No. That's wrong. Not just a single day if the magic is to be believed, but an eternity.

He nips the bottom of my earlobe with his teeth before pulling apart. "Are ya' ready far' ar' adventure?"

The words come out breathy. "I am. I just need to let *Birgit* know we're ready to leave and go over Dylan and *Buaf's* schedule with her," I say, already regretting having to pull out of his embrace to head toward the nursery. I find the ingenious *scathach* teaching our new page basic geometry by folding Dylan's nappies into different shapes. Both the boy and the dog watch her with rapt attention as she folds the cloth into a perfect octagon.

"His Lordship and I are leaving now, *Birgit*," I explain. "We should return by afternoon tea, somewhere around 4:00 PM. I left three nursing bottles for Dylan in the ice bucket in the parlor. He prefers his milk at room temp, though I expect he'll still let you know he's not fond of the rubber nipple. If you need to reach us for any reason, call for my husband's cousin, Duncan. Apparently, he knows where we'll be."

"Let yar' mind be at peace, dear Lady. All will be fine here," the nanny promises. "Enjoy yar' day with his Lordship. And may I say ya' look especially beautiful this morn," she adds with a knowing grin.

"Aye, Lady Rosie," *Buaf* adds. "Ya' look mar' prettier than any of the ole' grump's gardens. If ya' was a flower, ma' boy *Seamus* would surely pick ya' ta' dig up first. An' that right, gad' boy?" he asks the dog. The pup sits up and wags his tail in response as if he'd actually understood the meaning of the kid's words. Who knows? Maybe he does.

"Thank you. It's very kind of you all to notice." I bend over to pat the little terrier's head and receive a lick to my hand in return. "However, let's try to keep *Seamus* out of the estate's flowers, especially while his Lordship and I are away. When you take your 'good boy' for his training today, I suggest you take the long way to the kennels and not your usual shortcut through the formal gardens."

"As ya' wish, ma' Lady. I will stay clear of those wretched animal drowners," the lad says.

"Very good. And don't forget the assignments I left for you to work on as well, Master Page. You are to copy those letter blends three times each. If you learn them well enough, we'll play a little game when I return home."

"Aye, Lady *Mac,* I will print them all out correctly," the boy answers, the majority of his attention focused on trying to make the same octagon shape out of the diaper as the nanny. "What kind of game will we play? Will there be a *duais* (prize) for the winner?" he asks. "Because I will surely win it."

Good grief. Another overly competitive Nuada male, I think to myself, but don't vocalize the statement. I have my own opinions regarding the boy's parentage, but this is neither the time nor place to express them. As far as the "prize" goes, I don't know where Declan is whisking me off too, however, I'm sure wherever we go, I'll be able to find something that seems like a reward to an eight-year-old boy who has nothing. "Of course, there will be a prize." I reply. "What kind of game would it be if there wasn't a prize?"

Buaf tilts his chin up and pushes his little-boy chest out. "Then I will practice those letters 'til ma' hand falls off, Lady Rosie, because no one shall have that prize but me." And if I ever wondered what the Tax Man was like as a child, the answer is sitting right here in front of my eyes.

"I'm counting on it, Master Page. Be a good boy and don't get into any trouble while I'm gone. Both of you," I add for the dog's sake.

I meet my husband in the parlor and though it's on the tip of my tongue to mention *Buaf's* competitive nature, I bury the thought. This day belongs to my Eternal Mate and me. I refuse to let anyone or anything else take center stage. "All yar' important business is settled?" the Tax Man asks.

"Yup. I'm ready to leave," I reply. "Do I get any hints as to where we're heading?"

"Nay. Not a single one. 'Tis a surprise, Love." He gestures for me to come to him in a spot where he's pulled away a corner of the rug and folded it over. Once I'm standing facing him, Declan takes a piece of chalk from the pocket of his breeches and draws a large circle around the two of us. I'm relieved to find that we're not traveling by horseback or carriage, both of which take far too long. I don't want to waste any part of this day just bouncing around. At least not on a horse or carriage bench, if you get my drift.

"Hmmm. Magic travel," I comment. "The plot thickens." Honestly, my money is on us heading toward "our spot" on a hidden hilltop near a small stream within

Nuada lands. It's where we had our first "date," days before it became "official" that we were each other's *Mo Shiorghra*. It's also where we spent the night together after our handfasting. I smile when Lord *Mac* pulls a scarf from the other pocket to use as a blindfold. My Tax Man is going all out today. His grin is the last thing I see before he ties the cloth over my eyes and I feel the magic wash over us.

To my mind, it seems to take longer than I expect to get to the mountain top and when we finally arrive, I find the air I'm breathing to be lighter than what I've become accustomed to these past four weeks. "And now far' yar' surprise, Lass," Declan says as he unties the blindfold. I blink in the darkness of early dawn, ribbons of purple and orange light filtering through the blinds. I stand bewildered and completely in shock at the unexpected familiarity of our living room in Salem, Massachusetts.

The coating of light dust on the side tables stands testament to the month the house has been closed up and empty. Still, it's home. My home. Our home. With all of its intimate, lovingly chosen pieces and parts. My mouth hangs open an extra second or two before the words come out. "Oh, Declan! You brought us home! But how? I thought the Black Knight was adamant about you staying out of the Mundane world?"

"The Queen's Hand is no too happy with me far' insistin' on havin' ma' way," he admits. "But Herself offered me a boon when I returned from North Korea. 'Tis not ma' way ta' ask far' royal favors, but for this special time alone with ya' I was willin' ta' make an exception."

It is an amazingly sweet gesture and I throw my arms around his neck. "You are the absolute best *Mo Shiorghra* ever. This is so romantic, Tax Man. Us alone in our home." An unwelcome thought crosses my mind. "Wait. Is it even safe for you to be here? I was under the impression that you were a lab rat to those assholes. That they'd do anything to get you back so they could see what..." I let the words trail off, not even wanting to say what those evil bastards want with my Eternal Mate.

He lowers his hands so they rest on my behind, pulling me closer so that I'm tightly pressed up against him. All of him. "Part of the deal was her guarantee that we'd be absolutely safe here," Declan says. "The house has been 'security warded' by The Morrigan's own spell. She promised no one would even know we are here. Ta' the Mundane senses, this house will appear completely empty of any life. There is, however, a six-hour time limit. After six full hours of Mundane time, the spell will weaken at a rapid pace. I had ta' swear ta' Her Majesty that we'd be safely back in *I Idir* before then. She told me I must make good use of ma' time,' then gave me a most indecent wink. She is vera' cheeky far' a goddess, but I did vow I would use every moment ta' ma' best advantage." My newly bonded Eternal Mate begins to press soft kisses down my decolletage as he murmurs, "T'would not be a wise move on ma' part to ignore ma' Queen's orders, now would it Lass?"

"Vera' unwise, indeed," I reply in a breathy, mock brogue. "We musn't disobey Her Majesty's directives." I step back and take him by the hand with the intention of leading him upstairs to our bedroom, but he holds back. "Time's a tickin', Tax Man," I prod.

"Not upstairs," he replies. "Not yet."

I'm confused. Standing as close as the two of us just were, I can't miss his sizeable...enthusiasm. "You're not interested in getting this little party started?" I ask.

"I'm vera', vera' interested," he drawls, rolling every single "r" because he knows it drives me crazy. "Just not upstairs."

I grin. "I see. You have another idea in mind then?"

"Aye. Several of them, actually. I feel the need ta' christen ever' room in the house before our adventure ends far' the day."

"You do remember we've already 'christened' every room in this house, as well as some in my dollhouses, right? Before we even handfasted."

"I remember. But ya' have gone and changed everything around, Lass. Added new rooms. That means the first time no longer counts. There be rules about these sorts of things," he explains with the best serious face he can muster in the enthusiastic state he's in. Leather breaches are very telling.

"Well, I wouldn't want us to break any Eternal Mate rules. Do you have anywhere in particular you'd like to start?"

"I do. Yar' husband always has a plan, Lady *Mac*," he says as he draws me back close to him and begins an attempt to unlace my corset strings. Unfortunately, the ribbon has a knot on the end and won't easily loosen, so the man with the plans pulls out the knife from the inside of his boot and slices the ties clean through. Taking my hand again, he leads me to the sofa parlor. "I think it best we start right here, ma' Lady," he instructs as he settles himself down across it.

When he tugs on my hand to join him, I hesitate. "Let me make sure I'm understanding you correctly, Tax Man. You want us to explore our racing carnal desires…right here? On the new sofa? The same sofa you spent six weeks picking out and personally declared off limits for food of any kind? That sofa?"

"Aye, Lass, this sofa is where we start," he replies as he pulls me down on top of him.

WISDOM 38

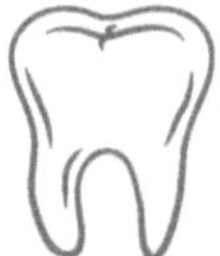

Bad News Travels Fast

MORE THAN THREE hours passes before we actually make it upstairs. At this point, I'm pretty sure there is no dust left on any hard surface of the lower level of our home, as most of it has been scattered or wiped clean by one body part or another. Granted, some places were more accessible and comfortable than others, but when the Tax Man has a plan, he is vera', vera' thorough.

Lack of passion has never been an issue between my *Mo Shiorghra* and I. From our first night together we simply "meshed" when it came to sex. No doubt the magic that produces fated mates has a lot to do with our unique intimacy, as if the Universe is giving its decisions a boost in order to keep destiny on track. I wish I had someone I could share my very personal questions with, but the only other couple that I know brought together by fate, and seemingly to have this same intense intimacy bond, would be the Lady Dear Heart and her

Black Knight. You can just feel "it" when they're in the same room together. They give off a certain vibe. Still, I can't see myself asking the *Banphrionsa* of *I Idir* or the Queen's Hand how often during a set period of time they "do it."

I will say this: since we've added the "Eternal" part to our mate bond, the Universe has certainly upped its gifts. Even his Jr. Lordship, who we all know has been around the block a few too many times when it comes to women, admits that he's never experienced this type of ecstasy with any other partner. If I wasn't feeling the same thing myself, I'd probably think the Tax Man was feeding me a line so I would feel less anxiety about his extensive sampling of the female population, but after these past few hours, I whole-heartedly believe him.

Currently, we're in a discussion as to whether we should use any of our remaining two hours and forty-five minutes to take a short break and have a bit of needed sustenance or just move to another spot on the second floor. We still have the loft, nursery and new guest room left to "christen," though my husband is leaning towards skipping that extra bedroom altogether, as it's the one his Dragon Mama stayed in when she was here and he insists her energy still lingers within its four walls, thus making it a definite mood buster for him.

Suddenly, Lord *Mac Nuada* pops up into a sitting position. "Feckin' hell!"

Startled, I shoot up as well. "What? What is it? What's wrong?"

"My damn cousin is downstairs. I told him we were not to be disturbed unless the feckin' world was on fire!"

Naturally my brain immediately jumps to my baby. "Dylan? Is something wrong with our son?"

"Nay. The first thing he said was that Dylan is fine." He struggles in the tangled sheets and heads to his bureau looking for some pants to put on, as the ones he arrived in are somewhere downstairs. He pulls on a pair of running shorts and moves toward the stairs. I get up to look for a robe but he turns to me and says. "Don't get up, Lass. Stay right where ya' are. I'll see what's up and then get rid of him. We still have a good two hours left."

Declan goes down the stairs and I ignore his order to stay in bed. I clamber over the mattress and streak to the bathroom where I know I'll find my old tatty robe on a hook just inside the doorway. I throw it on and hustle to the hallway so I can eavesdrop on their conversation, feeling guilty that I forgot to ask about *Buaf*.

Duncan has my sympathies. Cranky Declan is not a pleasant host. "This better be feckin' important, Cousin, or else I will feel the need ta' kick ya' in the arse and send you back to *I Idir*," he growls. "I ordered ya' not to disturb ma' Lady and me unless it was a dire emergency."

"I am sorry, ma' Lord. I know you wanted yar' privacy, but I come on the Black Knight's orders," his cousin explains.

"Well, ya' can just tell the *Ridre Dubh* (Black Knight) I have a good two hours left. Guaranteed by Her Majesty. Whatever he's in a snarl about can wait until we return to the Otherworld."

"I'm afraid it ken' no wait, ma' Lord." I can't see Duncan's face from where I'm hiding, but I can hear the timbre of obvious worry in his voice.

"Then spit it out, man! What the feckin' hell is so important that the Black Knight must renege on the Queen's own promises."

The words coming out of Duncan's mouth nearly make my heart stop. "They found a woman's body at the bottom of *Carraig an Bhroin* (Rock of Grief). Her neck was broken and her skull smashed. Ma' Lord...the woman is Marcy Kilcrabtree."

WISDOM 39

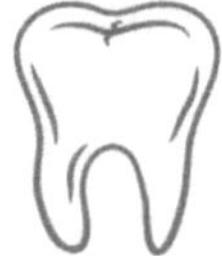

Something to Cry About

WE RETURN to the *Nuada* ancestral home an hour before we had originally planned. I had refused to leave Salem without at least taking a quick shower, so the Tax Man and I take it together to save on time. It was surely not the shower "experience" my *Mo Shiorghra* had planned for us, and between having to cut our special afternoon short and his worry over what Duncan's awful news would mean to our lives, Lord Declan *Mac Nuada* is in a foul mood when we return to the parlor of our family quarters at *Dun Siorai. Birgit* is walking the floors with a howling Dylan and *Buaf* is sitting at the dining table practicing his printing, the dog curled up under his chair. The boy's eyes and nose are red, and when you add in his sniffles, it is obvious he's been weeping.

In his current mood, I hated to ask the Tax Man for any help, but I can't handle both children at the same time. "Do you want the baby or the kid?" I ask.

Understanding my question, he sighs and says, "You take the wee *bairn*. I no have the titties that are required ta' soothe him. I'll deal with the lad."

In between our conversation, Duncan joins us in our quarters, anxious to talk with my husband in private, but Declan waves him off and sits in a chair at the same table with *Buaf*. "I would vera' much like to know why ya' are cryin', Master Page," he asks.

The boy wipes his nose with the sleeve of his shirt. "I am no cryin', ma' Lord. I am too big ta' weep like a *bairn*. Ma' eyes and nose water like this whenever I be angry."

"Then perhaps ya' should tell me what has ya' so angry that yar' eyes and nose are leakin'?" Lord *Mac* asks.

The boy looks away. "I am angry because I must print these letters and 'tis too hard," the boy fibs.

"'Tis not honorable ta' lie ta' yar' Lord, Master Page. I donna' believe these letters are behind yar'...anger. I was hopin' ya' would always be truthful with me," my husband tells him.

The kid blinks several times, then his sniffling turns into full sobbing. He slides off his chair and falls at Declan's feet, wrapping his arms around my husband's ankles. "Oh, ma' Lord...I am cursed forever now. I touched a dead witch and now I will forever be unclean. Even me own *Seamus* will shun the likes of me. I will have ta' move far' away from *I Idir*. Away from ya', and Lady Rosie and wee Dylan and Lady *Scathach*. I will be all alone. Livin' with a witch's curse." The boy put his head up and wailed even louder.

Lord *Mac* picked the sobbing child up off the floor and

tucked him in his lap. "You will go nowhere, *Buaf.* You will stay right here. I give ya' ma' word."

"But ya' donna' know what I did. It was horrible, ma' Lord. Her eyes were milky and evil and har' head was sittin' on har' neck all the wrong way. I sat on har', ma Lord! I used the dead witch like an old seat cushion and now she will put a forever curse on ma' par' soul."

"Are you speakin' of the unfortunate woman at the bottom of *Garraig an Bhroin,* lad?"

"Aye, ma' Lord. I be the one who fond' the dead witch," the child explains.

"I'll want ta' know how ya' came ta' find the par' woman, Master Page. But far' now, I want ta' know who told ya' she was a witch."

"One of the House's own guards warned me. I do not know his name, but he was the one who told me I was forever cursed," *Buaf* whimpered.

"I know of only three practicin' witches livin' here in *I Idir,* lad" Declan relates. "And they are all old women. Most of the powerful ones fled to *Asgard* when Her Majesty put an end to the use of soul magic. I donna' believe that the par' lass ya' sat on was a true witch." The boy didn't look all that comforted by my husband's words, so he adds, "But…if it be a true witch layin' such a dreadfal' curse on ya', then I will ask the Lord Merlin to come to *Dun Siorai* and remove it from you."

"Ya' know the Merlin, Lord *Mac?*" the boy asked, his eyes wide with amazement.

"Aye. I know him well. We have often spent an afternoon fishin' for *Iasc Dearg* (Red Fish) up in the mountains. I am sure he'd be willin' to remove an evil curse from ma' favorite page." *Buaf* looks up at my husband with such admiration and affection, I can barely keep from melting on the spot. It's hard for me to put into words how much I love this kind, honorable man. "Now," his Jr. Lordship continues, "I think ya' should take yar' printin' to the bedroom ta' work on so ya' won't be distracted. I will come check on yar' progress in a wee bit. I need ta' speak ta' Master Duncan now."

The boy slips off Declan's lap and gives a proper bow. "Thank ya', ma' Lord. I will do as ya' ask." He takes a few steps then turns back to my husband and bows again before scampering off to his room.

"Ya' have made a loyal friend far' life, Lord *Mac*," Duncan comments.

The Tax Man shrugs. "I feel far' the par' lad. He's had a vera' rough start ta' his short life. Somehow, I was not aware of how mean-spirited the estate's staff has become over the years. I remember as a boy how it seemed everyone at *Dun Siorai* was pleased and grateful ta' be part of House *Nuada*. I do not feel that same thing these days." His cousin doesn't answer, so my husband continues. "I think ya' better tell me all ya' know about Marcy Kilcrabtree's death. I have a bad feelin' this tragedy will dog ma' Lady and I. 'Tis common knowledge there is no love lost between us and that damn woman."

The way Duncan is rubbing his hands over his thighs and the furtive way he keeps giving me quick glances out of the corner of his eye has me on edge. I know my husband's cousin is not telling us the whole story. I just can't figure out what he's not saying or why.

The worried *gancanagh* relates the sequence of events

as he knows them. It seems *Buaf* and *Seamus* were returning to our quarters after their training session with the Hound Master. The kid sat down to shake a pebble out of his boot when the dog grabbed the leather shoe and ran off with it. Not wanting the dog to damage his new boot, the boy chased after him and both of them somehow ended up on the treacherous cliffs of *Garraig an Bhroin*. Their combined weight was too much for the rocky outcrop they were perched on and the ledge broke away, sending boy and dog down to the bottom.

"Oh goddesses!" I exclaim, still pacing the floor with a whimpering Dylan. "They could have both ended up dead themselves! Or severely injured! It's miraculous that they look no worse for the wear after such an experience."

"Aye," Duncan agrees. "Boy and dog managed not to hit any other ledges on the way down before landing on the Kilcrabtree woman's body. That's what the lad meant when he said he sat on a witch. The body broke his fall."

I shake my head over thoughts of what might have happened to that poor, orphaned child and his dog. Throwing caution and common sense to the wind, I interject, "I would like to say that I have some tiny sense of sympathy for what happened to that evil woman, but, truthfully, that would make me nothing more than a hypocrite. What happened to Marcy Kilcrabtree was Karma, pure and simple, and I refuse to have one iota of grief over the fact she's gone from this world and our lives as well."

"I do not disagree, but please, Cousin Rosie, whatever ya' do, do not repeat those words should someone come askin' about yar' whereabouts today," Duncan says, a look of terror on his face.

"That's a weird thing to say, Duncan. Why should anyone care where I was today? Besides, I was with Declan in the Mundane world all morning. Even the Black Knight knew where we went."

Duncan looks away and mutters a Gaelic obscenity under his breath causing Declan to lose his patience. "Just say what ya' have to say, Dunc, and get it over with. I've had a feelin' ya' been keepin' things from me the moment ya' showed up in Salem."

His cousin glances first at me and then back to Declan. "Ya' know I am no fan of Otherworld gossip, ma' Lord. Most of that *cac* (shit) is no more than nonsense. But this time it's serious. Vera' serious. I have heard it said by several sources that witnesses have come forward and spoken to the Black Knight. People who say they saw… someone above the spot on *Garraig an Bhroin* where the woman was found dead."

"Who?" I ask, suddenly feeling a growing wave of fear rise up from my soul.

The *gancanagh's* expression matches my own gut feelings. "It's you, Cousin Rosie," he admits. "The witnesses say that they saw you on the Rock of Grief this morning and that you pushed Marcy Kilcrabtree to her death."

WISDOM 40

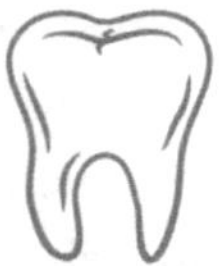

When The Other Shoe Drops

My voice comes out in a piglet-style squeal, sheer panic tightening my throat muscles. "Me? Someone is saying I killed Marcy Kilcrabtree? That's ridiculous! I won't deny I hated the woman for what she put Declan through, but I sure as hell didn't kill her! I'm a dentist, for goddesses sake! We don't go around pushing people off cliffs!"

"Of course, ya' did no such thing, ma' Love, and anyone who says ya' did is a filthy lyin' bastard and will answer ta' me," my Tax Man states, calmly pouring himself a finger of *Uisce Beatha* ("Water of Life"-whiskey) into a short, crystal tumbler. His voice resonates with no sense of urgency. However, without warning, the matching ice bucket next to him shatters into a fountain of broken glass and ice. The explosion startles us all. I jump while the noise and the sudden jerky movement causes Dylan to let lose a piercing wail. Duncan is up and out of his chair, dirk in hand, and *Birgit* seems to come out of nowhere straight into the center of the parlor, battle-stance ready. Even *Buaf* and *Seamus* stick their small heads out of the bedroom door to see what has happened.

His Lordship appears more annoyed than embarrassed over the incident. "Ya' all are far' too jumpy when there's no good reason far' ya ta' be so," he scolds. The wet mess dripping off the serving buffet to the carpet below completely disappears with a wave of my husband's hand. "Maybe ya' all shud' consider joining me," he adds, raising his own glass and tossing the contents back. "Calm yar' high strung nerves a bit," he says as he grimaces in response to the bitter taste I know he doesn't care for, then wipes his lips with the back of his hand.

I catch Duncan's eye out of the corner of mine, and it's hard to miss the *gancanagh's* concern. The *scathach* slides her own long bladed knife back from wherever the hell she's pulled it from within the bodice of her gown. She drops a respectful curtsy and puts her arms out to take the crying baby from me. With everything going on in this room, I need to be in attendance, so reluctantly, I hand my son to the nanny. "I'll come to the nursery in a few minutes to feed and bathe him, *Birgit.* I need to speak to his Lordship first."

"Vera' good, ma' Lady. Shall I order the afternoon tea?" she asks.

The late day respite is a welcome idea. Declan and I never did have anything to eat or drink while home in Salem. Plus, I'd rather not see my *Mo Shiorghra* tossing down any more whiskey on an empty stomach. "Have the kitchen plan for tea at 4:00 PM," I instruct. "That will give me enough time to finish up here and spend some time with Dylan before the meal arrives."

"Aye, Lady *Mac*. I will do just that," the nanny replies as she exits the room.

I, on the other hand, don't move from my spot. Rather, I hold my ground and give my husband the true wifely "stink eye." Initially, the Tax Man ignores my silent observation, but then my staring gets to him. He puts the tumbler down on the table with an echoing bang. "Far' the love of *Lugh*, Rosalinda, ken' ya' just stop scoldin' me with yar' eyes? I am vexed enough as it is."

I drop a low, overblown curtsy in response to him calling me by my full first name, something he knows annoys me. "As you wish, oh gracious Lord. We would not want you to be vexed any further, lest we are all forced to drink all our liquids from paper cups," I reply, not bothering to hide my sarcasm.

The Tax Man answers with a dramatic sigh. "Please, Lass, this is neither the time nor the place," he comments, throwing a glance toward Duncan.

"Why?" I ask. "Because Duncan is in the room? I'll wager all the crystal you haven't already shattered that your cousin already knows more about what's going on with you then I do."

Duncan remains outwardly silent, taking his cues from his Liege Lord and honorary brother, but I have no doubt they're communicating mentally, leaving me out of the discussion. I try not to have hurt feelings. Mate or not, I've known Declan Fitzpatrick for the incredibly short period of ten months. Duncan, on the other hand, has known and loved the Lord *Mac Nuada* for his entire life. They have a history together that I'm not part of.

Whatever his cousin is saying must sway my husband's mind. He runs a hand through his hair several times before answering. "I dinna wan' ta' tell ya' this way, Lass, but since North Korea, I appear to have much stronger magical abilities than I had befar' I left."

"Yes. You and Robyn have both already explained that might be the case. And as I said to you multiple times before, we'll deal with whatever comes with that. All of it," I say. "Is the breaking glass some kind of side effect of the extra magic?"

"More than just a "side effect," Love. It is a physical manifestation of the new power I donna' seem ta' have the ability ta' control. The changes the North Koreans made in ma' frontal cortex not only gave me this phenomenal wealth of power, it changed my emotional ability to hold it in check, at least currently. It sometimes…overwhelms me. So far, no one, not even the Merlin, nor The Morrigan, have been able to find a method to help control my newfound…gifts. But I still have hope they will offer some workable solutions." He picks up the empty tumbler. "Until then, it seems only the use of alcohol dulls ma' reactions ta' certain situations, especially when anger or rage is ma' encompassin' emotion. He adds to my mind only, *"And, as I have just discovered this vera' day, sex also keeps it in check, as I so happily fond' out this mornin'. Ta' ma' mind, a much mar' enjoyable outlet than drinkin', Lass. It seems as if makin' endless love ta' ya' will save me from myself."*

Endless? A warm rush of heat works its way throughout all my lady parts. The Tax Man's mental revelation does a lot to explain the heightened experiences of our past hours in Salem and his new found exceptional… drive. *"Wow. Good to know,"* I mentally say. *"I'm gonna have to do some extra research on how to build my own stamina if I'm gonna keep up with you. For the sake of our stemware, of course."* I can hear his laugh in my head and it makes me happy during a time when there is little to laugh over.

I kiss my beloved husband with extra exuberance, ignoring Duncan's presence. "Whatever it takes, Sweetie. Your North Korea experiences…the lies being told about me…*Buaf's* mysterious past…we'll work through all of it together. I've already sworn to it. Eternally. Now, if you'll both excuse me, I need to tend to our youngest Lord before our tea is served."

* * *

By the time I finish with Dylan's afternoon ritual everyone else has gathered in the dining room, including Duncan who it seems has decided to hang around in the Otherworld. Despite the shocking news that I'm considered a possible suspect in the murder of Marcy Kilcrabtree, I'm famished. I can't help it. The effects of breakfast being eight hours earlier plus all the extra strenuous "exercise" this morning is making my stomach grumble with complaints about its emptiness and I am looking forward to some needed sustenance. Afternoon Tea in *I Idir* is traditionally a hardy spread that fills in as a late lunch, or for some folks, a lighter style, early dinner as opposed to the formal evening meal which is usually served after 8:00 PM. The Otherworldly version of Afternoon Tea is closer to the Mundane British definition of High Tea. As one would expect, there are the scones, pastries and small finger sandwiches that everyone expects, but you'll also find heartier dishes containing eggs, cold meats and seafood in smaller-than-dinner-sized-portions. Since our move to *Dun Siorai*, the Tax Man and I have found that most days, we both prefer Afternoon Tea in lieu of the heavier, richer evening meal, so we usually forgo lunch and opt for that variation of an earlier dinner.

After everything that has gone on today, I look forward to having a quiet meal and retiring to bed early to rest up for what's sure to be a difficult day tomorrow. However, in the way these things usually go for me in the Otherworld, that's not what I get. When *Birgit* answers a sharp rap at the door, I expect it to be a member of the kitchen staff with our much-anticipated afternoon tea. It's not.

Even from the dining room, I have a perfect view of the imposing ensemble gathered in my doorway. The unwelcome group consists of my father-in-law, two of his security people, two unknown Fae folk, and the Black Knight of *I Idir*, Ted Beckett. Declan is out of his chair and across the room in a handful of steps with Duncan right behind him. *Birgit* immediately leaves the table and heads straight for the nursery where I just laid our son down for his nap. The tension in the room is tangible, a living, breathing force that has me up off my feet and heading that way as well.

Oddly enough, it's the Black Knight that takes the lead, an unusual turn of events when the ever- pompous Lord *Nuada* is involved. Ted speaks directly to Declan, ignoring me standing next to him. "I regret having to intrude on your afternoon, Lord *Mac Nuada*, but I come under difficult circumstances. May we come in?"

My husband ignores his own father, also out of character for Declan. "You are always welcome, Lord Knight. Won't you all come in? We were just expecting our Afternoon Tea. I can send word ta' increase the number of guests."

"Thank you, Lord *Mac*. That's very gracious of you, but I'm sorry to say this is an official visit," the Knight says.

I've met Ted Beckett on several occasions; in his role as Sheriff of Essex County, as the Black Knight of *I Idir*, and as my husband's superior and good friend. The man officiated our Mundane wedding, for Pete's sake. I'd like to think he's a friend of mine as well as Declan's. But today, standing here with my husband's *athair*, he hasn't bothered to address me at all. In fact, I'm getting nothing but icy, stern vibes from him, causing my anxiety level to shoot through the roof. "I assume you've heard that we've found the body of Marcy Kilcrabtree at the base of *Carraig an Bhroin?*" the Hand of the Queen says.

"I've been informed. I'm not sure why this brings you to my door, Lord Knight," my husband says, not bothering to hide his own icy tone. His response seems odd to me. The Tax Man is part of the Black Knight's tight inner circle. He would have undoubtedly been included in the investigation of Marcy's death even if we had not had a connection to the vile woman.

"I'm afraid we have reason to believe that House *Nuada* might bear responsibility for the unfortunate woman's death," says the Lord Knight, unblinking, his jaw tight and his expression stern.

My father-in-law interrupts, so angry that sprays of spittle fly from his lips. "Not House *Nuada*! Only that tooth fairy *deamhan* (demon)!" he says, pointing a finger at me. "Ya' have brought nothing but *mi adh* (bad luck) and trouble ta' ma' House, *Tarraingeoir Fiacail* (Tooth Puller)! I mourn the day the Universe mated ya' ta' ma' long cursed heir. T'was no secret ya' despised the Kilcrabtree woman. All of *I Idir* saw yar' ugly brawl at the *Ostara* Faire! Ya' needed ta' finish up what ya' started that day by pushin' that defenseless woman off that cliff to her death below. But ya' won't get away with it, ya' death monger. We have witnesses that saw ya' do it!"

In my fury, I take a step towards the nasty old man, but Declan puts his arm out to stop me. Through my rage, I hear my mate say in my head. *"Let me handle this, Love. I understand ma' athair better than you do. Keep yar' mouth closed and yar' shields up as tight as ya' ken. Ya' must trust me Rosie, like ya' never had ta' befar this moment."*

"What proof lies behind these treacherous accusations?" Lord *Mac Nuada* blandly asks. "Keep in mind befar' ya' fling these untruths at us that this woman is ma' fated mate, ma' *Mo Shiorghra*. I will defend her at all costs. However, I am first and foremost a reasonable man, heir ta' House *Nuada*, and thus willin' ta' hear all the facts."

The Black Knight turns his attention to me. "If I may ask, Lady *Mac Nuada*, where were you this morning?"

I look at Declan and he nods his approval for me to answer. "I was with my Lord Husband all morning, Your

Lordship. In the Mundane world collecting on Her Majesty's boon to my mate."

"Is this true, Lord *Mac Nuada?*" the Knight asks Declan.

"Aye. We were together from mid-morning until mid-afternoon until ma' Liege Man brought news of the woman's unfortunate death."

"Mid-morning, you say? Approximately what time did you leave *I Idir?*"

"We left the Otherworld a few minutes after 10:00 AM and arrived in the Mundane world in time to witness the sunrise of the day befar'," my husband answers.

"Lady Rosalinda, did you leave *Dun Siorai* at any time before your departure from *I Idir?*" the Black Knight asks me.

I start to say no, then I recall my morning outing. "I did leave the estate for a short time to gather these flowers to wear in my hair," I explain, reaching up to pull a few blooms out to show them. Then it dawns on me that all those delightful little petals are probably lying somewhere on the floor of our parlor in Salem where the Tax Man plucked them out during our passionate sofa rendezvous. "I guess I left them in the Mundane world," I admit.

"How very convenient," Lord *Nuada* says. "I don't understand what more you need, Lord Knight. We have two witnesses! What else could convince you?"

"If you have proof of ma' Lady's guilt, Black Knight, then I demand ya' provide it immediately," Declan says.

I feel his rage, barely in control, and I pray to every goddess I worship that the stemware doesn't start popping in the background. I don't know who is aware of what happened to my husband in North Korea and I'd rather not have his inability to control this new magic become public knowledge. However, I'll be honest when I say I'm more than a little annoyed that the Tax Man uses the words, "my Lady's guilt" rather than "my Lady's 'assumed' guilt. Normally, Declan, like most of the *Tuatha De Danann Sidhe*, is very exact in his choice of words. Something about this whole scenario bothers me beyond the fact that I'm being falsely accused of murder.

The two Fae folk standing there step forward at the Black Knight's command. "Is this the female you saw with the dead woman on *Carraig an Bhroin* earlier this morning?" he asks.

The shorter of the two, a pixie, if I had to guess, replies, "Aye, Lord Knight. We was checkin' the snares for *lioncs* (lynx-type cat) we set up last night on the cliff. We heard loud voices arguing. Female voices. When we investigated where all the noise was comin' from, we saws the Lady *Mac Nuada* slappin' at the dead woman's face. Then the Lady here grabbed at the other woman's ear and tugged. It must have hurt somethin' terrible 'cause the lady shrieked at the pain and put a hand ta' her bloody ear. Then, before we could do a thing, we saw Lady *Mac Nuada* give the poor defenseless woman a hard shove. Pushed her right over the side of the cliff."

The other man, a *Dokkalfar* (Dark Elf), most likely from *Asgard,* added, "It right chilled ma' blood, Lord Knight, to see a noble woman doin' somethin' heinous' like that. After she pushed that poor woman, she turned and stomped off, wearnin' a face belongin' to a *Surtur* (Nordic demon).

It suddenly becomes absolutely clear to me what's going on here. Thus, I am not at all shocked when the Black Knight holds out an emerald earring. It's the match to the one I found that day in the dungeon. The very one that is sitting in the jewelry box on top of my bedroom bureau. "Have you ever seen this earring, Lady Rosalinda?" the Knight asks.

I look our supposedly "good friend," Ted Beckett, straight in the eye. His face is entirely blank. "I'm guessing you already know that I've seen that earring, Lord Knight," I say. "In fact, you'll find it's mate in my jewelry box. But I swear on my son's life, I didn't kill Marcy Kilcrabtree."

I see Declan's face go white. To swear on someone's life is akin to calling bad Karma on yourself, as only the Universe holds a soul's life force. Across from me, my father-in-law's face goes red. "How dare you swear on the life of House *Nuada's* heir, you wretched whore!" He turns to the Black Knight. "You have your proof, Hand of Justice! As a leading member of *I Idir's* Ruling Council, I demand you hold this woman responsible for the murder of one of its citizens."

The Lord Knight puts a heavy grasp on my arm. I expect my husband to spring forward to my rescue at the sight of another man's hand on me, but to my unending shock, the Tax Man stands stone-faced. "Lady Rosalinda Fitzpatrick *Mac Nuada*, I'm taking you into custody for the murder of Tooth Fairy Marcy Kilcrabtree. Under *I Idir* law you are entitled to counsel, and counsel shall be provided to you free of charge by the Throne. I am hoping you won't make this any more difficult than it already is by causing a scene. I promise you fair justice under the tenets of Her Majesty and the Ruling Council of *I Idir,*" the Queen's Hand says, his blue eyes boring straight into mine.

Every part of me goes numb and I'm having trouble breathing. Or even thinking straight. As I am being led away, I turn back and call out, "Declan...please." But unbelievably, my beloved Tax Man, my One and Only, my Eternal Mate, turns his back on me. Grief hits me like a giant wave and I can physically feel him cutting the mental connection between us. My knees wobble beneath me and if the Black Knight hadn't been hanging so tightly to me, I might have dropped to my knees.

Somewhere in the midst of this all-encompassing sense of loss and confusion, I think to myself how ironic it is that Marcy Kilcrabtree has gotten the better end of this whole, raw deal. Because now that she's dead and presumably gone on to the Afterlife, the Old Ways teach that the wretched tooth fairy feels nothing more of the raw treachery that must have been wrought upon her. But me? I'm still here in the Land of the Living, carrying enough grief and brokenhearted betrayal for the both of us, as I am unceremoniously led away from everything... and everyone... I hold dear.

* * *

Find out what happens to Rosie, Declan, and their beloved family in Book 5 of The Tooth Fairy Chronicles: Toothpicks And Wicked Tricks

Also by Victoria Rocus

The Tooth Fairy Chronicles

Tooth Decay With A Side Of Fae

Toothaches And Wedding Cakes

Baby Tooth And Tangled Roots

Wisdom Tooth And The Awful Truth

Toothpicks And Wicked Tricks

More from Serenade Publishing

Songbird Series

By Sarah Williams

Songbird

Brigadier Station Series

By Sarah Williams:

The Brothers of Brigadier Station

The Sky over Brigadier Station

The Legacies of Brigadier Station

Christmas at Brigadier Station

Heart of the Hinterland Series

By Sarah Williams:

The Dairy Farmer's Daughter

Their Perfect Blend

Beyond the Barre

The Outback Governess

By Sarah Williams

Primrose Series

By Tanya Renee

Prairie Sky

Prairie Nights

Prairie Fire

Prairie Hearts

Prairie Sound

Prairie Rain

The Spring of Love Series

By Virginia Taylor

Forever Delighted

Forever Amused

Forever Heartfelt

The Ancient Fire

By Ellen Read

A New Page

by Aimee MacRae

It Happened in Paris

By Michelle Beesley

For more information visit:

www.serenadepublishing.com

About the Author

Victoria Rocus is a retired educator, accomplished miniaturist, and full-time author living near the home of country music, Nashville, Tennessee, USA. When she's not writing new adventures for her imaginary friends, catering beach parties for mermaids, or finding homes for orphaned dragons, she's building and rehabbing one-of-a-kind dollhouses and accessories, just like her favorite character, Dr. Rosie Parker. Many of her multiple miniature buildings are 1/12 scale replicas of settings from her unique fantasy stories.

Victoria started her writing career as a weekly blogger while still teaching middle school language arts. Now retired from the educational field, she's been able to make writing a full-time adventure, penning several fantasy and romance stories she hopes readers will enjoy with both a sigh and a smile.

Find out more at: victoriarocusauthor.com

instagram.com/victoriarocusauthor
tiktok.com/@victoriarocusauthor

Acknowledgments

This book, like the three that came before it, is a monumental joint effort. Special thanks to Sarah Williams and the whole team at Serenade Publishing. You make it all look so easy and I am forever in your debt for giving me a chance to make my dreams a reality.

Without the constant input from my regular Beta team, this endeavor wouldn't have seen the light of day. Much gratitude to Carol Peden-Fuller, Donna Gentile-Ruth, Michele S. Kaspar, Daniel Caddigan, and Kaia Viney, along with my dear friends and fellow authors, Arla Jones and K.C. Nord. No amount of thanks is sufficient enough to convey my appreciation for your support.

To my dear family, my own "One and Only," Victor Rocus, our children, Steven, Michael and Allison, as well as my darling, little granddaughter, Valerie James, and the very special Kaia Viney; I hope you feel my love for you all in every word I pen, especially within this book, a story so centered on the meaning of family. *Gloanna na fola!*

Last, but certainly not least, a big heap of gratitude to you, my awesome readers, for letting me share the characters I love with your own imaginations. You guys rock my world! Thank you so much for your continued support of my work.